ABOUT THE AUTHOR

Andrew Gallix is an Anglo-French writer and occasional translator, who teaches at the Sorbonne and edits *3:AM Magazine*. His work has appeared in the *Guardian, Financial Times, Irish Times, Stinging Fly, New Statesman, Independent, Literary Review, Times Literary Supplement, London Magazine, Apollo, Aeon* as well as on BBC Radio 3, and elsewhere. He is the author of *Unwords* (Dodo Ink, 2024) and the editor/co-author of *We'll Never Have Paris* (Repeater Books, 2019). He also co-edited and co-wrote *Love Bites: Fiction Inspired by Pete Shelley* (Dostoyevsky Wannabe, 2019) and *Punk is Dead: Modernity Killed Every Night* (Zero Books, 2017). Andrew is neurodivergent. He divides his time between Scylla and Charybdis.

www.andrewgallix.com

Dodo Ink, an imprint of Dodo Publishing Co Ltd
66 Mayford Road,
Levenshulme,
Manchester,
M19 3DP

Cover painting: Felicity Gill
Cover design: Andy Soameson
Copyediting: Simon Thacker
Typography and typesetting: Ben Ottridge

ISBN: 978-1-0683351-7-4

This book was produced with the kind support
of Arts Council England

Printed and bound by TJ Books, Padstow, Cornwall

LOREN IPSUM

ANDREW GALLIX

CONTENTS

Let's go somewhere, he said, that makes miserable a look, that smiles only when it absolutely has to.

'Paris,' she said.

- Nicole Flattery, 'Parrot', *Show Them a Good Time,* 2019

« Zut, zut, zut, zut. »

- Marcel Proust, *Du côté de chez Swann,* 1913

Chapter One
ON MOONING CONSIDERED AS ONE OF THE FINE ARTS

Still glowing with postprandial bonhomie, Sostène Zanzibar hailed a cab and slurred his words all the way back. Or so he would have us believe. In point of fact, he had failed to navigate the Uber app – his habitual port of call in such circumstances – on account of being fully half cut. *This* he deeply regretted when, looking up from his seatbelt, he discovered the driver's masked reflection in the rearview mirror. Was a whole face really too much to ask for these days? It was foolish, he knew, but he could not help viewing this abbreviation as retribution for inebriation. A wrong turning taken – a minor deviation from customary practice – and the whole fucking world was half cut too.

'*Alors, on va où*?'

Good question. Zanzibar tried to assume an expression of benign amusement – like a father surveying his offspring's latest eccentricity – but all he could muster was a creepy rictus, which remained etched on his features long after he had given up all pretence of a grin. In future, smiling would have to be divined from the appearance of crinkles around the eyes, or a slight elevation of the ears (should said appendages be substantial enough). He thought of Loren's teeth in the wild. Their arctic whiteness. The thrilling pinkness of her raspberry tongue. The warm sweetness of her breath, up close. He thought of Loren, though she thought not of he.

'*8 bis rue de Douai, dans le 9ème, s'il vous plaît.*'

He disclosed the location slowly, reluctantly, as though there were no coming back from where they were going – a sentiment not wholly inaccurate when considered in the round. In his mind's ear he could hear the jaunty airport chime, followed by the sound of his address being spoken repeatedly in mellifluous yet robotic tones. Echoing over the imaginary tannoy, it felt like a terminus rather than the mere destination it usually was. And never a home. Home is what Zanzibar caught glimpses of through the bright windows he walked past on cold evenings in the run-up to Christmas. Yes, home is where the hearth is. He pictured Loren curled up on the floor by the open fire, her flared ultramarine skirt like an Yves Klein swirl lapping at her bare ankles; her face concealed by the book she was reading out loud – something heart-rending about the blue yonder you can never possess. Home was always somewhere else in a constantly deferred future. Now in late middle age, he had spent his adult life staving off adulthood; striving not to become one of those people Elizabeth Hardwick described as 'set up at last, preparing to die'. Yet he knew that the future could not be postponed eternally. The hearth is where home will be, 7.5 billion years hence, when the expanding sun swallows up the earth, having boiled alive all the wild swimmers in their streams of self-consciousness and laid waste to the pelargoniums cultural critics flaunt on Instagram. Before that, in the not-so-grand scheme of things – at micro level, if you will – Zanzibar would ride off into the sunset. In what could be construed as a dress rehearsal for the grand finale, he would vanish into that blue yonder – but not just yet. In the meantime he lived surrounded by cardboard boxes containing most of his earthly possessions. 'I need to maintain a degree of discomfort in the world,' he once told a journalist. Every five years or so, he would relocate, along with all his boxes, to a new rented apartment. Casual visitors assumed he was in the process of moving in or out, they could never tell which, and their uncertainty was to him like a reserve of potentiality that had escaped actualisation. He intended to go on dwelling in this grey area – this Schrödinger's flat – for as long as possible, although he often wondered if life had not in fact already passed him by. Particularly right now.

Small talk was not Zanzibar's forte at the best of times, but the driver – desirous to go the extra mile – broke the ice by enquiring about his journey.

'A flight of fancy curated by Air France,' he chuckled, immediately warming to the subject. The safety demonstration had proved one of the most poignant he had ever been privy to. Something about the flight attendant. The way she committed to her role despite an inauspicious start. No sooner had she stopped going through the motions than the motions started going through her. It was really something to behold. Zanzibar closed his eyes. She crucified herself wingwards, he said, fired two-finger guns down the aisle. In raptures, suspendered in mid-air on this astral plane, she writhed before the passengers. It was uphill from there on in – until the aircraft began its descent. Zanzibar opened his eyes again. The driver clearly could not see what he was driving at, so he raised his hand, palm downwards, and mimicked an aeroplane landing. He even produced a little whistling sound effect to accompany the gesture. An aural flourish. The driver's ears did not move one iota. Not a crinkle in sight.

Zanzibar suspected his words were coming out all wrong because he had wet his whistle. 'Did you know that Wittgenstein was a virtuoso whistler?' he free-associated, although it was the drink talking. 'An interesting titbit in and of itself, but one that takes on a whole new dimension now that this jovial pastime is regarded as a musical protolanguage. Whereof one cannot speak, thereof one must warble... Never be afraid of something you can whistle... That's Burt Bacharach.'

A barren pause ensued during which Zanzibar became acutely aware of a high-pitched sound, as though a delay effect had been added to his prior trilling. Notwithstanding, he racked his befuddled brain for prejudices they could feasibly bond over for the rest of the ride. Slurs he could slur all the way back. Failing to place the driver's accent (foreign is as close as he got) turned the exercise into a minefield, but he finally hit upon a recent *fait divers* that would provide a suitably gruesome, yet relatively safe, topic of lamentation. An old dear who had been strangled in broad daylight with her Hermès scarf near the Champs-Élysées. The motive of the crime remained a complete mystery prompting prominent columnists to brush up on their Gide, eager as they were to frame this putative *acte gratuit* with lots of Lafcadio. There was no CCTV footage. No witnesses. None of the woman's expensive jewellery had been stolen. The wads of banknotes she was in the habit of carrying about in her handbag were all there too and all too there. Not only was their non-theft ostentatious, even downright provocative, but rumour had it that a couple of extra bundles had been bunged in for good measure – that is, presumably, as compensation for the murder. A tip of sorts. Her quiddity for a few quid, or the equivalent in euros. Stranger still, forensics had found breadcrumbs lodged, hither and thither, in the biddy's extravagantly-lacquered bouffant. They believed the victim was beaten about the head with a *baguette tradition bien cuite*. Whether this had occurred before, after or, less plausibly, *during* the strangling, remained a moot point at this stage. One school of thought argued that the criminal had planned to kill their easy prey with this incredible – and indeed edible – weapon, before consuming it, *justement*, thus cunningly disposing of exhibit number one. In the event, however, the crusty bread had proved insufficiently crusty, hence the scarf as gateway to the blue-rinse yonder. Hermès. Her mess, indeed.

The only real clue, and a rather cryptic one at that, was a note pinned to the corpse's coat, which read NOTHING

IS LOST in English and in all-caps Helvetica Neue. A death sentence.

'I reckon the bastard meant her life was worthless,' ventured the driver in his enigmatic accent, visibly sickened by the whole sorry affair.

'Or life in general,' said Zanzibar, before adding, 'Maybe we're missing something here. Maybe it's nothing we're missing. I mean, as soon as you write down *nothing* it turns ipso facto into *something* – especially in all-caps, right? So: what is lost when *nothing* is lost? When it becomes *something*.'

Something about the flight attendant. The way she reminded him of Loren Ipsum.

The phone woke him up. He had overslept.

'Can you hear it?'

'*Allô! Loren?*'

'Can you hear it?'

'Hear what?'

'Go out on the balcony.'

Zanzibar opened the French windows and walked out in his boxer shorts. He leaned over, looking up and down the deserted street with his penis peeking shyly through unbuttoned flies. Some 600,000 Parisians – a quarter of the population – had fled the city to sit out the plague in the provinces. Everything, including Le Sans-Souci (where he drank his first coffee in the morning and last beer at night), was closed. There was no traffic whatsoever. Scraps of paper and a plastic bag fluttered in the wind like tumbleweed. A crow was perched on a bin, loitering on litter. Another, clearly up to no good, hopped onto the bonnet of a car. Nature was healing.

'Can you hear it now?'

'What?'

'Nothing.'

'I need to maintain a degree of discomfort in the world,' he told the pretty journalist with her white teeth and raspberry tongue. Mme Ipsum – '*Appelez-moi Loren*' – who had come all the way from London to interview him for *The Observer*, seemed a little perplexed at first by the cardboard boxes piled up higgledy-piggledy. 'I dwell in possibility,' he said by way of explanation, 'a fairer apartment than prose.' She seemed unimpressed. 'The minute you're done building your house, the melancholy attendant on any completed task moves in. That's what you're left with, observes Nietzsche – that and a house, of course.'

'This reminds me of a Lydia Davis story – one of her really short ones,' said Loren. 'It's called "The House Plans". Not sure if it's been translated into French, though. Have you read it?'

Zanzibar admitted, sheepishly, that he had not, and tried to regain the upper hand by enquiring if she was familiar with the work of Bachelard. Without waiting for a reply, he informed Loren that he would look up a quotation and send it to her – which he duly did the following day. Here it is: 'Perhaps it is a good thing for us to keep a few dreams of a house that we shall live in later, always later, so much later, in fact, that we shall not have time to achieve it'.

It was going to be an in-depth, career-spanning profile ahead of Faber's release of the French author's entire back catalogue with matching jacket designs. Some titles had never been published before in the UK; others were to appear in brand new translations. Zanzibar spoke at length – and for the very first time – of the breakdown he had experienced in 2009 when, after deleting the novel he had been working on for years, he took a taxi to Denfert-Rochereau, uncovered a manhole, and disappeared down the labyrinthine catacombs. There, he listened to the same album track over and over again on a ghetto blaster rumoured to have once belonged to Don Letts. All-girl trio Les Péronelles always maintained that they had rounded off their 1983 classic, *Trois fois rien,* with a hidden song, but most critics dismissed this as a joke, adducing the ten minutes of taped silence with which the record concluded. After a few days, Zanzibar was able to recognise every hiss, hum or crackle on the track – what Loren would describe in her piece as its 'teeny-tiny tinny tinnitus quality'. By the middle of the second week he was convinced that a melody was beginning to emerge from the static: it was just out of earshot; a mere whisper away.

'I thought I was poet of *la música callada,*' he said, essaying Spanglish in a bid to achieve greater intimacy. 'Like – how to say? – Jean de la Croix. I was very sick man.'

Then he got up to refill her glass and, instinctively, she got up too and now they were kissing, deep and slow, their tongues going round and round and round like the ground bass number in the background, and he gently lifted up her floral frock as the melody soared over the looping bassline and she found herself reclining in a Le Corbusier-style chaise longue. '*J'aime quand ça s'incarne,*' she croaked, a frog in her throat, drawing him hither with her long legs.

Interruptus being Zanzibar's favoured mode of coitus, Loren enquired as to what had just happened. She was feeling confused, if not a little gaslit. 'Something has more or less happened,' he explained, 'both more and less.' In this manner, he stated, his desire for her would never be sated: was not *she* the lucky girl?

'Thanks,' she said, upon leaving, shortly thereafter. Zanzibar stared at her outstretched hand. 'For having me?' she explained, but the high-rising terminal turned her statement into a question. A final probing question that she left dangling like one of Pat Butcher's earrings as she departed with a toss of hair and rustle of chiffon.

They went on to become friends. Loren moved to Paris to research her monograph on Adam Wandle, a reclusive author who was hiding out in the French capital. She lived just down the road, on rue des Martyrs. The more Zanzibar found out about her, however, the more inscrutable she appeared, which was truly mystifying. Loren, it seemed, had a heart of frosted glass. She was all blurred features and radio static. In other words, there was a deep mystery at the bosom of her inner *penetralium*; a patina of opaque non-disclosure. Although she remained a closed book, what Loren reminded him of was not so much a text one could read, if only the book were open, as a pretext designed to delineate a space where nothing but place took place. She was both that space and that taking place. She was a happening. The space where everything happens. Something along those lines. A rapturous event. Something like that. He could not quite put his finger on it. Not quite. Never quite. Not quite ever.

Loren grew up in a big solid house near Box Hill, where the floorboards were always joyously strewn with old hardbacks and Scandinavian-style wooden toys. As a sultry but surly teenager in Surrey she had liked nothing more than to walk up the hill, all alone save for the odd bunny, past the tombstone indicating that Peter Labilliere was buried 'head downwards' in 1800, and right to the top, where – from the viewpoint on the other side – she would gaze upon a chocolate-box country railway line straight out of Edith Nesbit. On occasions so rare that it always seemed like a mirage, a toytown train would suddenly materialise, snaking along the tiny tracks at a leisurely pace, as though operated by some spectral model enthusiast. Beyond, a game of cricket was invariably in progress. Loren liked to think it was always the same one: always had been; always would be. She had a recurring dream where she sauntered downhill through romantic aromatic fields, vividly verdant and full of long-stemmed wild orchids – with their pink flowers and delicate purple Morse-code markings – deep into the real, the arboreal; deep, deep into the past, where she was when she was not; hobbling along, ageing at an alarming rate and now, breathless, she could just about hear the sound of leather on willow and make out the long shadows on the cricket ground and, groaning in the gloaming, by the railway line she lay down and rested and died. When the cricketers found out, possibly the next day, they all stopped playing to pay their respects. One of them – Rupert Brooke – declared that she had had a good innings. 'From the Ashes to ashes,' he half-whispered; some of his fellows nodded gravely although it was doubtful whether they had actually heard this terse eulogy. They carried her slender body back up the hill for a rather jolly topsy-turvy interment. Bumbling bumble bees buzzed around the solemn procession of young men in their immaculate cricket whites; butterflies fluttered by: Purple Emperor, Painted Lady, Adonis Blue... Once she had been laid to rest, restless tea ladies produced the crisp cucumber sandwiches and scrumptious Victoria slices they had brought with them in wicker hampers, and they all drank lashings of fortifying builder's brew. Then, following an appropriate interval, the cricketers made their way down again – Rupert Brooke, hands deep in his pockets, whistling a jaunty little tune of the naughty nautical variety – and the game resumed as though nothing had happened. It was at this juncture that Loren usually woke up, feeling her luxuriant locks still putting down roots, but the game went on regardless without her. Always had done; always would.

Loren's father was an architect, who had worked with Richard Rogers; her mother, a renowned landscape gardener once described as a 'visionary plantswoman'. She had three sisters and one brother. It was the latter,

Athelstan, who had taken the picture that was proudly displayed on Zanzibar's kitchen corkboard: Andromeda, Lunula, Phylloxera, and Loren, all stark naked, on a Cornish beach (a re-enactment of the famous 1914 shot of the Olivier sisters). Loren was studying at Oxford (Lincoln College) when this photograph was taken. After graduating, she worked briefly in a posh London art gallery while doing some modelling (she featured in two Boden catalogues) before going into journalism and producing several successful children's books, which (of course) she both wrote and illustrated.

Her first novel, *Fifty Shades of Grey Matter,* was published, to great acclaim, by Galley Beggar in 2019. A few months later it was released in France, under the title *Les Yeux de merlan frit,* by Éditions de l'Olive. The translation, courtesy of Victorine Gribiche, was singled out for praise by all the reviewers who had not – or could not – read the original. Those who could and had observed that the French version only bore a fleeting resemblance to the urtext, 'which shines through, on the rarest of occasions, like a very faint watermark' (*Le Courrier Picard*). Gribiche told Loren that they had completely missed the point. She even made a sweeping whoosh gesture indicating that her approach had gone right over their puny heads. 'I always mount a strong resistance to the tyranny of origins,' she declared. 'Translation is essentially an act of betrayal: it amplifies a process of corruption already at play in the source text. The original is metamorphosed: its essence remains the same but all the rest is up for grabs. *Traduttore, traditore* – I fully embrace the Italian dictum. *Qu'ils aillent donc tous se faire foutre!'* The two young women could often be found, giggling away over a cheeky spritz, at La Fourmi, following their Pilates class. Sometimes Jarvis Cocker would drop by.

Loren contributed to numerous publications including the *London Review of Books, Brixton Review of Books, Oxford Review of Books, European Review of Books, New York Review of Books* and *Los Angeles Review of Books*. She liked the American desert, most of the Cyclades – those former sea nymphs an ill-tempered Poseidon had turned into rocky islands – and Antibes, where they owned a charming family home (bohemian yet comfortable) with a sizeable swimming pool. Her favourite photographer was Francesca Woodman (although she also had a fondness for Saul Leiter and Cartier-Bresson). Her favourite Frankfurter, by a long chalk, was Theodor Adorno. Her favourite Teletubby was Dipsy. Her favourite film was *Berberian Sound Studio*. Her favourite filmmaker was Stan Brakhage. Her favourite actor was Dirk Bogarde. Her favourite animal was the hedgehog. Her favourite party trick was making an omelette without breaking eggs (this, admittedly, was still a work in progress). Her favourite artists were Bridget Riley, Lee Krasner, Dorothea Tanning, Helen Frankenthaler, Linder Sterling, Pauline Boty, and Nina Childress (in this order). Her favourite gallery was the Serpentine in London. Her favourite bookshop was Shakespeare and Company in Paris (she had all their totes). Her favourite living writers were (in no particular order) Anne Carson, Kathryn Scanlan, Deborah Levy, Lavinia Greenlaw, and Tom McCarthy. Her favourite dead writers were growing ever more numerous. Her favourite park was Cannizaro in Wimbledon Village, close to her two favourite pubs, the Crooked Billet and the Hand in Hand (she preferred to drink in the former and dine in the latter). Her favourite city break was Amsterdam. Her favourite comedians were the Marx Brothers. Her favourite biscuit was a digestive (McVitie's, plain). Her favourite crisp flavour was officially salt and vinegar (but really cheese and onion). Her favourite beverage was Yorkshire Tea (Gold). Her favourite wine was white. Her favourite colour was blue. Her favourite music was barely audible.

Loren, you see, was a fan of musicians who piped to the spirit ditties of no tone. She was a sucker for attenuated sounds that trembled on the edge of self-erasure, gesturing to the silence from which they had sprung and would promptly return. The minimalist soundscapes she inhabited were in fact so minimal that a considerable amount of time often elapsed before Zanzibar was even able to detect their presence. He would be sitting there, in her apartment, and suddenly realise that the noise he had just overheard was part of some lengthy composition that had been playing all along in the background, rather than a flushing toilet, say, or creaking pipes. On one occasion he enquired, before going out, if she had forgotten to turn off the music, only to be informed it was a neighbour's vacuum cleaner – how they laughed! 'Music is the space between the notes,' she said, arching an eyebrow and citing Debussy (citing Mozart). She went on to explain that Maurice Maeterlinck had a theory according to which silence is actually more musical than sound. Vladimir Jankélévitch's definition of *pianissimo* as the '*nearly* insensible form of the supra-sensible' was even deployed at one crucial point.

The last time he paid her a visit, prior to the pandemic, Zanzibar had done his homework. When the music manifested itself, he recited (*en anglais dans le texte*) a section from a Wallace Stevens poem he had painstakingly committed to memory: 'I do not know which to prefer, / The beauty of inflections / Or the beauty of innuendoes, / The blackbird whistling / Or just after'. Loren, who was exiting the room to retrieve her phone, looked round, stuck out her raspberry tongue at him and flashed her knickers with a dextrous flick of the hem of her pleated miniskirt. Orchestral drones had never sounded so wistful.

Music, according to Jankélévitch, is 'the silence of words, just as poetry is the silence of prose'. Zanzibar often revisited this idea during the first weeks of lockdown, while working on his new book, *Le Sot dans le vide* – a sequel to his bestselling 1986 debut, *Je suis la Femme Bigorneau*. Or rather while contemplating working on his new book. Or at least attempting to do so. Confinement had muted the habitual circumambient city noises, allowing other sounds to come to the fore: birdsong, church bells pealing in the void, the neighbours' lusty lovemaking, the tinkling of spoons in coffee cups, the daily applause for health workers every evening at eight... He could even hear the traffic lights, down below, clicking fruitlessly from amber to red, and then on to green. *Yes, let's go. They do not move.* His audition now fine-tuned to a level of shell-shock sensitivity, Zanzibar could hear for miles and miles and miles and miles and miles...

A background hum, almost imperceptible at first, but which – once tuned into – could no longer be unheard, surfaced too. It grew louder when he walked towards the large mirror and would go on uninterrupted for hours, climaxing in a rumbling that seemed to make the walls and floorboards vibrate. At such times he felt like he was trapped in a Van Gogh painting. Every single particle within and without him was pulsing. Everything was swaying. Everything was on fire. He was connected to the fucking national grid. And then it would stop and there was almost nothing again, but he could not relax and concentrate on the matter at hand – be it writing or sleeping – for soon enough some thermostat, somewhere, would fire up the power units again. During these lulls he would approach the walls warily and place his ear against them, listening to the slumbering monster on the other side – its fresh breath of eternal rehashing – as though he were back in the catacombs. Sometimes he placed his sweaty hands flush with the wall on either side of his head and they would leave imprints resembling prehistoric cave paintings. His daily state-sanctioned one-hour walks within a one-kilometre radius of his home (that was not a home and had now become a living hell) offered him ample opportunity to contemplate whether he was suffering from auditory hallucinations, misophonia, or hyperacusis. Perhaps he was tuning into Very Low Frequency radio transmissions – unless of course he was picking up high-frequencies habitually only distinguished by kids and hounds. But who was he kidding? Nobody was hounding him, high *or* low. This was the hum of being – the tinnitus of existence – from which there is no escape in this life. He called Loren. She told him that John Cale, in his La Monte Young days, used to tune into the hum of the refrigerator, which he described as the drone of Western civilisation. Not knowing what to do with such information, Zanzibar just hung up.

On some days, when he got back, the humming was already perceptible from the ground floor and his heart would sink. On others, all was quiet when he stepped into his apartment until he started noticing the creaking floorboards, the rumbling of the plumbing system, not to mention the leaking cistern. Soon the entire building was a vast sound installation curated by some devilish conceptual artist. *Le silence a été assassiné. Il n'y a plus de silence nulle part.*

In the dead of night, Zanzibar goes round and round and round in circles, with bees in his bonnet and butterflies in his stomach: Purple Emperor, Painted Lady, Adonis Blue... He can hear cicadas too. In the distance, but growing louder. In the distance in the dead of night. All the cardboard boxes stare at him. He begins scratching at a wall until it is smeared with blood. By dawn there is a big hole Barbara Hepworth would have approved of. He contemplates it with satisfaction. The sun shines through. A kind woman, dressed in a white lab coat, smiles at him. Zanzibar wonders if he is in heaven.

'What have you lost?' she asks.

'Nothing.'

'So what's the matter?'

'I can't find it anywhere.'

The kind woman accompanies him to his bed.

Others will dream that he is mad, and he will dream of Loren Ipsum.

Chapter Two
THE SENTENCE CANNOT HOLD

She cracks the spine, making him flinch. There is something indecent about the way she holds the book splayed wide open. He imagines the text squirming with embarrassment under her stare.

'Once upon a time...'

The sentence is sentient.

She can feel it.

She can feel it feeling her.

If you can read this, you're too close.

She looks up.

'Lie down now, there's a good boy, or there'll be no bedtime story.'

Her voice is stern but soothing. Soon it will speak from some secret wound, secreting senseless squander. And then what? What happens when mute speech is sounded – when nothing becomes something?

Running out of wriggle room gives him such a thrill that he ignores her present request in anticipation of the final summons. This one would brook no argument. Resting his head on his hand, he gazes at the illustration in the middle of the page, noting that no attempt is made to conceal it from him. He charts the blue island, covered in lush palm trees and surrounded by a swirl representing the ocean. It occasions a sharp pang of longing in his chest, as though his heart had been stabbed with a pirate's cutlass. *As often as not, we are homesick most for the places we have never known.* Who said that? He tries, and fails, to recall. His eyes drift back up to the opening sentences, which, to his dismay, he finds himself unable to parse. However much he squints, the words remain illegible squiggles – a preliterate child's impression of writing as ludic abstraction. Just as he notices the resemblance with the swirl on the drawing, the word-doodles he last alighted upon start dissolving like sugar in absinthe. Entire paragraphs give way and now he is all at sea, having lost his footing. Grasping its hideous head with both hands, he strangles a particularly perplexing sentence while dodging the sting in its flailing tail. He then crawls through the scrawls awhile, swimming against the current, before drowning, exhausted, in the wide inky-blue yonder. Giant crabs throw him sidelong glances. Tentacles twine, like tendrils, around his legs and testicles. Water nymphs, following some ancient sushi recipe, are wrapping his erect penis in seaweed. And just out of earshot, the unspeakable sound of behemoths rutting amongst the flotsam and jetsam of idioms, both dead and yet unborn. Somewhere impossible worlds are being mapped somehow – and there he is bound, on his bouncy bed with his stripy pyjamas and incarnadined buttocks. *It is not down in any map; true places never are.* Her lips part: somewhere is a mere whisper away. Tales of strange voyages to enigmatic climes are about to pour forth; unmoored, rudderless. Shivering all over from sheer delight, he snuggles up under the eiderdown

down

down...

'Are you lying comfortably? Then I'll begin.'

She pauses for effect. He is hooked: reel him in.

'Once upon a time...'

Chapter Three
THE SQUIDDY DANCE

There was a mermaid on the beach – a beached mermaid – just across the road from where Loren and Océane were sitting. She had swum all the way from Cornwall, fleeing 'the fucking surfers and Hooray Henrys' who invaded her picture-postcard village during the summer months. Deborah (for that was her name)[1] squealed with pleasure when a galant young man in a crisp white uniform rushed to pick her up from the shingle, where she lay helpless – Undine undone. For an instant there, she thought she had washed up on the shores of heaven.

Is it her body I hold in my arms or the sea?

'Mind my scales, shipmate,' the bleached mermaid murmured in his shell-like, feigning loss of squiddity whilst draping her arms around his neck and clinging on tighter than was strictly necessary.

In the course of being conveyed to the nearest sun lounger, she tilted her head back, catching a scrumptious glimpse of pink gelato dome. From such dizzy heights she

1 It never suited her.

soon tumbled, however, when the young man – having discharged his load – marched away without saying anything. Not a dickie bird. Deborah scrutinised his fast receding posterior and dorsal musculature with mixed emotions: her knight in shining armour was also a beastly bounder, who evidently had bigger fish to fry. She turned her melancholy gaze to the horizon, which the young man seemed to have wiped away with a sponge, like yesterday's specials on the blackboard. *How was he able to drink up the sea?* Shielding her aquamarine eyes, Deborah peered into the distance in search of the literal littoral and a little anchorage. A little courage too, if truth be told, now that she had been cast away on a sea of troubles, and a terrible sense of foreboding was rising, threatening to engulf her from within. Imagine that: drowning in yourself! 'Focus, focus, hocus-pocus,' she whispered, closing her eyes, still pining for some underpinning; still unsure of the treacherous shore – where it ended and started and started and ended... She opened her eyes. Tiny triangles bobbed up and down, shimmering in and out of pure abstraction – a fleeting fleet on the wavering waves. Leftward, a fancy ferry was heading for Corsica at a leisurely pace. A plane suddenly loomed large – its orange and white livery in plain sight – having just taken off from the airport in the opposite direction. The roar it let loose, as it caught up with the vessel, was ferocious, prompting Deborah to raise her eyebrows and purse her lips, producing a little whistling sound in appreciation. At this very instant, some passengers were doubtless looking down upon other passengers looking up at them. Whether their paths would ever cross again was most doubtful. Such things happen in one second and last forever. As though to illustrate this elegiac mood, a forlorn figure glided gracefully overhead beneath a gilded canopy; Deborah followed its iridescent descent across the azure sky of the Mediterranean. *Ceci est la couleur de mes rêves.* Nice that Yves Klein should have hailed from Nice, where cerulean rules the waves, she thought. None of that snotgreen slop she often had to wallow in along some stretches of coast back home – naming no names. The Greeks did not have a word for it. Blue. Homer describes the sea as 'wine-dark', or so a drunk sailor had once told her.

A grizzled old man, his skin tanned to leather, waded out of the foam as life itself must have done in the year dot. He stared at her shamelessly while she gathered her peroxide hair into a ponytail with a pink scrunchie she had been sporting as a bracelet. He stared at her brazenly as though he were king of all he surveyed, but he was labouring under a gross misapprehension. This fishy kind of woman was not his subject – oh no. If anything, the reverse was true. Refusing to be subjected to his objectification, she began singing a song under her breath, ever so quietly, stitching up this skipper like a kipper. As if sleepwalking, the ancient mariner drew closer and closer, mesmerised, until he was standing beside her lounger, with his hands clasped in front of him, concealing the spectre of sceptre haunting his Speedos. He had no idea how he had ended up there, rooted to the spot, with demented thoughts eddying round his head and tears streaming down his ravaged face. A sudden breeze lifted his combover to one side like a paper crown at a skew-whiff angle. He attempted to speak a few words – garbled to the point of unintelligibility – but the words were speaking him. Is not this what the waves had been whispering all along? '*Die Sprache spricht*,' confirmed a German tourist, channelling the voice of the abyss while sporting a walrus moustache. He gave a cheery thumbs up as he sauntered on towards Mont Boron.

'*Gesundheit!*' said Deborah, before resuming her chant.

Though he knew not why, the old man longed to hear the song, which was just out of earshot; a mere whisper away. He longed to inhabit it. To merge with it. They all did – and then they all died. The melody mimicked the unmistakable sound of a corpse, covered in coral and barnacles, being dredged up from the deep. It was a traditional shanty about a foolish young buck – a buccaneer-type – who refuses to marry Time, ending up shipwrecked on the scrotum-emptying She. It conjured up a world where the advent of music was inevitable. The lyrics, frankly, made little sense; attempting to parse them was like glossing glossolalia. They had been dismissed as 'full fathomless five' by a particularly dense columnist, who simply could not comprehend that sometimes you have to sing what you cannot say. According to mermaid lore, these were lyrics that passeth all understanding. Incantatory lyrics. Magical lyrics. Part of some sort of ritual or hex – sirens remained evasive when sounded out on the subject. The long and short of it is that you had to allow the words to wash around you and just go with the flow:

I see men, seamen, semen,
Stresses, mistresses,
The tresses of enchantresses,
And the wives back home,
Yearning and yarning,
And the wives back home,
Scrying and crying,
In their aviaries of ovaries.

Shanty shanty shanty.

The mermaid's thrilling trilling trailed off into humming, then ceased altogether. Now that the spell was broken, the man tiptoed gingerly over pebbles – suddenly cutting a curiously epicene figure – back to the safety of his lounger, where he pursued his naval gazing from behind a copy of *La Stampa.*

Many men are human beings above and fish below. Yet each one represents an attempt on the part of nature to create a human being. Deborah's mind was on other things – these words from Hermann Hesse in particular. She was pondering (as she often did) why her ancestors had remained frozen midway through metamorphosis. Had they been too timorous to relinquish their subaqueous condition? A growing number of young mermaids fully identified as fish, eschewing their human halves, which they regarded as an evolutionary aberration and a betrayal of their origins. They called for a return to the depths, arguing, not without reason, that mankind was responsible for most evils perpetrated on our planet. Others claimed to be fully-fledged women, rejecting their roots (was not such a word a misnomer?) as backward-looking nostalgia with 'fishistic' overtones. Some went as far as to deny the very existence of their tails (which they deliberately misspelt as 'tales' and covered up with overlong overcoats). Deborah belonged to a third category: mermaids who fully embraced their hybridity. We are liminal creatures, she frequently declared – a bridge between nature and civilisation. She would never chop off her tongue in exchange for legs, but recognised that the latter might come in handy now and then. It would be disingenuous not to. If only she could borrow a sturdy pair for the evening to go and inspect that pink dome at closer quarters! She pictured Nietzsche, with thyme on his side, ascending fragrant Mont Boron to the cacophonous accompaniment of chirruping cicadas. Perhaps she would bump into him as she mooched about town from swerve of shore to bend of bay. He might introduce her to vermouth and try to persuade her, after a few glasses, to take the ferry with him to Corsica. And from thence, they could sail on to Sardinia, he would suggest, squeezing her thigh while mutely ordering two more glasses with a V-sign to the *garçon*.

The waiter in the crisp white uniform returned brandishing a tray. He bent down, proffering a cocktail crowned with a jaunty yellow parasol.

'*C'est offert par la maison,*' he explained, once he was able to remove the pen that had been lodged between his teeth like a pirate's cutlass.

'Ahoy,' she said, raising her glass in the direction of her prodigal saviour. Deborah then toasted the old man, who was being stretchered away, now toast himself. She soon ordered another libation and then another and then quite a few more for the road.

'*Ben alors, ça tourne pas rond?*' enquired the waiter, looking increasingly concerned.

'*Au contraire,*' she replied, 'I'm fine as long as I remain in the shallows of tipsiness. I stop imbibing when I feel the world spinning again. Anticlockwise.'

Swishing her tail to the music[2] she was listening to on her earbuds, Deborah started performing a discreet, vaguely oriental dance with the graceful limbs at her disposal. Supine, piscine, and more legless than ever, the beached mermaid was now having a whale of a time.

---

2 'Rock Lobster' – the original 1978 version on DB Records.

Chapter Four
THREE IMAGINARY GIRLS

Zanzibar! High on the agenda as well as psychoactive drugs. Would it be insensitive to send him an invitation knowing that, in all likelihood, he would not be in a fit state – or perhaps even at liberty – to attend their annual get-together? Or would the failure to receive one exacerbate his sense of exclusion and rampant paranoia? Having failed to reach a decision, they moved on to the next item – the menu – which would require several follow-up meetings deep into the summer. It always did. That was the point.

Loren Ipsum and Océane Ciboise were sitting side by side outside Le Balthazar, just in front of the scrub of grass from which sprung a mighty palm tree bisecting their view of the Promenade. You had to crane your neck and squint into the blinding sun if you wanted to embrace its full height. Loren fancied there might be a castle up there amid its spiky fronds, that resembled a firework frozen in mid explosion. The lair of a giant bloodthirsty cannibal strewn with gnarled bones, perhaps, or a Gothic Revival villa inhabited by a wicked vicomte with a library full of exquisite books bound in human skin. There was a cluster of three other palm trees, of smaller stature, on the island dividing the two streams of traffic in the middle of the road. They seemed to be looking back at daddy palm tree, stranded on the other side. It was a heartbreaking tableau when viewed from this angle. Loren, who was in a patch of shade, had pushed back her sunglasses on top of her head and was extolling the merits of *penne al dentata*, a radical dish of her own devising inspired by yoni iconography. She felt overdressed in her party frock – part Mondrian, part Battenberg – especially combined with the golden eye shadow modelled on Grace Kelly in *To Catch a Thief*. Glistening in the sunshine, Océane listened politely while staring ahead at a point equidistant between two street lamps vaguely reminiscent of tridents. Loren was going on and on and she was listening, glistening...

'*On va quand même pas leur servir un plat de pâtes,*' she said, finally standing up, wiping her brow, and smoothing down her skirt. '*Tu imagines un peu la tête de Blandine?*' Blandine de Blancmange: what had possessed her to pick an Englishwoman as co-hostess of this year's dinner party? She loved Loren dearly, she really did, but – to paraphrase Jacques Chirac – how can you ever trust a people whose cuisine is so bad? Especially when it comes to food. I mean, honestly. With patriotic pride, Océane pictured the late President's statue, which had recently been unveiled down the road. She shuddered to think what culinary abomination her friend would come up with next.

'But the penne is mightier than the sword,' said Loren, resuming their habitual bilingual banter. 'Oh well, back to the drawing board then. Shouldn't we be concerned, though? Our current menu is menuscule!'

'*Mais non, on a encore tout le mois d'août,*' said Océane, smiling at her joke, before repairing to the ladies, where ladies repair themselves.

Loren put her sunglasses back on and beamed into her iPhone. After contemplating the picture quizzically, she deleted it and took another, almost identical, which she immediately posted on both Instagram and Twitter (as it was then known). *So looking forward to @firminlepiador's party tonight!*

On her way back, Océane picked up the copy of *Nice-Matin* that had materialised on the bar, as though someone had noticed her scanning the tables on her way in. The local rag's whereabouts were a daily source of mystery, sending the regulars on lengthy rescue missions that frequently turned into wild goose chases. Beaming, Océane sauntered out holding up the Holy Grail by its top corners, tilting it from side to side as if to say: *ta-da!* Loren scanned the sensational headline on the front page. Holidaymakers, it screamed, were being terrorised by a dangerous sea creature. Océane handed over the paper:

Il fait plusieurs victimes chaque jour: on a plongé sur les traces du mystérieux poisson mordeur de nos plages.

Experts agreed it was most probably an ill-tempered triggerfish (they went on to explain that there was, in fact, no other kind). Its size, however, varied wildly from one account to another. Fifteen people had been bitten over the past three days alone in Antibes, Juan-les-Pins, and Vallauris.

'By the sound of it, the Riviera's turning into Amity Island,' said Loren, glancing up from the compendious article. 'It's what we call the silly season: they've got nothing better to talk about now that everybody's sick of Covid.'

'Apparently, it attacks people in shallow waters near the shore.'

'That's good to know,' said Loren, who was now perusing an update on the Champs-Élysées murder.

The victim's identity, which had been kept secret for unspecified reasons, was revealed as Solange de la Turlute, the controversial boss of one of France's largest family-owned publishing houses. She had been most accommodating to the German occupier during the war despite professing radical left-wing views. Mme de la Turlute came out of all of this largely unscathed due to her numerous connections in high places. After making herself scarce for a couple of years – travelling throughout Latin America, mainly – she had returned upon her husband's premature but timely death to take charge of the business.

Without a word, Loren closed *Nice-Matin,* folded it in half, placed it on the small table by her side and stretched theatrically as if limbering up for some imminent exertion. When Océane reached for the paper a few minutes later, knocking over a long-stemmed glass of rosé in the process, she decided that this was her cue.

'I shall see you later, then,' she said, taking her leave. 'Fat Mermaid. Eightish.'

She turned left on the Promenade des Anglais, then left again through the arches on Quai des États-Unis, past the Stygian statue of Jacques Chirac, and on to Cours Saleya, whose Italianate façades – bright yellow and terracotta – always put her in mind of fondant fancies. Were she a giantess, Loren would bite a big chunk out of each one of them, scattering crumbs of crumbling rubble all over the square while diminutive figures ran for cover or stood frozen, amid toppling masonry, staring up her statement dress. Instead, she walked at a fair clip towards her favourite gelateria – arms crossed over her cleavage, head bowed against the sun – where she joined a long queue of tourists outside. There were far fewer holidaymakers this year, due to the travel restrictions, but they all seemed to have congregated at this precise point in space and time. As she reached the entrance, a man with a moustache resembling a household paintbrush dipped in purple emulsion squeezed past her – *Entschuldigung!* – proudly brandishing his cone. She eventually ordered two exotic scoops of lavender and violet amid the polyglot cacophony: snatches of French, English, Italian, Russian, and Swedish, all merging into a babel of babble. From there, Loren ambled in the direction of the Promenade du Paillon, licking the melting cream already trickling down the cone's shaft. When some of it splashed onto her bare leg, she fumbled for a tissue in her handbag, bending down to stem the pink flow – which had almost reached her ankle – while holding out the ice cream in her left hand, as if inviting passersby to have a lick. By now the gelato was melting on all fronts like glaciers in the Arctic; spilling over onto the pavement drip painting-style. Outside the botanical park, on Place Masséna, she produced a small bottle of Volvic (or Vulvic, as she preferred to call it) and poured water all over her stickiness. She then went fishing for another tissue and, finding none, resorted to drying her hand on her dress. Looking up, she caught sight of the walrus-whiskered man perched on the open-air upper deck of a tour bus.

Loren sat down on a bench in front of the fountains that spouted water intermittently, as though issuing from a shoal of subterranean cetacea. She messaged her brother on WhatsApp. Athelstan should have landed by now, but you never knew with him: everything might still be up in the air. Once, he had arrived at Gatwick five hours ahead of departure – just to be on the safe side – only to fall asleep after check-in, eventually missing his flight to Nice. That was Athelstan all over. In his twenties, he had made a mint in the sun-dried tomato racket, but was ousted from his position as CEO when a tabloid reported that the fruit he had been peddling for more than a decade had never seen the light of day, let alone sunshine, in blatant contravention of the Trade Descriptions Act. He was now a merry-go-round inspector of international repute. His job involved verifying that British gallopers revolved clockwise while Continental and American carousels did not. The origin of this quaint equestrian custom was mired in controversy. Some contended it was because English gentlemen used to mount their steed from the left, encumbered as they were by the sword they sported on the right. Others said it was because, in Victorian times, advertising messages were posted on the rounding boards. This explanation most appealed to Loren, who imagined an endless yarn you would read until you got off your high horse once your number was up. Then the story would go on as it had begun – without you – like the cricket match of her adolescence. Athelstan ingratiated himself with his foreign collaborators by describing planet Earth as a merry-go-round on which the British alone persisted in going the wrong way round – merrily, merrily, merrily, merrily! At this juncture, someone would invariably bring up left-hand driving, and then Brexit, and everyone would fall about laughing. Loren sent her brother a second message. They had just enough time to take in the Archinard exhibition before meeting up with the others. If all went according to plan, that is.

A tall dark figure enters an art gallery bathed in blinding light. Your average white cube. The room is bare save for an unmade bed. Presumably Tracey Emin's. The figure she now recognises as Sostène Zanzibar gets into bed amid all the debris and effluvia. A woman appears, preceded by the sound of her heels on the marble floor. Her face is pixellated, or rather smudged, as though by Francis Bacon's thumb. She sits on the edge of the bed, then picks up a book among the flotsam and jetsam. You can make out the illustration of a blue island on the cover. She crosses her legs.

'Are you lying comfortably? Then I'll begin.'

The woman starts reading to him but, oddly, no sound issues from her blurred lips. Her voice could be pitched at a frequency Loren cannot tune into, unless a whole new speech – as yet inaudible – is slowly emerging from its own utterance. *For last year's words belong to last year's language and next year's words await another voice.* Loren thinks she can now detect a very faint whisper, like a librarian's shush caught in a shell. The woman may be reading out low, as if from some sacred text, breathing the words into hushed life rather than merely mouthing them. Sostène closes his eyes. Others will dream that he is mad, and he will dream of Loren Ipsum.

Loren is on a train, somewhere in Surrey, it seems. That must be Box Hill through the dirty window. The train slows down. An announcement informs passengers that, due to a short platform, they must – please – move forwards to alight at the next station (should they wish to do so, naturally). Loren is perplexed. She looks round, but there are no fellow passengers to confer with. She knows full well that she boarded the first carriage and that there is therefore no next one to walk through to. Moving forwards is not an option – surely they can see that. What is this? The Charge of the Light Brigade? The exact same announcement is repeated but there is a subtle shift in tone this time. More persistent, even a little menacing. Loren gets up and walks to the other end of the carriage, craning her neck; attempting to peer through the small window on the door, which, by the by, is just as filthy as the previous one. She observes that there *is* another carriage ahead of her now. Wondering how the dickens it could have got there, she opens the door and walks through just as the train comes to a standstill. Mind the gap. She steps onto the platform, only it is not a platform, is it? Why, of course not. Screaming children are weaving in and out of water jets gushing from the pavement, hoping to avoid getting soaked while clearly relishing the dreaded prospect.

How predictably unpredictable! It occurs to Loren that there is nothing more tiresome than other people's dreams, especially in bloody books. I mean, how much pointless made-up pseudo-surreal slash absurdist shit can you stomach, for fuck's sake? And, please – please, *please* – do not get her started on dreams within dreams.

Uh-ho.

She is sitting down on a bench, looking shattered. It must be the heat.

Or some rare disease.

Or too much to eat.

She is tired, she is weary.

She could sleep for a thousand years.

Loren closes her eyes.

Oh, here we go.

Her breathing grows louder.

Wait for it.

She is out for the count.

Quelle surprise!

Ensconced in the arms of Morpheus, she dreams that Sostène is waking up. There he is in all his morning glory – yawning and stretching and scratching his balls – but, hang on, where does this leave her? If Sostène is dreaming that she is dreaming that he has woken up, he is, ipso facto, no longer dreaming about her. It is a truth universally acknowledged by John Berger that women dream of themselves being dreamt of, but Monsieur Zanzibar is evidently too busy to honour this fine tradition. Sostène is indeed presently enraptured – and not a little aroused – by the spectacle of the woman in the diaphanous lab coat storming out of the gallery. Her heels make sounds like gunshots, such is her wrath.

Having read somewhere that cartographers describe blank spaces as sleeping beauties, Loren wonders if she has not become a blank space. She certainly feels like one, now that she finds (or rather, loses) herself in this ontological pickle. I am not even enough of a presence to become an absence, she muses; I simply am not there. Sostène taps her on the shoulder. If he thinks he can come on to her now – now that his appetite has been whetted by *her* – he's got another thing coming! Some playful prodding and poking ensues. Can't he take a hint? She grows dimly aware of the cicadas. Their unceasing deafening drone in the background, like the tinnitus of life. There is no escaping their mating game – it is positively obscene. Sostène caresses her shoulder again. He even shakes her gently. The man is insatiable!

'How's it going, sis? Having a little snooze in the shade? Good for you.'

Loren squinted at her ~~brothersome bother~~ bothersome brother, whose bushy beard had grown at such an alarming rate that he could give Toby Litt a good run for his money.

'Oh it's *you,*' she said, yawning a yawn so wide that it threatened to engulf the entire French Riviera or (at the very least) dislocate her jaw. 'You made it.'

'Of course. Party on a yacht. In the Med. What's not to like? Welcome to the waking dream!'

The exhibition, *L'appel du vide*, was billed as something of a departure for Édouard Archinard, who had started out producing works specifically designed to be hung in waiting rooms. Psychotherapists seemed inordinately fond of them. He then painted a series of controversial self-portraits. When people remarked that he appeared in none of them, the artist would (depending on his mood) either retort that this was precisely the point or that the author of the remark had not been looking properly. Archinard's third period stemmed from his observation that pictures of paintings in the press almost always included a young woman – usually viewed *de dos*, with an abundance of hair – contemplating the said artworks. Alternatively, she would be shot traversing the length of the canvas; a blurred figure of glamour against a clear, colourful catwalk. This inspired his 'honey-trap paintings' (or 'pantings') which were supposed to attract female admirers and even conjure them up out of thin air (as he claimed, somewhat extravagantly, in the catalogue).

Athelstan told his sister that the void had long been one of the artist's major preoccupations despite accusations of frivolity. The pieces included in Archinard's *Éthernité* exhibition – all based on the Renaissance technique of *non-finito* – seemed, he said, to have been composed on shifting sands. He likened them to the treacherous shore: 'never quite itself; always in the process of becoming and unbecoming'. Were figures emerging from the searing light or being obliterated by it? Were these works in progress or regress? Was that a mermaid in the distance? At Tate Modern, Archinard had filled a narrow corridor with dense blue fog. So dense, in fact, that several visitors had vanished, as though vapourised, never to be seen again. Making people appear or disappear was clearly his USP. It was on the strength of this lapis lazuli peasouper – a homage to Yves Klein – that Claire Iris had commissioned a retrospective in the latter's hometown. Archinard had taken over a large gallery in a palazzo during the first lockdown in order to hang his most famous paintings in secret when no one, crucially, could see them. He then went on to exhibit the discoloured spaces that remained on the bare walls once they had all been removed. Loren was anxious to find out if the execution was as thrilling as the audacious concept. A looped recording of *Symphonie Monoton-Silence* – a D major chord sustained over twenty minutes followed by twenty minutes of titular silence – provided the soundtrack to this hauntological experience.

Fittingly, the exhibition was empty save for an elderly French couple who seemed to have ended up there by accident after taking a wrong turn. A turn for the worse by the look of it. The diminutive husband retreated to the entrance twice to check the introduction label printed on the wall, only to return to his spouse with an expression of utter dismay on his face. The second time he was even shaking his head and shrugging his shoulders, although not simultaneously.

Loren and Athelstan were admiring the final discoloured rectangle – a little verdigris tempera number – when

Océane texted to say Manuella had arrived. They had just ordered two glasses of Whispering Angel and would make their way through the latticework of tiny streets to the Fat Mermaid once they had drowned them. Athelstan smiled at the typo, wondering if it was deliberate.

En route, Loren noticed the magnificently moustachioed man again, this time aboard the little tourist train. He seemed to be going round and round and round in circles. Anticlockwise.

Chapter Five
THIRTY TWO FEET PER SECOND

They hand you a newspaper. The latest edition of the *TLS.* Hot off the press. You recognise it by scent alone. It has that warm bread and freshly-ground coffee aroma. A breakfast at the dawn of the world kind of vibe – which is ironic given the circumstances. You know what they are going to ask you next, but the suspense remains undiminished. You wonder how they manage to do that, from a technical point of view. *Ask* is not the right verb, though, is it? Tell not ask. They *tell* you to hold up the newspaper while they take pictures of you holding it up. You understand that you must remain silent throughout. There is an understanding between you. The tender-looking bruise on the side of your face attests to this. Show don't tell. *You know all about that,* they say. *Tricks of the trade,* they say. Their tone is pitched midway between mirth and menace. As a connoisseur, you appreciate this brand of comedy – the shades of early Pinter.

You assume there is a nifty backdrop behind you. Perhaps a red-and-black star with the name of their outfit underneath in big bold letters. Yes, that would be just the ticket. You wonder what kind of typeface (or is it font?) they might go for. Something heroic but low-fi: a stencil-type affair, evocative of urban guerrilla, would be fitting, no doubt. You hope they have gone to the trouble now the trouble has come to you. Might as well do things properly, right? Besides, it would reflect badly on you if it turned out they had not made the effort. Your status as a VIP hostage could well be downgraded as a result. The very length of your obituaries is at stake, for crying out loud! Figuratively speaking, of course, as no actual speaking – let alone crying – is permitted. There is an understanding between you. Your bloodied broken nose attests to this. Recalling the sobering tale of Orpheus in the Underworld, you dare not look round. It might give the wrong impression, signalling that you are not taking this kidnapping lark with the degree of seriousness it warrants. It might even make you look deceitful: lyre, lyre, pants on fire! 'Don't smile,' one of them says with opportune timing, but you cannot see who as you are blinded by an interrogation lamp. You have seen the light and now you cannot see. For all you know, it may be the lamp talking. Anglepoised to pounce, should you fail to stop gurning like a cretin. You do your best Hanns Martin Schleyer impression. You can do a mean Hanns Martin Schleyer. After all, you are a luvvy at heart. Not many people know that. You were even an understudy in a Tom Stoppard play at the National Theatre – once upon a time. You make a mental note to add this nugget to your Wikipedia entry should the opportunity arise. It is a facet of your rich and complex personality that must be shared with your fans. You owe them that. The world has a right to know. Inwardly, you take a little bow. You wish they would let you choose a more flattering angle, though: let's face it, you are not getting any younger. You suspect the harsh light will spoil the pictures anyway, but realise, on reflection, that it may also lend them a cool, bleached-out arthouse feel. Yes, you can see this now, very clearly, as in a vision.

An East Village apartment in the early eighties, straight out of an Amos Poe movie. Empty save for a couple of chairs on either side of a small rickety table (found on the sidewalk) and a black-and-white TV set that is permanently on although no one ever watches it. Very much like a backdrop, come to think of it. The TV set sits on the paint-splattered floorboards; an integral part of the spartan furniture. It is just there like a stone or the wind or the sea and its very thereness troubles you. In one of your novels, it would immediately become symbolic of something or other: the modernity of American society, say, or its mindlessness. Who cares, as long as it means something, right?

Minimalism does not even begin to convey the sense of utter desolation at large between these thin walls. Everything is bare including the tall, lean-limbed young man by the window, looking at the snow now falling on St Mark's Place. Not an ounce of fat on him, although he never exercises. His pallid skin is almost translucent –

possibly betraying a drug habit – in stark contrast with his luxuriant dark hair. It is so damn thick you might be tempted to grab a handful and then feel compelled to give it a good tug and shake his head about a little.

As you did with your bride when you first rode her like a horse, using her ponytail as a bridle; geeing her up with those sharp little slaps on the rump she so enjoyed. You re-enact this scene every month after entertaining your friends, who always compliment Spirulina on her slinky party dresses that shimmer, in a certain light, like sharks underwater. All evening they admire the configurations her body describes as she performs her meticulously-choreographed domestic duties, placing her cleavage at eye level when she lays out new dishes or bending over, at a perfect right angle, to retrieve the dessert from the refrigerator. Her commitment is commendable. Admirable, even. Bent on bending, she goes above and beyond. You are there too, of course, doing your bit – passing the plates, closing the fridge door behind her – but nobody feasts their eyes on you in quite the same way. While Spirulina is whetting appetites, a full factory reset slowly takes place as you rediscover your spouse through the prism of your friends' concupiscence. And when the last guest has finally departed – only dimly aware of having played a part in the renewal of your nuptials – you look around in wonderment and think:

Is this my beautiful house?

Is this my beautiful horse?

You both clear the table and put things away, as though nothing had happened but you can feel the filly by your side champing at the bit, growing more and more frisky until she starts trotting – clip-clop, clippity-clop – around the kitchen and galloping through the dining room, neighing all the while, and you run after her to the bottom of the stairs, where she waits for you to catch up and smack her backside and say, 'Giddy up you giddy mare!' Soon enough you are holding on to her tight ponytail for dear life and she is whinnying like billy-ho and bucking bronco-fashion, sometimes even unseating you, whereupon you both bray with laughter, bringing horseplay to an abrupt end.

The reset only fails to materialise on those rare occasions when, for some reason, you browse her brows for too long. Truth is, you believe women have serious eyebrow issues these days. Put simply, there is either too much of them or not enough; an oscillation between totality and nothingness you would find fascinating if applied to more philosophical considerations. You do not buy Charles Le Brun's contention, in his celebrated 1688 lecture, that eyebrows – and particularly their motion – express the truth of the human soul. Never have done. Can Roger Moore be described as a particularly expressive actor? At times, Spirulina affects the fuller, Frida Kahlo/Denis Healey look – that puts you in mind of her untopiaried pudenda – only content once she can run a comb *à rebrousse poil* through the thickets of those bushy uplands. At others, she shaves them clean off the face of her face before pencilling them back in again. You know this style was all the rage during the Elizabethan era but sense there is something a little aberrant, if not downright French, about viewing nature in this manner, as a mere draft to be improved upon through human artistry.

There is nothing striking about the young man's eyebrows. You cannot even observe them, presently, as he is still staring out of the window. He has spotted Richard Hell gingerly crossing the road down below, almost slipping on an icy patch at one stage of his perilous progress to the other side, where Andrew Wylie awaits. It is so cold in the room, but the young man – who cuts a fine emaciated Egon Schiele figure, you can see this now – seems totally oblivious. He is all pinched nerves and cold tobacco, this one. Spindly and sinewy; as snake-hipped as he is tight-lipped.

'Don't move,' says a kidnapper, presumably the one taking the pictures. You struggle to place his accent – West Country, you think, but would not put any money on it. That will be the next step, you wager. What font (or is it typeface?) might they use for the ransom note? Something generic like Times or Times New Roman? A cool collage of cut-out letters *à la* Jamie Reid is probably too much to ask for. You hope they do not cut off any of your extremities instead – send them to your publisher in an innocuous-looking manilla envelope. Would they go to such extremities? Would not that be a tad too Grand Guignol? Or simply too clichéd? Then again, they *are* operating within a very codified format. You wonder if they intend to renew the genre or embrace its constraints, either ironically or creatively. Ah, to be a laboratory rat building the labyrinth through which it plans to escape! Your arms ache from holding up the paper. If only you could just glance down for a second to see who is on the cover this week. You are dying to see who is on the cover. Your arms are killing you. You picture all the unread issues of the *TLS* piled up on your desk at home and think it is a hopeless cause. You are overwhelmed by a feeling of exhaustion, no longer merely physical. Exhaustion and futility. Didn't Lydia Davis write a story about speed-reading her back issues of the *TLS*? You wonder what time it is now. Would the kids be home yet? At what point, if any, would Horatia look up from her mobile and interrupt Cosimo's video game to enquire where you are? And where is Spirulina? Is she horsing around? Someone switches off the lamp. You hear the door open and people filing out. Nine or ten? You hear the door close behind them. You are all alone, holding up the paper in the dark.

The young man looks round. A young woman has appeared wearing a towel turbaned around her hair and another wrapped – rapt – around her waist. Her breasts are as pert as his dick is limp. Not so much pert as angry. Her breasts, you can see this now, are glaring at him. They are fucking livid. The young man turns his gaze back to the snowscape outside, where Richard Hell is getting up and dusting himself down.

Neither of them pays any attention to the cartoon on television, where a little boy is putting the final touches to a snowman while his daddy looks on, camera at the ready. Whenever the latter is about to take a picture, his son motions him to wait while he adds a carrot for a nose or an extra coat button. Once there is nothing left to add, the little boy asks him to wait, and then wait some more, while the corpulent snowman slowly deliquesces, like a poem riding on its own melting, until the hat, carrot, and buttons are bobbing in a big icy puddle at his feet.[3] *Now that the snowman has become a noman, the little boy finally gives his father the go-ahead. He smiles at the camera while the credits roll.*

The door opens. How long has it been? Someone prises the paper from your rigid digits. You can barely feel your arms, they ache so much – an intimation of rigor mortis. The interrogation lamp is turned on again. A woman with a strong German accent starts questioning you. Her command of English is so good that you wonder, at first, if the accent is not put on for purely comedic purposes.

'Mr Titterington-Jones – may I call you Jonathan?'

Shielding your squinting eyes with your hand, you nod in agreement.

'My name is Astrid Strumpfhosen.'

'May I call you Astrid?'

'Of course.'

'That's a relief.' You can tell she is smiling.

'Enough banter, Jonathan. Let's cut to the chase. You stand – well, sit – accused of middlebrow crimes against literature and aggravated champagne Marxism.' She pauses an instant to let it sink in before resuming. 'Creative writing students always want to learn *how* to write and *how* to get published, but the question isn't *how*; it's *why*. Now, tell me: why do you write?'

'Well, I've been doing it for almost – what? – forty years now. So it's just what I do, really.'

---

3 'All art aspires to the condition of snowmen,' according to the Shakespearean scholar T. J. B. Spencer.

'It's just what you do? Really? Well, that won't do, will it, Jonathan? Surely you can do better than this.'

'Above all, I write to express myself, I guess.'

'You guess? You're not sure? Are you a gambling man, Jonathan? Do you think it's wise to gamble in your present predicament? Aren't the odds heavily stacked against you?'

You remain silent, assuming – rightly – that these are rhetorical questions.

'So – to express yourself, you say?'

'Absolutely.'

'The sense of a separate self is only a shadow cast by grammar.'

'I'm sorry?'

'I was quoting Wittgenstein.'

'Oh, I see.'

'Do you? Do you really, Jonathan? I hate to break it to you in this way, but' – and here she starts whispering – 'there is no self to express.'

You hold your peace, unsure of where this is going.

'Now, a work of art, or a work of literature, expresses itself. In fact, it expresses *nothing but* itself. Art isn't the embellishment of a message, Jonathan; it *is* the message.' She pauses as though pondering something. 'This young man who's distracting you: he's your alter ego, right?'

'What young man?'

'The naked one looking out the window.'

'But he's in my head – how can you see him?'

'Just answer the question: is he your alter ego?'

'Yes, I suppose he is.'

'Thought as much. Evidently, an idealised version.'

'What makes you say that?'

'His dick.'

'That's about the size of it,' you concede, sheepishly, after a moment's hesitation.

No reaction. A lone voice in the wilderness.

'The long and the short of it,' you add, interrupting the eternal silence of infinite space that scared the bejesus out of Pascal.

The young woman absents herself again. No sooner has she left the room than the young man strides to the cassette player on the table, his long, flaccid penis slapping nonchalantly against his thigh. He presses play and returns to the window. The music now emanating from the tape sounds like On the Corner*-era Miles Davis performed by a totally inept No Wave combo. All New York City artists worth their salt are in a band at this point in time and the young man is clearly a painter, you can see this now – I mean, just look at the floorboards. Contraband have played a couple of ramshackle sets at venues like the Mudd Club or CBGB, tearing their hearts out in front of a smattering of indifferent spectators waiting for the main act. On the strength of this demo, you draw the conclusion that they have hit the sweet spot where rank amateurism and preternatural proficiency merge, becoming almost indistinguishable. This lengthy instrumental is called 'I Lost My Heart at the Peppermint Lounge' in homage to the night, almost a year ago, when the young man first met the young woman. She was dancing in front of a stack of TV sets showing music videos – mainly repurposed black-and-white films from the silent era. He was standing at the* *bar, observing her while nursing a scotch and trying to act cool. It took four whole tracks – 'Too Many Creeps', 'Stand and Deliver', 'I Know What Boys Like' and 'Rock Lobster' – for her to notice him, but when she did the attraction was immediate.*

'Okay, so let me guess: you write in order to make sense of the world.'

'That's right – spot-on.'

'Do you think the world makes sense of you?'

'Excuse me?'

'If you knock on a door and get no answer, do you assume that nobody's home, or that there's someone inside who doesn't want to see you?'

'I don't quite follow.'

'Is nobody home?'

'What do you mean?'

'When you look at the world, does it look back?... Well, does it?'

The young woman reappears in a tight blouse and dark pencil skirt, holding a small suitcase. She glances at the young man, who is feigning to ignore her, before turning on her vintage kitten heels. Trash and Vaudeville. The front door closes. The young man can still smell the scent of her perfume in the room. He can hear her receding footsteps in the corridor.

'Is the corpse the truth of the body?... I'll tell you something for nothing, Jonathan. Without our intervention, you'd just end up in some care home, unable to remember you'd ever written anything. Unable to even read. You'd just be shitting there all day long, staring into the middle distance. Festering in your own faeces. Muttering incomprehensibly to people who died years ago. Calling out to your mummy, who can no longer make it better. Waiting for it to end as soon and as painlessly as possible. We're doing you a favour, really. Your execution will be a personal as well as a public service. We're going to put you out of your misery, pre-emptively. Think of it as a mercy killing, Jonathan. Think of us as benefactors.'

'So you've already decided you were going to kill me?'

'Oh yes – your demise is *de mise*, Jonathan. Very much so. Big time.' She grins, maxing out her maxillary. 'I fear you may find what follows a little triggering.'

'Unthinkable!'

'Unsinkable? You're already plumbing the depths...'

'No, no – un*think*able. It seems impossible,' you say, shaking your head like the diminutive husband at the Archinard exhibition.

'Nothing is impossible, Jonathan – by which I mean nothing is a distinct possibility. I'm sure you're familiar with Heidegger's notion of death as the possibility of impossibility. Well, I'm with Levinas on this one. He sees death, conversely, as the impossibility of possibility...'

'What's the difference?'

'In your case? Frankly? Absolutely none. Zilch. *Nada*. Nowt. Sweet FA... Expect no succour you sucker! Compassion is doubtless an important asset in a writer, but not in a terrorist.'

When the young man was a little boy – no older than the one in the cartoon – there were two different ways to go to school, both equidistant. Had he read Proust he may have drawn a parallel with the côté de Méséglise *and the* côté de Guermantes, *but he was only a little boy back then, remember. Every day, he and his brother would split up outside the school gates and race to get home first.*

'I'd love to discuss philosophy with you all day, Jonathan, but I must crack on with the interrogation. Hope you understand. Now – do you recall how you (and I choose my words carefully) ended up here?'

'Yes, I think so. Up to a point. It was most peculiar, to say the least.'

'If only you did say the least,' she sighs, 'if only you did, Jonathan. In your books, I mean. Perhaps the word "corpus" would be more fitting now to describe your body of work – but please proceed.'

'Well, I'd reached an impasse: a plot hole I couldn't fix in the new novel (a page-turner with heart). So I decided to take a constitutional upon the Heath, nearby. Anyway, I was walking at a brisk pace, deep in thought, when I found myself in this dark forest. Dante, etc. Pretty Grimm – double m. Had no idea where I was although this is, as you know and as it were, my neck of the woods. I realised I had lost all sense of time...'

'Time is temporary. You were experiencing the encroachment of the actual upon the potential.'

'...I was still thinking, but no longer *about* anything in particular. Actually, it wasn't so much that I was thinking, but rather that thinking was taking place within me – I was the locus of rumination. Let me put it another way: something within me was ruminating, possibly rumination itself. I really don't know how to explain it any better, sorry. Perhaps I had acceded to a higher state of reflection. Fuck knows.' You shake your head in bewilderment again. It is becoming a habit.

'Go on.'

'Clouds of unknowing were gathering overhead...'

'Where else could they possibly gather?'

'...The leaves in the trees started rustling in the breeze. After wandering aimlessly for a while, listening to this rustling, I got my bearings and, as I made my way home, I noticed that the rustling was following me – was now *within* me. It was relentless, let me tell you.'

'Rustling never sleeps when it becomes whispering; when it taps into that language that isn't quite language and its fresh breath of eternal rehashing. How much of it could you make out?'

'Very little ... almost nothing. Most of it was inaudible or incomprehensible. The only word I could distinguish was *modernism*, which seemed to crop up regularly. Turns out it was *Mordenism*.'

'Did that ring a bell?'

'Not at first, no, but then I remembered Adam Wandle.' You scoff. 'I once attended a strange reading by Stewart Douglas-Home...'

'Is there any other kind?'

You laugh.

'This was years ago, at the Crypto-Amnesia Club – Wandle was there. His friends used to call him Lord Biro. Very odd chap, very odd. Probably has some kind of syndrome. He was drinking heavily to offset what I took to be an extreme form of social anxiety. He was being very provocative, making all these grand pronouncements: "Literature is a hate crime, or it is nothing" – that kind of nonsense.'[4]

'Is it nonsense, though? I mean, Walter Benjamin describes the "birthplace of the novel" as the "solitary individual", right? A free agent, cut off from tradition, who can no longer claim to be the mouthpiece of religion or society. Is it any wonder, then, that the modern writer should have become a sociopath? Is there really any other option in a destitute time of absent gods and silent sirens?'

'I'm not sure he made that much sense, frankly. He kept repeating "I'm a cell of one", "I'm a cell of one" like a fucking Dalek...'

'Well, there you go. A cell of one. Precisely. He had a great enthusiasm for devilment in those days, I'll grant you that. The theft of toilet-rolls from public lavatories, pens from post offices; the obscene telephone calls... He'd give a wrong time, stop a traffic line.'

'Well, he didn't impress me. In fact, he cut a rather pathetic figure, banging on about this bloody Mordenist movement he was going to launch. Some kind of working-class literary avant-garde, apparently. He claimed the renewal of fiction would come from the wrong end of the Northern Line.'

'And *you* lived at the other end.'

'That's right. Still do, of course.'

'Like bookends. How symbolic! Did you ever meet him again?'

4 It is doubtful whether Adam Wandle would have used the expression 'hate crime' at the time.

'Just the once, I think – a festival with readings, performances by artists and live music: Subway Sect, Billy Childish… A good decade later, I'd say.'

'Where was this?'

'At the Horse Hospital.'

'I should have guessed.'

'The place was packed to the rafters with landfill indie writers. By then, of course, he was involved with *3:AM Magazine* and all that early online literary scene. What did they call themselves? The Offbeats – that's it. Yes, he was one of the Offbeats. Bunch of muppets, most of them, if you want my honest opinion. Wandle stumbled on stage looking very much the worse for wear, glared at the audience with his manic Johnny Rotten eyes, and decreed that if the world couldn't be beautified, at least it could be destroyed. Deadpan delivery.'

'Classic Wandle!'

'He then proceeded to read an extract from a work in progress – a rather abstruse piece of prose poetry about a blue island. I believe that was actually the title: *The Blue Island.* Legend has it that it turned into a *magnum opus*, which Wandle then whittled down to its very essence over several long years until there was nothing left.'

'When nothing is left, it is no longer lost,' Astrid interjected.

'The weirdest thing is that *blue island* were the only other words I could make out, as I was walking home this morning. I've only just made the connection.'

'You see, it's all beginning to make sense, Jonathan.'

'I wouldn't go that far.'

'So, you're walking home...'

'I'm walking home. This blue island business is fast becoming a leitmotif, and suddenly I start hallucinating. I see myself on a tropical beach. There I am, on all fours, sweeping the sand aside with my open hands to reveal monumental Moses-type tablets entirely covered in some kind of abstract calligraphy. The words may be illegible squiggles but there are thousands of them and they're literally written in stone. The message is clear: here lies a gift from the Muses. A ready-made double decker. Triple even.'

'*Sous la plage, le pavé!*'

'Indeed. So, breathless, I open the front door and make a beeline for my desk. The words are already there, 'written in invisible ink and clamoring to become visible', as Nabokov put it. They're swirling round my head and start pouring out as soon as my stubby fingers land on the keyboard, but I only discover what they are once I've moved on and see them up on the screen in my peripheral vision.'

As he opens the window, he thinks of the future that could have been: the children they will never have together. Every day, they will split up outside the school gates and race to get home first. The young parents will hear their offsprings' footsteps coming up the garden path lined with shells from trips to the seaside – Rockaway or Redondo Beach.

'The words come as easily as leaves to a tree, sentence upon sentence appearing fully formed. I am typing to dictation in a frenzied fugue state. I am played upon like an Aeolian harp. I am ventriloquised; spoken through...'

'And who is speaking through you?'

'A voice.'

'And what is this voice saying?'

'It says follow me to the blue yonder. Follow, follow until my words echo hollow, hollow in the distance as they merge with the reality of things and fall silent. Then you shall enter a world where nothing is known in advance.'

Standing on the windowsill, he pictures her winding down the flights of stairs, suitcase in her hand. Jack is in his corset, Jane is in her vest. And me, I'm in a rock 'n' roll band. There are two ways to go home, both equidistant, but his is the quickest.

'Open your eyes, the voice says, and take a look around you. There is no mystery, yet all is mysterious. There are no miracles, yet everything is miraculous. There is no subtext; no beyond. Stop writing and open your eyes. Bask in the Edenic simplicity of life. Our present task is to *unexpress* the expressible. We must murder language because language is murder... So I stop writing and look around me, and see everything as though for the first time.'

'Louise Glück is right: we only look at the world once, in childhood – thereafter it's just recall. That's why Baudelaire describes genius as "childhood recaptured at will". That's why Picasso claims it took him four years to paint like Raphael, but a lifetime to paint like a child... But please continue.'

'All the words are vanishing. I am Adam in reverse.'

'Mada?'

'No. Anti-Adam. Whatever I gaze upon is unchristened, set free from the tyranny of preordained meaning. I am the verbal decoloniser re-enchanting the world. It is beautiful. Everything is beautiful. *You're* beautiful.'

'Steady on, Jonathan!'

'I haven't quite finished. There's more.'

'You're not related to Scheherazade by any chance, are you?' Astrid says, stifling a yawn.

'Now for the weirdest bit. The grand finale. Language returns with a vengeance, asserting its materiality and autonomy in a most aggressive manner. Instead of referring to things, it has become a thing, like a stone or the wind or the sea...'

'I'm not sure these things really qualify as things, but I get your drift.'

'As a toddler, I used to scribble page upon page of senseless script, pretending I could write. Signifiers without signifieds, signifying nothing; communicating nothing but communication itself. Ah, the doodles of yesteryear!...' You are lost in reverie. You snap out of it. 'Anyway, there are words, words, words left, right, and centre now – all over the bloody shop – but reading them is like peering through a filthy train window in a dream. A swarm of illegible words. A plague of opaque words. Words overprinting other words in thick impasto sediments. Words scuttling across the screen at great velocity and in all directions as soon as my eyes alight upon them, resisting all attempts to parse.'

'They shall not parse!' Astrid says, punching the air.

A smattering of *Ahoys!* emanates from the obscurity of the room.

'Remember what Roland Barthes said: "For writing to be manifest in its truth (and not in its instrumentality) it must be *illegible*"... Please proceed.'

'Something is happening right there on the screen of my laptop. Language has somehow come alive. It is performing; doing what it cannot say. The overprintings begin to form patterns. Soon I can make out silhouettes looming in the inky darkness; faces staring back at me, and then – suddenly, inexplicably – you are no longer behind the screen but in my study with your hatred and your guns...'

The snow falls. The young man falls with the snow and then the snow falls on the young man, covering him up; making the world new again.

You doubt whether your blood will look as decorative as his once it is splattered across the wall and that backdrop, assuming there is one. Even his blood is more attractive than yours. You can hear Charles Trénet's 'La Mer' – very faintly, in the distance – and it reminds you of your childhood summer holidays. Your father used to sing along to it in the car (making up most of the lyrics). It used to drive you mad. It was so hot in those car rentals. You remember a Simca 1000. It is so hot now. The questions keep coming quick and fast and you seem to be answering them without hesitation and in great detail, although you have no idea what you are saying. You listen in. 'Alain de Botton', apparently. Fuck's sake!

Passersby, no longer passing by, congregate around the naked body that lies on the sidewalk close to where the rickety table was found. The young woman howls mutely

– Munch, Eisenstein, Britten, Bacon – as though acting in one of those silent movies at the Peppermint Lounge. She drops her suitcase dramatically and kneels by the prostrate young man. There are no words. Words are meaningless. Her thoughts turn to God. God is what's left when nothing is left. God and the snows of yesteryear.

'Say Alain de Botton again. Say. Alain. De Botton. Again. I dare you. I double dare you, motherfucker. Say Alain de Botton one more goddamn time...'

You are suspended, weightless, in a pause in time.

Goddamn time.

A shot rings out and continues to ring in everyone's ears except yours. You hear the blackbird whistling but not just after. Astrid places the gun on the table and turns to face the audience. 'We must sail to the Blue Island,' she declaims to what lesser writers would describe as rapturous applause. 'We must sail to the outside of everything!' More clapping. Cheering. A few whoops. She raises her arms like a preacher and the assembly falls silent. 'A toast,' she says, removing the miniature parasol from the cocktail glass that has replaced the gun on the table. 'To Mr Titterington-Jones' new headshot!' She tosses the parasol over her shoulder. It lands on the space – now largely blank – where Jonathan's face used to be. 'Ahoy!'

'Ahoooooooy!' comes the collective echo.

The TV screen is now covered in snow – a blizzard of static. A fin glides through the electromagnetic waves left over from the Big Bang. The sun is rising above St Mark's Place. There is a breakfast at the dawn of time kind of vibe.

Chapter Six
QUEEN MOB

The Marquise went out at seven. It could have been at six, of course, or even at five; indeed, it usually was. That day, however, it was at seven, on account of her husband – a *romancier à succès* and former diplomat – being frightfully late. Consistent is the life he leads, said the maid, who often likened him to the ever punctual *pater familias* in *Mary Poppins*. You could set the time by his comings and goings; indeed, everybody did. At five o'clock sharp, the maid would start dusting, scrubbing, mopping, and ironing as if propelled by the velocity of a hard day's work. At five on the dot, Madame la Marquise – freshly abluted and made up – stood poised to greet her husband like a domestic goddess, who would never dream of spending the afternoon in the company of young bell boys with the stamina of Duracell bunnies. No, it really was not like him at all, said the maid, shaking her head; totally out of character. Lost in thought, the Marquise gazed out of the window, blinking into the blinding summer light that was still streaming in. She was fiddling with her pearl necklace, as though it were a rosary. You always know where you are with him, said the maid. And what about without him? Lost *tout court*, the Marquise gazed out of the window, blinking into the blinding light that was streaming in from long, long ago. I have seen the light and now I cannot see. She was fiddling with her pearl necklace, as though rolling testicles between thumb and forefinger. Her late husband was in fact so late now that it could only be *too* late. He would never be coming home again, not least, of course, because he was lying in a pool of blood with a gaping hole where his heart once was – or should have been. Dinner would be ruined now.

Chapter Seven
THE FAT MERMAID

'A-thelstan!' Océane exclaimed. 'It's been too long – really. Mwah! Mwah! Loving the beard, by the way.' She turned to Manuella, who was sitting by her side at one of the turquoise tables on the tiny terrace. 'This is Athelstan, Loren's brother. *Bel homme, n'est-ce pas? Il est dans les manèges.*'

'Lovely to meet you,' said Athelstan, almost bowing, and extending his right hand before promptly retracting it. 'Sorry, I forgot! Keep forgetting.' He slapped his wrist.

'Don't worry, me too,' said Manuella, performing a semi-circular wave as though cleaning a dirty window. She then trained her socially-distanced smile on his sister.

'And this is Loren,' Océane said. *'Elle a vraiment hâte que tu lui parles de cette soirée où tu avais rencontré son bonhomme là, machin chouette...'*

'Adam?'

'Oui, c'est ça: Adam.'

'Ravie de faire enfin votre connaissance,' said Loren.

'*Moi aussi. Depuis le temps qu'Océane me parle de vous. Loren par-ci, Loren par-là...*' She laughed. '*Vraiment top le maquillage! Comme Grace Kelly dans le film d'Hitchcock, n'est-ce-pas?*'

'*Exactement!*'

'*Bon, les enfants, vous pourriez peut-être commencer par vous tutoyer,*' Océane said. 'We need to switch to English anyway, otherwise Athelstan's going to feel excluded. *Il va se barber, le pauvre!*' she said, pretending to stroke a long phantom beard. 'Sit down, sit down...'

Loren and Athelstan took their places on the other side of the table, with their backs to the steady stream of holidaymakers looking for refreshment and sustenance in the old town. The street was quaint but so narrow that people kept brushing against them, causing Athelstan to scrape his chair forwards and look round in exasperation.

'It's funny,' Loren remarked, 'how we seem fated to lose our bearings around here despite always knowing more or less where we are – as if our sense of space were being ever so slightly recalibrated each time.'

'Yes, I know what you mean. The minotaur tries to wrong-foot us at every corner. He likes to keep us on our toes.' Océane reached for the bottle of white wine and poured out two generous glasses for the newcomers. 'Cheers!' she said and they all went clink. 'So, Manuella's real name is Emmanuelle – Emmanuelle Lavinasse – but all her friends call her Manuella.'

'Call me Manuella,' said Emmanuelle. 'Are you guys staying in Nice?'

'In Antibes,' Loren said. 'Our parents have a holiday home there. They bought it twenty years ago when Dad was building villas at Eden-Olympia – you know, the science and business park above Cannes. He's an architect.'

'You're so lucky! I love Antibes – and, like, you won't have far to go after the party tonight. By the way, did you guys hear about Firmin's wife?'

'No,' said Océane.

Loren shook her head.

Athelstan scraped his chair forwards.

'She, like, went for a fish pedicure *in Monaco yesterday? Eh bien, vous allez jamais le croire,*' she said, turning to Océane, 'someone had filled the tub with piranhas – it was, like, a bloodbath!'

'Like, literally,' Loren said under her breath.

'Oh my God! Is she all right?' Océane shrieked, covering her mouth with her hand in shock.

'Let's just say she won't be dancing tonight.'

'Actually, my sister Marine-Alizée has sent me a long text about the incident,' Océane said, squinting at her phone. 'Only just seen it. So, here we go... The culprit was a young woman. Not a member of staff. Never seen her before, blah, blah, blah. She shouted "Language is murder" before fleeing. Interesting... An accomplice was waiting in a getaway car outside. An old Simca 1000... Probable link to the Champs-Élysées murder – no shit, Sherlock!... That's about it.'

'Firmin was clearly the real target here,' Loren said after they had all ordered, her eyes lingering on the departing waitress's shapely buttocks. 'He must be busy tightening security on his yacht and hiding away his stash of sternutation porn.'

'What?' Manuella's curiosity was piqued if not aroused.

'Oops! Didn't you know? Firmin has a massive sneezing fetish. It's common knowledge in the publishing industry. The spasmodic eruptions of the female form hold no secrets for him. He can distinguish a Chinese sneeze from a Norwegian one with his eyes closed – a true connoisseur.'

'What do you mean, a sneezing fetish?'

'Well, he collects films and photos – even paintings – of attractive women in the process of sneezing. They're often naked, in sexy lingerie or a bikini, but sometimes fully clothed in everyday attire.'

'How bizarre!'

'I know! But strangely benign at the same time. Spray a plume of salivary droplets in his vicinity and Bob's your uncle. He's a man of simple, if esoteric, tastes is Firmin. Sure, it's a bit niche...'

'So, like, how does it work?'

'He uses all sorts of devices – sunlight, pepper, snuff; that kind of thing – to engineer a sneeze or, even better, a whole series of sneezes. The more the merrier, right? He also seeks out women who suffer from allergies but draws the line at colds or viruses because, let's face it, it's not a good look, is it? Especially in this day and age. The holy grail is a spontaneous sneeze, but that, of course, is a notoriously capricious and elusive phenomenon. As with so many fetishes, there's this impossible quest for authenticity at work – or at play.'

'Can he tell the difference between a spontaneous sneeze and, like, one that isn't?'

'Probably not but he knows, you know, and that makes all the difference. The power of faith and all that.' She paused, unsure whether to pursue. 'Between you and me,' she said, lowering her voice, 'I've modelled for him on a couple of occasions. Not for money, I hasten to add – just for fun. I've even featured in *Atishoo,* his invite-only quarterly newsletter. Tagline: "God bless girls who sneeze".'

Océane raised her eyebrows.

Athelstan coughed nervously, scraping his chair forwards.

Manuella looked bereft, like a child whose parents had forgotten to collect her at the end of the day. 'What does he, like, you know, *get out of it*?' she asked, peering through the railings of the school gates at two little boys tearing away in opposite directions.

'I think it's mainly the sudden loss of self-control that turns him on,' Loren explained.

'It's the same convulsive beauty André Breton writes about at the end of *Nadja,*' Océane remarked. '*La beauté sera convulsive ou ne sera pas,* remember? But it's also quite problematic: he collects all these powerful ladies – writers, artists, business leaders; even politicians, I'm told – and what excites him is their momentary loss of power.'

'Firmin's a naughty boy, that's for sure,' Loren said, wagging her forefinger. 'He'll get cancelled one of these days if he's not careful... We love the old scoundrel though, don't we?'

'Lepiador, j'adore!' said Océane, draining her glass. She gazed mournfully at the empty bottle.

At this very instant, Manuella sneezed thrice in quick succession, sending (*inter alia*) a ripple of incredulous laughter around the table. Making deft use of his napkin, Athelstan dabbed at the expiratory ejecta that had just landed on his elegantly dishevelled, but hitherto immaculate, white shirt. It was difficult to tell which of the two was most embarrassed: Manuella, who was feigning innocence, or Athelstan, who was trying to spare her blushes by being as discreet as possible?

'Great expectorations!' Océane quipped, before adding, 'Sorry, couldn't help it.'

'Moi non plus, figure-toi,' Manuella hissed in a bid to ward off any more teasing.

'What are the odds?' said Loren, still smiling but suddenly pensive. 'The Greeks believed a sneeze was a sign from the gods: I wonder what they're trying to tell us.'

They all observed the looming waitress juggling three plates with the recklessness of a seasoned tightrope walker.

'Manuella resided for several years in New York,' Océane explained, once they had rearranged the table to accommodate the food and ordered another bottle. This accounted not only for her fluency but also her vocally-fried accent, which she knew Loren would find particularly grating. It was one of those unspoken private jokes that cemented their friendship. Like many of her compatriots, Manuella affected the languorous delivery prevalent across the Atlantic these days – the croaky voice of late capitalism. This rootless *reductio ad absurdum* of

English was so easy to mimic that it had been adopted universally and now sounded for all the world like a foreign language, even when spoken by native US citizens. As such, it was the ultimate *lingua franca*. According to Loren's back-of-the-envelope theory, everybody was American today except the Americans: this was the price to pay for globalisation. Loren had many such theories. For instance, she harboured a sneaking suspicion that the French had never got over the Treaty of Paris and that the anti-Yankee sentiments they frequently professed, so performatively, were partly designed to conceal their *ressentiment*.

'Yes, I went there on vacation when I was, like, sixteen, in 1981, and stayed on illegally for, like, *years*,' Manuella said, as though speaking through some opiate-induced catatonia. 'I dated a young painter who was also in a band,' she continued. 'He was, like, a promising artist but he sucked at music, you know? Sucked at life too. It's kinda sad. We broke up after, like, a year and he jumped out the window. Smashed his stupid skull.'

'Talk about overkill,' said Loren, smiling coyly at the waitress, who had reappeared with Athelstan's plate and the new bottle. Her mind turned to Alfred Agostinelli, Proust's Icarus-like secretary, who drowned off the coast of Antibes in 1914, after falling from the plane he was piloting. She followed his iridescent descent across the azure sky of the Mediterranean. It's raining men – hallelujah! Loren then pictured the painter Nicolas de Staël in 1955, leaping from the terrace of his apartment on the city's old ramparts while someone else was eating or opening a window or just walking dully along. Those who live by the coast die by the coast, she mused.

'We'd, like, broken up a bunch of times before, so why did he, like, jump? For sure, he was, like, taking multiple drugs and I was, like, sleeping around with Richard Hell, etc. but, you know, we were, like, always taking drugs and sleeping around, etc.'

Loren was expecting her to say 'oftentimes' or 'anyways' any minute now. It was just a matter of... well... time.

Goddamn time.

'Anyways, oftentimes I wonder what would have happened if, you know, I hadn't, like, you know, *dumped him that day?*'

'He probably would have committed suicide at some point,' Océane opined cheerily, eager to avoid any unnecessary melodrama. Emoting, she firmly believed, belonged between the covers of hybrid works of creative non-fiction. The kind that deftly weave trauma-adjacent memoir with disquisitions on the likes of Louise Bourgeois, Virginia Woolf or Sylvia Townsend Warner. The kind, in fact, that she frequently commissioned these days. 'Your first novel was based on all this, wasn't it?'

'Yes. *Huit semences.* It's about him, Richard Hell and six other guys – *über*-decadent guys – I dated while living there.' She seemed to savour every single word like a fine wine, swishing it around *en bouche* before spitting. Loren's latest on-the-hoof thesis was that this quasi-autoerotic enjoyment of the signifier was inversely proportional to the triviality of the signified. Some of her theories were, admittedly, more convincing than others, but it was difficult to tell which.

'It's the portrait of a time and place as refracted through all these men who explored, with varying degrees of success, the then largely uncharted territory of her body,' Océane explained for Athelstan's benefit. 'The book is divided into eight chapters, each one devoted to a different lover. But they're all interrelated in various ways – the chapters. Some of the lovers too, actually.' As she spoke, she admired this force of nature – this hulking hipster Heathcliff – sitting diagonally across the table. They were like a couple of noughts or crosses awaiting the third iteration that would complete their row. Was a threesome in the offing, then? Was that the gods' message? She glanced discreetly at Manuella, sizing her up, but the very thought made her stomach churn. She then glanced at Loren, wondering if she might be game tonight, after a glass or two. *Ada* was one of her favourite novels, so it was not beyond the realm of possibility. Océane went through all the different permutations until she alighted upon the most acceptable scenario. *She* would do Loren while Athelstan watched, or pottered around in the background, then Athelstan would do her from behind while Loren watched. Loren would definitely watch. Waves of polymorphous passion pulsed through her body. *Oh Athelstan! Your rugged rock face could have been quarried by Emily Young and I, a mere Lilliputian in such a formidable presence, long to scale its sublime heights.* Drowning in desire, Océane felt oceanic. Tiny jolts made her jump imperceptibly. She was electrified.

She was bouncing up and down on a space hopper. She was sitting astride Athelstan's handsome visage wearing nothing but a pair of riding boots and it was impossible to say, with any degree of accuracy, where bush began and beard ended. *Oui, c'est ça, parle dans ta barbe; encore, oui, vas-y, vas-y, encore!* Now that she was grinding her crotch against his salient features, that his aquiline nose kept popping in and out of her prize orifices, Athelstan's discourse was largely inaudible and all the better for it, frankly. She wanted to move beyond surface meaning, to experience his words at a more physical – and yet more spiritual – level. That of muffled mumbles. Warm, moist exhalations. Visceral verbal vibrations. Epic poems licked onto her clitoris, one labial consonant at a time. 'Is this a fair description, Manuella?' she asked, breathless, a sheen of sweat illuminating her flushed features.

'Absolutely, one hundred percent. One of these guys was Teddy Huskinson, the English author and, like, playboy, who's coming to the party tonight. Teddy and Lepiador are, like, old buddies. They go way back.'

'Your Teddy may also have a sternutation fetish then,' Loren said, with a wink. 'We'll have to sound him out tonight when he's drunk. Personally, I tend to be wary of men who mainly write short stories,' Loren said, expounding another of her theories – she was on a roll. 'Men as opposed to women. You know, the adorers of Chekhov or Maupassant: they always seem to fall short somehow. A bit like Bob Dylan fans or Joyce scholars, or those tossers who take shelfies of their colour-coordinated book collections. You know the type.' She made a gagging sound. 'They'll boil the kettle but won't make the tea. I think it's because perfection seems within reach when you're writing a short story. Perfection within very formulaic parameters.'

She paused as a boisterous band of buccaneers – possibly on a stag do – stormed by amid a riot of eyepatches and plastic parrots. In between swigs of rum, they chanted scurrilous snatches of 'Good Ship Venus', filling in the blanks with some rather creative humming and arring. One of the swashbucklers waved in Loren's direction.

'Do you know him?' Océane enquired.

'No, I don't think so.'

'He certainly seemed to recognise you.'

'He was probably just flirting.'

'Maybe.' She looked sceptical.

Manuella then said something, but we shall never know what. Her words were drowned out by a swarm of shrieking she-pirates, belonging no doubt to the companion hen party. In their leggings and feathered tricorns, they resembled silhouettes cut from black card. One of the stragglers, whose haunted features conjured up Musidora, cupped her hand behind Loren's neck and kissed her before walking away in dreamy slow motion without ever looking back. They all stared at the beautiful conch shell the pirate had left on the table. Loren picked it up and put it to her ear. She could hear the sea in her ear. She closed her eyes and now she could see the sea too; how blue it was. Blue is darkness made visible.

'Was *that* just flirting?' Manuella asked.

'Anyway,' Océane resumed, 'what you were saying reminded me of Clarice Lispector, who, if I'm not mistaken, once expressed the ambition to write a book in which every sentence would be a climax.'

'That's the dream, of course,' Loren said. 'Multiple orgasms on an epic scale! I bet only a woman could write such a book.' She giggled. 'I was reading an interview with Joshua Cohen the other day – *Paris Review*, I think – where he wished every sentence could be as strong as the first one. Well, you can pretty much achieve that in a short story,' she continued, 'but in a novel you have to contend with reality. The vicissitudes of life. The lows as well as the highs. Tedium and mediocrity. Time and failure. Especially failure.'

'I expect this is also Wandle's point of view,' Océane said.

'Pretty much. Adam sees the history of literature as a gradual process of emancipation of the writer and privatisation of writing. The modern author is increasingly a free agent but this very freedom opens up a yawning gap between inspiration and execution. I'm paraphrasing on the fly here. So, in theory, a novel can be pretty much anything the novelist now wants it to be. Anything or everything, right? By this token, however, a book is necessarily a failed instantiation of the vision that gave rise to it in the first place. As James Baldwin put it, you never get the book you wanted; you settle for the book you get. But through this gap between the virtual book and the actual one, something *other* – some otherness – is secretly secreted. Something comes alive. The writing starts writhing on the page, transcending mere evocation. This, according to

Adam, is the rich seam that must be located and tapped into. You can't really control it, but you can try to conjure it up and then nudge it gently this way or that. Ideally, the author would disappear through this gap... In effect, that's what Adam's done, now I come to think of it.'

'Are your books successful, Manuella?' Athelstan blurted, 'I mean in commercial terms.' He had had quite enough of his sister's tedious lecture, thank you very much, and feared he was losing Océane's interest, which certainly had not gone unnoticed.

'She's huge,' Loren said, blushing a little as it dawned on her that this remark could be misconstrued as a reference to Manuella's embonpoint. 'Literature's a closed book to him,' she added hastily to deflect attention from her prior pronouncement.

'It's true,' Athelstan confirmed, holding his hands up. 'Until recently I thought a Thesaurus was a dinosaur!'

'I don't believe you,' said Manuella.

'No, really. I've found reading quite taxing since studying horticulture in Japan,' Athelstan explained. 'Our mum's a landscape gardener – she's big in plants – and I think she was hoping I'd follow in her footsteps, so she sent me over there. As you probably know, the space between trees is very important in Japan...'

'Didn't Rilke write somewhere that the space between trees is more sublime than the trees themselves?' asked Océane, showing off a bit now.

'Yes, something along those lines. Definitely rings a bell,' said Loren, a little put out. Her friend's verbatim quotation from *Nadja* still rankled.

'Well,' Athelstan continued, determined not to be blown off course, 'after a while, I began focusing on the space *between* words rather than on the words themselves. It's made reading very tricky indeed. Talking of reading...' He reached for his leather messenger bag from which he produced a chunky hardback. 'Here's the book you wanted,' he said, handing it to his sister, 'I got it at Gatwick.'

'Oh thanks! I just assumed you'd forgotten,' Loren said, placing it on the table.

Manuella looked intrigued.

'It's the new Will Self,' Loren explained.

'Oh, I met him once. He's very tall; like, you know, verrrry tall. As tall as Athelstan, I think. We were both talking at a literary festival in Lisbon. I've read one of his novels: *Requin*. *Shark* in English? Or was the original title, like, you know, totally different?'

'No, no – *Shark*, that's right. Did you like it?'

'I prefer Peter Benchley.'

'Will Self's fallen out of fashion back home. This one's of particular interest to me, though – been waiting for it for ages. It's called *The Haecceity of Sam Mills*: the protagonist – Sam Mills – is Adam's publisher and (I suspect) much more besides. It's based on her days as lead singer with the Velveteen Underground. They were the resident band at the infamous Mr Men Fetish Club in the mid-noughties.'

'Why infamous?' said Manuella.

'They were often depicted as a kind of cross between the Groucho Club and the Manson Family. Minus the killing sprees – as far as we know. There was that time

Lily Samson spanked a critic in public. On stage, over her knee, bare bottom! A fully-grown man! That was all over the tabloids, as you can imagine. She's known as the mistress of suburban noir now. A logical career move, I suppose.'

'I can't stand books about writers! They're so self-indulgent,' Océane scoffed.

'As opposed to all those autofictional memoirs you publish?' Loren snorted. She stuck her tongue out. Its very pinkness was a provocation. A poke at life. 'Your objection may have been valid in the past, when there were still proper – common – readers out there, but everybody's a bloody writer these days, including those who are yet to put pen to paper. They're all bookblogging, bookvlogging, BookTokking, Bookstagramming, Substacking, podcasting, organising Zoom literary salons, attending launches and festivals, enrolling for creative writing classes (preferably taught by people who have barely published anything), networking on social media (#writingcommunity) or telling the whole world that they're writing (#amwriting) while demonstrating that they're patently not. The rest of the time they're posting endless pictures of pointless piles of books – the new Towers of Babel – as if binge reading were something to be proud of. I mean, for fuck's sake!'

'Is this Sam a good publisher?' Manuella asked, sensing tempers flaring beneath the banter.

'You know *The Eejit,* Flann O'Brien's Hibernian reworking of *The Idiot*? She stumbled upon that manuscript on a trip to Ireland. Publishing it was quite a coup for a small press like hers. She's also a very successful author in her own right. *The Quiddity of Will Self*, her most famous novel, was described in the *Guardian* as a tale of "orgiastic obsession".'

'Wow!'

'Yes. And she's just published a collection – or is it a novel in parts? – called *Mrs Whippy and the Cat of Nine Tales.* Apparently, it revolves around a woman who chucks in her dead-end job flipping burgers at the local McGuffin's to become a professional dominatrix in a genteel English seaside resort, where she lives alone with her cat, Lyra. Can't wait to read it! I've heard that Lily Samson was the inspiration behind Mrs Whippy.'

'The one who...'

Océane looked up, startled, prompting Manuella to break off in mid-sentence, mouth agape. A waif-like woman of a certain age and uncertain character had stopped in front of their table. Too close for comfort. So close, in fact, that her sopping serpentine locks brushed against the back of Loren's chair. This feral figure with Greece in her hair resembled a corpse, covered in coral and barnacles, that had been dredged up from the deep. She was standing stock still, in high resolution, scrutinising the foursome from the eye of the storm, whilst tourists, all ablur, whizzed by behind her. The most unnerving feature was not the smell of putrefying flesh but the petrifying intensity of her gaze; its oracular, rather than ocular, inward turn. She was looking right through them, as if they were ghosts, at something beyond that was also somehow within herself. Something abyssal – abysmal – from deep, deep down where the hideous fishes hide.

No sooner had Athelstan resolved to shoo her away than the high priestess began humming, taking them by surprise again. She did so in a voice that was barely there at first, like silence rendered audible or Jane Birkin. All four instantly experienced a sharp pang of longing in their chests, as though they had been stabbed with a pirate's cutlass. Loren imagined the haunting melody, that tore at her heartstrings, emanating from the outer reaches of experience before emitting from this grotesque creature. She wondered if it was not itself a means of navigation, charting the distance to be travelled all the way back to our lost futures.

'L'île bleue, au creux de l'océan
L'île bleue, sous un soleil si grand
Perdue dans la mer
Comme un point, comme une larme
Bien loin de l'hiver et du temps...'

Although this was obviously a private recital, people stopped to listen, usually moving along as soon as they realised there was nothing to see here. For an instant, though, they mirrored the captive quartet being forcibly serenaded. Manuella was reminded of a shambolic concert she once attended, where the band played with their backs to the audience, not so much *à la* Miles Davies or in the spirit of a conductor, but out of sheer provocation. It had resulted, predictably enough, in a frightful fracas. The singer was wearing a tartan suit: she would never forget that detail. Océane, for her part, was attempting to conceal that she was weeping. As a rule, she frowned upon public displays of emotion and felt she was letting the side down.

Little did she know that there was not a dry eye around the table. Athelstan was sobbing uncontrollably.

'L'île bleue, tu la verras bientôt
L'île bleue, entre le ciel et l'eau
Plus loin que le monde
A l'abri des hommes
Tu la trouveras enfin devant toi...'

Still crooning, the crone began backing away, incrementally, until she was swallowed up by the crowd in a process of reverse parturition. The singer had now vanished into her song, whose lyrics and melody, increasingly faint, were returning to their point of origin. Athelstan was the first to notice the bottle an accomplice must have left, surreptitiously, on the edge of their table. It contained a message on a piece of paper, which he carefully unrolled and handed to his sister, who read it aloud.

'You can sing without words, but can you also write without them?'

'A riddle,' Océane said. 'That's weird. And in English too. Curiouser and curiouser. What does it say on the other side?'

'"*Levons l'encre!*" And look, underneath they've reproduced an old engraving of Captain Nemo aboard the *Nautilus*.'

They all scrutinised the captain peering, awe-struck yet defiant, at a giant squid through a large porthole.

Later, by magical candlelight, Manuella recounted how she had met Adam Wandle, back in 1980. The first time was at a band rehearsal. No words were exchanged on that occasion. Her best friend, who had a crush on the bass player, had asked her to come along for moral support. The members of the band were all pupils at the lycée Jacques Decour. They rehearsed during their lunch break in a small shop that sold musical instruments, nearby on rue Viollet-le-Duc. The owner, who had exceedingly long hair, wore round sunglasses with purple-tinted lenses and an abundance of shiny rings on his fingers. He let the kids use some of his cheaper second-hand guitars as well as the sole drum kit in his possession. Adam was initially the drummer, but had graduated to lead singer because he had a strong voice, wrote the lyrics in English, and was fully bilingual. He was shy, weird, skinny, and smoked compulsively. There was an aura about him, she said. An edge. Something out of the ordinary – almost otherworldly. Manuella walked past the shop on several occasions in the following weeks, hoping to see Adam again, but the whole band seemed to have disbanded or vanished into thin air. The second time was at a party, a few months later, towards the end of the summer term – she had no idea he would be there too. It was held in a grand bourgeois apartment on the second floor of a typical Haussmannian building. At daybreak, surrounded by dozens of other revellers, she fell asleep, and woke up, exalted, but also deeply melancholy. She instantly felt a strange nostalgia for the few hours which had preceded her slumber, as though she had mislaid an incipient something on the other side and could no longer find her way back to retrieve it. She had left something behind, she said.

There were tears in her eyes. It was impossible to tell whether they were tears of sorrow or joy.

Chapter Eight
HALF-HEARTED CONFESSIONS OF A GELIGNITE DOLLY-BIRD

Daintily, a faun-like figure stole across the cluttered room, pirouetting over the bottles and ashtrays that littered the splattered floorboards. She was the first to notice, having been awakened by a muffled squishy sound as of manifold foreskins peeled back in unison.

Manuella sat up and fumbled for her cigarettes, which she dimly recalled leaving beside a well-thumbed magazine. She pouted outrageously, mimicking Nina Hagen on the glossy cover, but feeling more like Mme Pompidou gone feral. Not that anyone could see her, of course; nor she anyone. Except when she sparked up, catching a glimpse of the other partygoers who had crashed on the rugs. The expensive Persian rugs with their expansive mindfuck designs: it was all coming back now.

Guy Debord in hot pursuit of a statuesque demi-mondaine modelling a lampshade hat. That fucking twat, with his sweater knotted around his neck, whose inanities were still audible above the U.K. Subs. Astrid surrounded by livid creatures of indeterminate gender lapping up the dark glamour of a voluptuous runaway terrorist. The lead singer with a pretentious Parisian band reclining on a Moroccan pouffe, drinking champagne from a shiny-shiny, shiny boot of leather. An amazon (with a blonde beehive and the blank expression of a blow-up doll) fellating an oversize banana in some dark (dank?) corner. Gilles Deleuze doing the twist to Martha and the Muffins: rather tentatively at first, then letting rip. Some obscure artist (with an impressive pompadour and an unresolved mother fixation) showing off his collection of individually-numbered potato prints. A boy who looked like a girl almost kissing a girl who looked like a boy before recoiling in sheer horror. Astrid astride an up-and-coming post-structuralist, who kept neighing and bucking bronco-fashion. Malcolm McLaren describing his new film project as Russ Meyer meets Blake Edwards. A statuesque demi-mondaine in hot pursuit of Guy Debord modelling a lampshade hat.

At some point, there had been a blackout. Matches were struck, candles were lit; she could remember that distinctly.

Probing eyes – disembodied, unblinking and bloodshot – trained on her, boring through. Bleeding gashes in the cloak of night.

Writhing couples – vertical, horizontal or higgledy-piggledy – their serpentine hips suddenly illuminated like quattrocento manuscripts. A torch flashed into the deepest recess.

Astrid, bent over a Formica table, Jackie O hairdo in disarray, retro ski pants concertinaed around her ankles, emitting unmistakably teutonic grunts while a rolly-polly pataphysician with a twirly moustache bobbed up and down behind her.

Wall-to-wall whizz kids, no worse looking than Johnny Thunders, every one a hip young gunslinger.

Marauding skinheads, among them Farid, the notorious leader of *la bande des Halles*, as skinny as he was unhinged. Sporting Onion Johnny berets, they outflanked the unsuspecting revellers – lithe, lank youths; all floppy fringes and flailing arms – making lightning incursions into their midst. Eyes were expertly blackened, heads duly butted and teeth promptly spat out amid a flurry of indiscriminate kicks, gratuitous punches, and failing arms – not waving but drowning.

Then the police arrived.

Then the police left with the skinheads, and dancing resumed.

Pointillist ponces in pointy shoes atomised under the strobe light, moonstomping to the B-52's like there was no tomorrow, although tomorrow was today. Today was tomorrow when Manuella's angelic features were bathed in gold, her halo melting like fondue cheese, and sparkling fruit carved in dewdrops dangled lasciviously from chandeliers like overripe testes.

How could she ever forget what it was like?

He had pounced out of nowhere and pinned her by the arms to the soft furnishings, his breath as fresh as a lungful of menthol, his greedy fingers foraging deep and she began biting his neck and scratching his back and making yummy noises and feeling guilty because she was rather enjoying this mock-ravishment, all things told, and the Buggles were on the stereo now, she could recall that distinctly, and she closed her eyes as video killed the radio star and mind and soul surrendered to body and the world melted all around like Dalí's watches on the poster above them.

'You can only take so much beauty,' Adam said, blowing a plume of smoke at the plaster putti on the ceiling cornice, where his sentence trailed off. Up close, he looked even more like Paul Simonon. Same fragile strength. Same studied abandon. A panther in a tonic suit. A pugilist cupid after a few rounds.

They slept in each other's arms, more soundly than they had ever slept since departing childhood and started kissing again, languorously, the instant they woke up, their eyelids still heavy, their movements leisurely like those of impassioned sloughs. Cheers from the living room greeted the opening bars of Lio's 'Le Banana Split' and Manuella – suddenly electrified; riding this collective surge of energy – straddled Adam, looked him in the eye (wondering what decorous cornice he had fallen from) and slapped him right across the face. Soundly. Resoundingly. *This,* she intimated, is what you get for even pretending to shag like a lord. Adam lifted his pretty head from the pillow, in shock, before cracking a boyish smile. Manuella smiled back, observing the rich blood trickle down from his nose over his lips and teeth and chin and onto his rumpled white shirt, whose buttons were undone (those that had not popped off). They embraced and kissed again, drenched in gore, like ghouls feeding off each other.

Later on that night, Manuella pictured Adam whizzing by at the speed of light on his shiny Lambretta, pork-pie hat cockily at half-cock, skinny tie lashing the air – high on hormones, bent on being. He was just wind in her hair now. A dot in the distance, merging with the background, at one with the cosmos. Pure life force. Just wind in her hair. She closed her eyes, but the world did not melt like it had the first time.

A man opened the door – *merde!* – and immediately closed it again. Around midnight, she would overhear him describing the scene in extravagant terms: '*J'ai ouvert la porte et Manuella se manuellisait*'. There were gasps and there were giggles. Little did they know, these people, that Manuella had triggered a chain reaction, but then neither did she. After closing the door, this person – who would remain a voice, twice heard but never identified – made haste to the lavatory, where he unburdened himself and delighted in the evocation of the vignette he had just happened upon. He applied himself most meticulously, painting a lavish tableau that was all lightness of touch – the kind that seems devoid of any gravity save for the odd tumbling cherub weighed down by its chubby backside or rosy cheeks. Manuella's foetal posture was a doddle: a doodle to be fleshed out with broad strokes, then filled in with layer upon layer of pigment. The grace and dexterity of her fingerwork put him in mind of a thereminist playing their instrument without any physical contact. Her hand seemed to hover, fluttering like a butterfly. Adonis Blue blue electric blue. Manuella's right arm reached right back behind her back all the way down to her behind and beyond so that she could tickle her fancy under her knickers that she had lowered just enough to allow entry. Drawing her drawers. Painting her panties. Panting. To be perfectly frank, he had not been expecting ultramarine undergarments, a colour traditionally associated with the Virgin's robes, and was shocked and aroused in equal measure. The black dress, hitched up above her waist, was easy enough to conjure, but those little red and yellow (or was it orange?) flowers – what were they exactly? He longed to name them with authority, as though for the second time, and this rather finicky attention to detail slowed down proceedings no end, as you can well imagine. The gradual realisation that what had been set in motion was a diminuendo led to a deeper sense of deflation, which he countered by going back to the beginning and replaying the whole scene several times in the hope of recapturing that initial intensity.

Opens door – *merde!* – closes door.

Painting. Panting.

Repeat...

Oh, but it was no use, though. All he could muster was a fading copy of a copy, whose original – itself already a copy – was locked away in the young woman's mind from which he was locked out. Painting the impossibility of painting.

'"Like" and "like" and "like" – but what is the thing that lies beneath the semblance of the thing?' Soon, Manuella would read the book in which this sentence features, and realise – upon reaching page 110 in her paperback edition (where it appeared right at the top) – that the book was reading her.

How could she ever forget what it was like? What it was like would never be forgotten, but what it was like was not what it was.

Yet her head still pounded to yesterday's pogobeat. An English voice said, *Nobody's ever been this young*, whereupon Astrid Strumpfhosen and her fawning retinue retired to a café-tabac across the road from Le Palace. In the metro, they mingled with the vanguard of the rush hour, disjointing time. Overground, daylight was already competing with sodium. Several other revellers had awoken to the dinky farting sound of the faun darting around. As their eyes adjusted to the semi-obscurity, it transpired that he had been dipped – stark naked save for a bow tie – in greasepaint. It also dawned on them that he was stealing everything his slender frame could carry. They all looked on, entranced, as though he were a cross between Arsène Lupin and Vaslav Nijinsky in his slivery silvery livery. A smattering of applause accompanied his final exit while tears rolled down Manuella's eyes. In that instant, she sensed she had lost something she had never found.

Chapter Nine
THE EMBRACE OF THE OCTOPUS

The lights burnt blue. It was now dead midnight. Partygoers were sipping their final cocktails on *terra firma* before the *Argo* set sail and the party really got going. The millinery on display was awe-inspiring; the skirts, long and lyrical. With a little wave, Manuella plunged into the bibulous throng, in search of Teddy Huskinson – he was bound to be in there somewhere. Océane began introducing Athelstan to all and sundry, as if displaying a hard-won trophy husband. Loren visualised her in vintage hunting attire, one foot resting triumphantly on her brother's recumbent figure. She made her way to the bridge deck, where a donnish fellow stood admiring a gaggle of callypigian naiads frolicking in the hot tub. He was puffing away on his pipe, transfixed: a glutton for glutes. Still no sign of Firmin Lepiador. Loren surveyed the beautiful people slowly coming on board, then ventured below deck, where she heard animated voices emanating from his suite.

The door was wide open, revealing a cacophony of rococo curios and exquisite exotica, as though washed ashore after a shipwreck. There were knackered old knick-knacks, books in piles on the floor propping up tables, but also priceless antiques uprooted from dark eras and savage circumstances. And Dalí's lobster telephone – the off-white version she once saw at the Minneapolis Institute of Arts. Loren perceived Lepiador's *Wunderkammer* as an annexe of the id. It was the site where the repressed – all the unsightly clutter modernism had brushed under the carpet – returned. If the yacht was a machine for lounging, streamlined like a shark, this space was more akin to a bloated walrus that had gorged on Victoriana and regurgitated the lot in some dark (dank?) corner. Each time, she had the same sensation – that of stepping into the realm of the unassimilable, the irreducible. The remainder that could never be remaindered.

'Ah, Loren! Come in, come in,' said Lepiador. 'These good people are trying to make sense of ... all this.' He gestured towards the posters plastered on every available surface. They had materialised in his absence, their provenance still shrouded in mystery. Seven distinguished artist guests – Suzanne Finissage, Julian Humbrol, Édouard Archinard, Monica Pittura, Joachim-Raphaël Boronali, Nat Tate, and Paolo Scarabocchio – were helping him decipher any potential coded messages.

'Now, this 1814 woodblock print,' said Scarabocchio, 'is a famous example of *shunga* erotica in the *ukiyo-e* mode that flourished in Japan between the 17th and 19th centuries...'

'Hokusai's *The Dream of the Fisherman's Wife,*' said Finissage, 'is an early instance of tentacle porn, which inspired the likes of Rodin and Picasso...'

'As well as countless manga artists,' said Archinard.

'It features in several episodes of *Mad Men,*' said Tate.

'Is it some kind of rape scene?'

'It was often interpreted as such by Westerners unable to read the lengthy Japanese text that surrounds the artwork,' said Pittura.

'Edmond de Goncourt, for instance,' said Humbrol.

'But things are a bit more complicated than that,' said Finissage. 'After all, it's a dream, a sexual fantasy.'

'A man's sexual fantasy attributed to a woman,' said Humbrol.

They all nodded in agreement.

'The woman depicted is believed to be a pearl diver,' said Tate.

'She reclines in the suckered arms of two cephalopods,' said Boronali.

'And is clearly in the throes of ecstasy,' said Scarabocchio.

'Not surprising,' said Finissage.

'The large octopus is performing cunnilingus,' said Pittura, 'while its smaller counterpart...'

'Its son,' said Finissage.

'Fondles the woman's left nipple,' said Boronali.

'And penetrates her mouth,' said Archinard.

'For good measure,' said Tate.

Loren was studying the posters, taking it all in. She recognised an illustration from a Jules Verne book depicting a giant squid menacing the *Nautilus* – possibly the same one as earlier.

'This ink wash piece,' said Boronali, pointing to an angry-looking octopus emerging from a Rorschach-type inkblot, 'was produced by Victor Hugo when he was in exile.'

'In Guernsey,' said Finissage.

'During this period,' said Humbrol, 'he relinquished writing in favour of political activism.'

'That's right,' said Tate, 'but he channelled his huge creative energies into hundreds of little artworks. He proved quite the dabbler.'

'He sometimes employed rather unusual materials like coffee grounds,' said Archinard.

'Indeed,' said Finissage, 'and he also adopted experimental techniques such as doodling with his nondominant hand.'

'I'm not sure about this text, though,' said Scarabocchio, scratching his big bald head. Clearly out of his depth, he turned to his colleagues, who looked equally perplexed.

Loren stepped forwards. 'I may be able to help here,' she said. 'It's a famous extract from *Mythologies* – a chapter devoted to the *Nautilus*. Roland Barthes argues that Captain Nemo's submarine (which he opposes to Rimbaud's Drunken Boat) is a symbol of bourgeois domesticity – of womb-like containment and contentment – rather than adventure. The antithesis of wanderlust, if you will. The solution, he argues, is to get rid of the captain so that the vessel is no longer Man's vassal but, as he puts it here, "a travelling eye, which comes close to the infinite"'.

'A "travelling eye" – love that!' said Finissage. 'Are you familiar with *Bergensbanen*, the Norwegian film that captures the entire train ride from Bergen to Oslo?'

Loren shook her head.

'It's more than seven hours long!' said Boronali.

'And made up of a single shot from a camera installed in the driver's cabin,' said Scarabocchio.

'A parallel can be drawn with Warhol's films, but the big difference, I think, is motion: the point of view seems to be that of the train itself,' said Tate.

'A subjectless gaze,' said Scarabocchio.

'"*Dieu sans les hommes*",' said Archinard.

'Balzac!' said Humbrol.

'Wasn't that Kunzru?' said Finissage.

'Where there is nothing, there is God,' said Tate.

'Yeats?' said Loren.

'Yay!' said Tate.

'Simone Weil longed to perceive the world with impersonal clarity,' said Humbrol.

'So that the beating of her heart would no longer "disturb the silence of heaven,"' said Finissage.

'Oh, for fuck's sake!' said Lepiador. 'Can we please focus on the matter in hand?'

'Yes, of course,' said Loren. 'Sorry, we got a bit carried away there.'

They all mumbled an apology.

'So, let me get this straight,' said Lepiador, 'feeding my wife's toes to peckish piranhas wasn't enough, now they want to get rid of me?'

'It's a distinct possibility, Firmin,' said Loren, kissing him on the cheek. 'After all, you are the captain.'

In the corridor, Loren knelt down to stroke Beppo, Lepiador's cat, who had miaowed enthusiastically upon seeing her. Further along, two people were locked in a furtive embrace, their silhouettes producing dramatic chiaroscuro effects. Angling for a tummy rub, Beppo rolled over on to his back, wantonly purring and stretching lasciviously. A light came on. Loren looked up again, recognising Lily Samson. As their eyes met, Lily spun her partner round so that it was now she whose back was against the wall. Loren let out a little gasp. It was Sam Mills.

Chapter Ten
I SAVE MY UPPER DECKS FOR YOU

A kiss of thanks and a flash of my breasts. A large black-and-white butterfly was bobbing about and I had to coax it to the window. A lot of lurching goes on. A threesome, where someone ends up dead. About to board. About to eat sea bass. About to leap onto a train at Blackfriars. Also sometimes when the cats miaowed there were subtitles! Am at gas mark 9 – overbaked. Am in the Costa where we brought the Christmas tree on our way home. An angry wasp is flying about. And you and I are still mysteries to each other, slowly revealing ourselves. Another chilly willy day here. Are there any days you can't do? Are these kisses helpful? Are you writing? If so, may the muses flow. As I walk, my heels make sounds like gunshots, such is my wrath. As you know, I much prefer autumn. At times I think of your bottom. Ate a delicious scone. It was one of the best I've ever had. Autumn trees stripping off.

Bathed in glorious light and filled with soup. Being in your epigraph is like doing a little dance at the start of your book. Bit bleary. Bits of Finn are based on you. Have you noticed? Finn being sexy, shy, charismatic. Blowing goodnight kisses. Blue skies here in superior England of pastures green. Booked my taxi for Monday. Bought a book! Bought a hat! Bought us a treat in Fortnum's. Btw I found the spider in my suitcase. It's living there now. Not even paying rent! Cheeky. But what time? Lacuna hasn't told me. But you can still give me a piggyback. Bye-bye rainy Paris. The clouds are weeping as much as me.

Can we drive to the Corniche for research? The fact that we can't drive would enhance the danger. Can you bring one of my converter plugs? Can't wait for Monday! 'China Girl' is playing. I associate all Bowie songs with you. Choosing a dress online for the launch. Could you translate this sentence into French? It's for my domestic thriller. Couldn't pronounce 'Dickensian' for some reason. Otherwise it was successful.

Daffodils ablaze across Sutton. Debating whether to go to Carluccio's or Tiempo. Definitely weaving *The Rite of Spring* into the book. Did I ever send you the peacock painting that I did some years ago? Did I lay the egg? Do my best writing in mornings now. It's the magical time. Do not make any remarks about the above mistake. I warn you. Do you like Swinburne? Do you pain in your cock still? Do you think it's good enough to go up? Dreamt I was carrying a bird that was half poodle. It had thin legs. It changed people's physiology – red dabs on eyelids and red straw tangled in their noses. Drinking a yuzu cocktail as it's so hot.

Earlier I was wearing a green roll neck, quite tight, and my breasts protruded provocatively. Eating a high-concept tiramisu. Eating pomegranate. Editing scenes set in Cannizaro Park. Egg protest. Empty islands. Enjoyable tosh. Exciting that we will be in Antibes this time tomorrow. Exploding unicorns carry a particularly heavy penalty.

Film so-so. Bit depressing. Finally booked a venue for the launch – what a palaver! Finally got a bus after a 90 minute wait. Finished copies of *The Watermark* are here! First day of detox. First they came for the apricot danish, then they came for the jasmine tea. Flew high and then ... I was naughty.

Getting amazing flow for second thriller! Finally coming together. Giggling. Glad my period is today. Glad you like the sketch so far. Going into Sutton. Going to buy some flowery things. Going to dive into my cheese sandwich. Going to wash my barnet. Goodie gumdrops! Got croissant in my hair. Grasshoppers on the line.

Had a bath this morning – your bad influence. Had a dream about you. All I can remember is telling myself to tell you. Had a powerful fly. Had nightmare that I was plugged into my laptop: definitely means I'm overworked! Halfway to Brixton the bus terminated. It was outrageous. Hate being housebound. Have just arrived at Heathrow Terminal 5. Have just realised the underlying plotline of my thriller is *Madame Bovary*. I haven't read *Madame Bovary*. Have landed in the UK. Time has been de-frogged. Have managed to cut 25 words from my book. A triumph.

I've cut 140 now. Thought the update would thrill you. Have sent final *Watermark* invites as my publicist was a bit anxious. Have typed up 2850 words today. Have you ever read *The Magic Mountain*? Have you scattered the ashes? Having a very good session with thriller. Having rosemary potatoes too. He is the opposite of his book, somehow. Heading for the South Bank. Heading north. Hedgehogs are horrifying. Here I am beneath a head of hair. Hired a sapling on Wimbledon Common to help with fact-checking. He is at my table with his own mocha. Dropping leaves. Hope you are celebrating the review of your book in the *TLS*. Hope you are not dreaming of unicorns. How red it was! How suave of you.

I also feel odd, finishing a book. Like destiny is being changed and I'm having a breakdown. I am curled around Lyra's purring furry fluffiness. I am ecstatic. I am half asleep or maybe three quarters. I am not a fox whisperer like you. I am on a double decker 164, which is a rare thing that brings good luck. It cancels out all single magpie sightings. I am still on the Zoom but I want to go and write. I am the Rothko vibrating on your wall. I am wallowing in bed, Vicomte, reading Cusk and examining my breasts with birdsong coming through the window. I associate grass verges in the sun with sex. I caressed myself this morning – I was thinking of being watched. I dreamt I could fly and I was with my mum, flying together. It was euphoric. I dreamt Lyra turned up. She had died, been buried, but dug her way out and come back home! I was so moved. Then she weed on the kitchen floor. I feel *The Watermark* has a strange magic. It doesn't care if I am tired. It's doing its own edits through me. There's magic swirling about. I feel truly alive when I'm writing – I'm an addict. I fell asleep in my evening meditation. It was very pleasant: a slanted drifting. I get the feeling there might be a subliminal message in your message. Or am I imagining? I had a blissful dream that I should write my Big War Book. I had a strange dream that our back garden had been commandeered by a neighbour wanting to push a wheelchair across it. They created a path, barriers, etc. I had a very intense dream about Lyra. I came home and she was on the stairs, safe and well. I stroked her. I had erotic dreams about wanting to photograph my breasts for you but I was stuck in a room of boring hotel guests. I felt very aroused in my sleep. I had my sundae and I got a shivery stomach and the giggles. I had strange dreams about a girl trying to attack me with a paperclip. Yet woke up feeling blissful, cleansed by nightmare. I had strange dreams about meeting ghosts. Ghost of a woman who lived on my road who died. She was mad. In the dream I gave her a hug and told her to learn TM! And another ghost was a Chinese woman. I had strange vivid dreams about missing a train and stroking an exotic bird. I had witnessing in sleep! I was awake and saw myself sleeping. I have asked my assistant to book you an appointment – a long slot. I have finished the thriller! It's 94585 words. I haven't slept properly in two months. It makes me want to curl up with you under a duvet and go into hibernation. I laughed out loud at last bit. I look surprised because the waitress came up just as I was taking it. I love you so very much. I miss being mad with you. I miss you very much. I ordered an aubergine schnitzel – big mistake. I planted the flowers but feel it's a waste of time when the slugs are on the prowl. I put eyeliner on every day. You don't always notice. I save my upper decks for you. I think I want the murder in part one to have a weird sexual undercurrent – an odd attraction between Emilia and the man she kills. I think there might be incest in this book too. I was with a strange group of people on an odd pilgrimage. I lost my luggage. I went for a Fiorentina of course. I didn't eat the egg. I glared at it. And complained to the manager. I will bend you over my strict attire. I wore my black sparkly top and long skirt with flowers. I would like to shower kisses across your cheek. Idea for a novel in five sections: in each the heroine's legs differ. In one her legs go swirly-whirly. In another her legs grow five feet. In another her feet fall off. Booker winner? In Benugos with a mocha. In my dream I had been renting a place in the North, as I used to. Only in this dream I'd been away a while and the landlady had moved someone into the spare room. There were amazing carpets. One was red with black swirls. Another green and swirly-whirly. In one I was flying. Another, I was giving job advice. In the toilet I accidentally weed on my ankle. Invoice info: bank details, SWIFT code, etc. A photo of your cock is also required. For identification purposes. Ironic emoji. Is a sock involved? Is the sleeping mask made of the finest silk spun by aristocratic spiders? It felt like a mouthful of whipped cream straight from the can. It has instilled an inner silence. It is a bit eerie leaving the mainland behind. It is a black jean skirt. Strict and dark and dangerous. And disapproving of misfires. It is easy to have cross-purposes on email. It is starting to thrill just as my Kindle is running out of battery! It is your duty to finish my fruit salads. It's a hairband with fetish issues. It takes discipline not to wake her with a kiss or a tummy tickle. It was very moving in a way I didn't expect.

Just bought a Lion Duo bar and you can't stop me. Just came up with big new plot plan for second half of thriller! Radical rewrite though. Just hoovered the bedroom: your carpet was drenched in champagne, sperm, caviar... You are a vicomte! Just jumping on a bus. Just near the bridge you think is Waterloo. Just shaved my legs and poked myself in the eye. Just signed 50 books at Goldsboro Books. Just thinking that I am excited to be engaged to you. Just thought up another amazing twist. Just woke up in the night thinking I was lying in bed next to you.

Keep being accosted by a beetle. Twice it has flown into my hair. Just before I got off the train it taunted me again by climbing into my book, but I got rid of it. Keep Wittgenstein! Not too much.

Last night's emoji was a ketteral. A ketteral is a fanged cock with wings. Leaking blood everywhere. Learnt a new word: fugacious. Using it in my essay. London looks even more beautiful now my perception has been heightened by this new technique. Looking up final bisexuality references. Lunching in Browns. Lyra just held my hand with her paw. As though she understands it's time to say goodbye. Lyra sat on the foam next to me, watching in amazement.

Making silly shapes with my mouth. Maybe because you associate air hockey tables with me bending over?

Meditating on the train. Meet at Les Vedettes? Miss you snoring very loudly next to me and feeling the walls tremble. Mocha madness! Must be the thoughts that blue tights inspire. My agent was lively. I spoke to various people who didn't seem particularly interested in talking to me. My American publisher has made a book trailer. My book is going out to 18 publishers! My books always consist of five parts. My breasts are being coy. They informed me they wish to be photographed tomorrow. They want to titillate you. Bit naughty of them. My breasts yearn for you. My carrot slice was inspired. My cooking is redemptive. My Dad was reading my memoir but fell asleep on first paragraph. The book tumbled to the floor. My doppelgänger's drinking a lychee juice and a cappuccino. My first draft of your portrait is attached – for comedy value. It's your eyes that elude me: I haven't yet pinned down some particular look in them. My hair is all squiddy. My hair is cut off in photo but it's actually down to my feet! My hair takes three hours to dry. My hair will see me through customs – it's very ebullient. My legs and arms will be crossed. My nail varnish is chipping away: less blue, like the tide is going out. My new boots are already falling apart. My perfume is a whisper on my skin. My phone's about to die. My publishers have sent flowers, which is nice. My quiche was stunning. My sandwich was boring. My scalp needs you. My tea has shades of strawberries. My toothbrush is sobbing. My tote bag was admired, so I said I had a wonderful lover who buys me totes. My train is delayed without rhyme or reason. Stuck in a waiting room in Wigan. My tree said hello.

Need to do my Day 8 test today. Nipples? No, I did mean Whitstable! Nothing beats your sexy Boots card. Now at Blackfriars, gazing at the water. Now in Foyles Charing Cross. Now on strict plaster regime – typing this with thumbs.

Odd feeling in house today as if my mum is close by. Oh dear, the number of women thinking they are in a relationship with you is quite high! It's the danger of online communication – it just becomes fictitious. Omelette off the menu. Making a crumble instead. On way we stopped at Asda and I saw a copy of my book. Only just coming up escalator at St Pancras. Opening chapters not pacy enough. Opening of *Chauvo-Feminism* was a mess, but after the retreat it all came together. Or a depraved swan. Otherwise I would have turned into ice and you would have had to collect me as a sculpture. Outrageous unicorn escalation!

Recall writing a bit of *Quiddity* on the way to have sex with someone dubious. I was full of fear. It was needed for the section. It helped it. He had a huge cock, which was uncomfortable. Red alert! This *scandaleux* has been spotted in the sea. Contact the authorities if you see him. Do not risk approaching him.

Scriabin good idea. Seem to be stuck in habit of heading for Piccadilly. She kept hovering about as though she might speak to me, but I moved away. She said that when I spoke about you, my face lit up. Six authors wrote under pen names. Mine is Chuck Valentine. Stupid name, forget why I chose it. Skimming sleep in a blissful way. Slept well, though I did wake around midnight thinking there was a witch in my room. Solved lots of plot issues. Some massive cunt reduced my rating yesterday. Sorbets are sobering. Sorry, I was in the bath! Soup was enigmatic. Starting on Basquiat research. What year did you meet him? Still a struggle to write about 'normal' couples but it's going quite well. Stuff like a character's knickers needing to be pulled down to make sense! Still waiting! Next one also late. Something about a cheese platter on the line. Suddenly remembered a dream from last night. I had a new pet, a small red creature, like a dinosaur. I was afraid of it but we bonded and I was able to stroke it. Swallowed some cat hair and now choking on it.

The bikini is halter neck with a tie at the top, so you will have to promise to behave. The book's pouring out of me in a deluge! The cheese is intense! Gnocchi is odd stuff. Like a plate of testicles. The film was appalling. The glow of shame. The hens said hello back. One wanted to date you but I said no. The husband in my domestic thriller drinks Yorkshire Gold, like you. There's a lot of emphasis on sympathetic characters in these kinds of books – fear the reader may lose sympathy as a result! The jerk chicken took ages. The leg situation is that I still have two. The parrot clung to my kirby grip, so I failed to notice it had come with me until it cawed. The pigeon flew across *la Manche* with a recording of your snoring and the squirrels are now listening to it, when they can keep still. The skirts are long and lyrical. The squirrels have decreed your snoring is marginally worse: you have 28 days to appeal this verdict. The threesome scene has been moved from a French chateau to Margate. The trouble I have, though, is that I am a mad writer. Trying to make it all convincing and sane is hard. The unicorn looked so odd – I did wonder. There is an awful woman on the bus constantly needling the driver. There is such a party atmosphere in London! It's the start of the roaring twenties. There's a squirrel in the garden. He says hello to you. There were four: I ate five. Think I have fixed my plot! This photo is all the evidence I need. Time to dive into the transcendent. Today feels too much like a Wednesday; it's an odd Tuesday. Today I included a grumpy trip to Sainsbury's. Such details help. Anchoring it before it all gets naughty. And wild. Today I learnt a delicious new word while researching Wilde/ Bowie: kaloprosopia, which means 'creating oneself as a beautiful character'. Today is a new moon btw. Today nature seems so serene. Lush greenery and calm sky. Tomorrow morning I have to travel into London early. I am learning an advanced meditation technique. There are four advanced techniques. Each is like a different drug and you don't know what it is till you get it. The last one did help *The Fragments of My Father*. It deepened my perception. Even my eyesight changed. Tomorrow we will meet. Tonight we fly. Trains are delayed, so just sitting in the station in the cooling breeze. Trains are in chaos: not sure I can get into Manchester. Typing with Book Antiqua 11.5.

Uncle Bulgaria had a frappé in Caffè Nero.

Very romantic of you. Vicomtes are vivifying.

Waited 45 minutes for a bus that never came. Was feeling weird before the film, like I was disintegrating. Was in such an exalted state when I went to bed! I could fix any problem in my book. Everything flowed. I was in that creative state where everything falls into place. Was on the top deck, missing you next to me. Was swiping through and we reached the one of you in your boxers and had to quickly hide it. Was thinking this morning of our trip to Tate Britain and we saw Turner and it was magical. And we ate outside in the cafe with rain droplets still on the table. Waterstones Piccadilly was virtually empty on the first floor except for another author photographing her book. Soon the only people in bookshops will be authors. We may create a bestiality side story for distraction about you and the Dodo having a hot affair. Then under the veil of it, we can be amorous in secret. Weird bounce as if Lyra had jumped onto the bed! Weird dream: you found a video on your phone of me masturbating. Well, here is a new draft of your portrait. I found it easier to draw your eyes when I realised you have similar eyes to Lucian Freud, who I've also been sketching (his ghost kindly sat for me). Well, I shall meditate now like a mountain sheep. What has Jonathan Coe got to do with my tea? What unicorn devilry is this? When I passed through St Pancras earlier, I remembered our trip to Oxford and how you would rip down my mask on the train to kiss me! Happy memories. When I was a child I liked making model villages out of cardboard and fine pieces of wood, e.g. for the detail on a Tudor cottage. I remember making a market stall, making all the little fruits and painting a glaze on them. Could make a sculpture of you with such materials but it would probably look too *Blue Peter*. When writing Emilia's section I became convinced I was going to be murdered.

Glad it's over. Who stole the hot water? Will you travel by horse and carriage? Woke up and read some more Cusk. Worn out from intense Dietrich research. Writing a blackmail chapter. Writing in Waterstones Piccadilly. Wrote on bus home!

You are not allowed to die. I'm glad we've established that. You have very good bone structure. You just need to learn your bridges. You looked ridiculously handsome on the call. You need to take some underwear photos of me. Your hard cock sounds hot. Your ring glitters on my finger. Your trousers don't need to be turned up; they need to be pulled down. Yours is the only toast I butter.

Chapter Eleven
VIV ALBERTINE DISPARUE

'Where's Viv? She seems to have vanished! Has anyone seen Viv? Viv Albertine? Anyone?'

Baek Jun-hwa, lead singer with the Ramens – a K-punk band from New Malden, heavily influenced by the Ramones – was panicking. The Ramens were scheduled to play a set, the highlight of which was to be a cover of the Slits' 'So Tough' with Viv as special guest on guitar. Viv, however, had not turned up for the sound check and they were on in half an hour. People were beginning to congregate in front of the small stage.

'Viv? I saw her snoozing in the main salon,' said a passing Arthur Cravan, 'I'll go wake her up.'

'Cheers mate!' He gave him the thumbs up and wiped his brow.

Baek had played in scores of bands over the years, mainly in the UK and US, but also in France, Belgium, Spain, and Germany, including A Cow Called Isis, Absynth, Alice Through the Testcard, Les Angles Morts,

The Anti Uglies, The Audible Gasps, Bad Fierce Rabbit, The Bad Pennies, The Baggy Monsters, The Beaver Shots, The Beer Goggles, The Belly of the Beast, Ben Ouais Quoi, The Birthday Suit, Bleurgh (a Blur cover band), The Blue-Arsed Flies, Les Bons Bougres, The Boojums, The Book Dummies, The Budgie Smugglers, The Buns of Steel, Busenaktion, Cahun-Caha, Canned Laughter, Cannot (a Can tribute band), Les Capotes Anglaises, The Cat's Mother, Cats Like Plain Crisps, The Charles Shaw Appreciation Society, Chaud Derrière, Chekhov's Gun, Chou Blanc, Close Third Person, Clotted Cream (a Cream tribute band), The Collywobbles, Comma Splice, Consensus Mou, Contraband, The Crannies, Cretan Hop, The Crib Sheets, The Criminally Overlooked, Les Croûtes, Damp Squib, The Dangling Participles, The Darling Little Spots, Das Nichts, The DBs, Dead Cock's Head, The Dead Silence, The Dirty Mac Brigade, The Don Drapers, Double Denim, Dross (a Bros tribute act), Dubito, The Dust Bunnies, The Dust Jackets, The Dusty Tomes, The Elephants in the Room, Les Éminences Grises, The Endpapers, The Erratum Slips, False Flag, Five to Midnight, The Flaming Nipples, The Flyleaves, The Fourth Wall, The French Flaps, Funny Peculiar, Furniture Music, The Gallic Shrugs, Gengivas Irritadas, Les Germanopratins, Gizmo (a Mogwai tribute band), Groom of the Stool, The Hairband, The Happy Endings, The Have-a-Go Heroes, He Do the Police in Different Voices, The Head Honchos, Heads Will Roll, The Hostages to Fortune, The Hot Potatoes, The Human Skittles, The Hurdy Gurdy Men, The Idle Hands, Les Illustres Inconnus, In Absentia, The Intractable, The

Invisible Bees, The Isms, The Jimmy Hendricks Experience, The Jolly Hockey Sticks, The Keelers, The Key Takeaways, Kif-Kif Bourricot, The Knowing Eyebrows, Kosy Krime, The Krayfish Twins, The Lame Ducks, The League of Liggers, The Little Englanders, The Living Brushes, The Lone Wolves, The Long Form, Lunar Sadness (formerly Lunar Camel), Les Machines Désirantes, The Magna Opera, Les Malandrins, The Metropolitan Elite, The Middle Distance, The Mixed Messages (formerly The Mixed Blessings), Mockney, The Modern Lovers of Debris, The Moths, The Mountweazels, La Musica Callada, Musical Differences, Les Musulmans Fumeux, My Giddy Aunt, No (a Yes cover band), Les Nombrilistes, The Nonplussed, The Nooks, No Shit Sherlock, The Noumena, The Old Duffers, Omnishambles, The Opening Gambits, The Orange Socks, The Overtones (an Undertones cover band), Les Paperolles, The Paper Tigers, Pat Butcher's Earrings, The Pedants, The Penceuls, The Penpushers, The Perfect Strangers, Le Petit Personnel, Les Petites Cochonneries, Les Petites Frappes, Les Petites Piques, Phwoar, Les Pipelettes, The Plus Ones, Point Barre, Poison Pen, Poxy Music (a Roxy Music tribute band), Quote Unquote, The Rabbit-Ducks, The Readymades, Recto Verso, The Retrograde Ejaculations, Revolver, The Rotating Power Tools, The Round Robins, The Safe Words, The Sawdust Caesars, The Scare Quotes, The Scarecrows, Scholarly Apparatus, Shadow Fruit, The Shakespearos, The Shallow Trolleys, The Sharp Elbows, The Shrinking Violets, The Sinkholes, The Sixes and Sevens, The Slush Pile, La Soledad Sonora, Some Minor Foxing, Squeaky Bum Time, The Sticky

Carpets, The Sticky Wickets, The Stopped Clocks, The Stragglers (a Stranglers covers act), Les Strapontins, The Sunny Uplands, The Supernumeraries, Taedium Vitae, Tarquin Superbus, The Tax Exiles, The TBR Pile (a Tom Robinson Band tribute act), Temper Temper, Les Tempes Grisonnantes, The Terrible Tusks, La Tête à Toto, The Things Themselves, The Thousand-Yard Stares, Tough Love, Tragic Pageant, Les Transfuges de Classe, Tutti Quanti, The Tweedy Top, The Twittens, The Ungodly Hours, The Unicorn Misfires, The University Twits, The Unknown, The Unmentionables, The Unreliable Narrators, The Unusual Suspects, Vehiculo Longo, The Velveteen Underground, The Verbal Asterisks, Via Negativa, The Vitrines, La Vizirette, Vulgum Pecus, The Wan Little Husks, The Wandering Wombs, The Weazel Words, The Whiteness of the Whale, The Whole Hog (formerly The Whole Shebang), Whoop Whoop, The Wimbledon Bardots, The Wordsmiths (a Smiths tribute act), Yves Klein Blue Monday, Les Zones Neutres, and now, of course, The Ramens.

Baek Jun-hwa was thrilled at the prospect of playing a gig on a yacht, not only because it was a novelty and the money was good, but also, more significantly, because it reminded him of the Sex Pistols' Silver Jubilee boat party. That ill-fated mini-odyssey had long fascinated him. He remembered reading about it at the time, in the *NME*, when he was only twelve years old. As for the enduring fascination it exerted, he had a theory. Bear with him one moment.

It went like this.

Stendhal's Fabrice del Dongo in *The Charterhouse of Parma* fails to understand he is actually taking part in the Battle of Waterloo. The battle, like the Faubourg Saint-Germain for Proust's narrator, always seems to be elsewhere. We are all Fabrice del Dongo, thinks Baek Jun-hwa. We are all in the thick of it and none of us can see the wood for the trees. The present for ever eludes us. Everything is in a state of flux; in the process of becoming or unbecoming, like Édouard Archinard's paintings. We are all lost at sea.

And there you have it.

The Silver Jubilee boat party, on 7th June 1977, was one of those rare occasions when you could accurately pinpoint where and when things were happening. They were happening *there*. There and then, on that drunken boat adrift upon the Thames. Baek knew, of course, that the moment had never truly coincided with itself, as evidenced by that oft-reproduced picture showing a very English queue of onlookers, who remained stranded on the Embankment, having literally missed the boat.

Recently, he had come across a photograph he had never seen before, which he found very moving. It gave him the feeling that the event was still pulsing, reverberating down the years, as if potentiality had not completely translated into actuality. He likened it to those live photos on iPhones that suddenly become animated when you touch and hold the screen. It was a little pocket of time past that had not passed.[5]

5 Adam Wandle once told him that discovering a 'new' single or album from his youth (he mentioned *One of Our Girls* by A. C. Marias) had the same rejuvenating effect.

Unlike most other pictures, this one was not taken on the *Queen Elizabeth*. Its purpose was obviously to show the doctored banner advertising the Pistols' new single ('God Save the Queen') in lieu of the monarch's jubilee. A cheeky act of *détournement* if not *lèse-majesté*. Six men – sombre-looking and ill at ease – can be seen huddled together at one end of the boat, smoking and drinking glasses of wine. They may be journalists or guests of Virgin Records. They are already too old and their hair is too long. They are on board but have missed the boat. Standing apart from them is a young punk, strikingly good-looking, with dyed jet black spiky hair. Elfin shades of Arthur Rimbaud. One hand buried nonchalantly in his pocket, the other nursing a can of lager, he comes across as the epitome of cool. He smiles straight at the camera, a smile of pure joy. It is the smile of one who knows he is in the right place at the right time: in the eye of the storm; at the still point of the turning world.

That day, the police had defeated the pirates. Tonight, the pirates would strike back. Baek could feel it. Something was brewing. Soon it would be now. Really now. The now of nows. He was biding his time.

'Where the fuck is Viv Albertine?'

Chapter Twelve
RISING INTO RUIN

There is, for every one of us, a void that can never be filled. Baek Jun-hwa learned this the hard way. I picture him as one of those cartoon characters who run off the edge of a cliff but only fall once they stop in their tracks and look down, having realised they're treading on thin air. They drop when the penny drops. I suspect Baek got ahead of himself in that split second when he decided to dive from the stage. Didn't think things through. Got a little carried away – or not, as it turned out. Had he forgotten that crowd surfing is predicated on the presence of a crowd? Otherwise, it's not so much surfing as crawling on the floor in a pool of your own blood. It was doubtless too late when he noticed that the spectators in front were a little thin on the ground. I'll grant him that. However, did it even occur to him that the rarefied members of his audience may not be attuned to the customs attendant on a concert of this kind? Not *au fait* with the rituals of the mosh pit. A bit – how can

I put it? – bookish. Besides, most of them looked too frail or too inebriated to withstand his not inconsiderable weight, even if they had been cognisant of entry-level stage-diving conventions. I don't know the guy from Adam Ant, but I bet he still sees himself as rake thin as he once was in the distant past despite incontrovertible evidence to the contrary. Evidence of porking out, so to speak. Sure, I'm just extrapolating – possibly embellishing a little, here and there, for comedic purposes – but it stands to reason, right? Ageing musicians like him have inflated egos to hide their expanding waistbands from themselves. They're almost as bad as writers, which is saying something, although what I cannot say.

In the event, Baek's rashness proved of little import, owing to a providential power cut. The lights died just as he dived into the audience – what there was of it. Consequently, nobody witnessed the prat's ill-judged leap in the dark. His epic pratfall. Apart from yours truly, that is.

I tend to go unnoticed at parties but I notice everything. *Ceci expliquant cela, sans doute.* On those rare occasions when my presence is acknowledged, people usually fuss over me for a minute or two before resuming their conversations. Being on the periphery, I'm always in the midst of things; snooping about incognito, mingling unobserved. A lithe black form in the corner of the eye is all they usually register, but I'm there, don't you worry, lapping it all up – omniscient.

Things had got off to an inauspicious start. The country was going to the dogs. Children no longer obeyed their parents, and everyone – *everyone* – was writing a book. Firmin spent an inordinate amount of time in his suite with a group of artist friends, which was rather unusual. He resurfaced looking worried, straining to conceal his concern under his habitual jocularity. The wind had been taken out of his sails. And then there were the piranhas – on everyone's lips, but spoken of in hushed tones behind Mme Lepiador's back, as she was pushed around the main salon in a wheelchair. The invalid hostess, whose exsanguinous features bespoke shell shock, served as a grim reminder to all present that the threat was growing closer. Naturally, speculation about the terrorists' identity, modus operandi, and latest outrages was rife. Were they, as some claimed, in the habit of gargling with their victims' blood before speaking at their secret meetings? Had Wandle been co-opted as a kind of guru – their slogans were, apparently, all culled from his obscure works – or was he actually their *éminence grise*? Was it true that he had been arrested at Le Hareng Rouge and pulled in for questioning? Why on earth did the Marquise de Perlimpinpin shoot her husband? Was she – with her twinsets and pearls – an unlikely member of the terrorist cell? Could anyone confirm that a critic had been electrocuted after describing a lacklustre novel as 'electrifying' in his latest review? And what of that other hapless hack, who had used the adjective 'lacerating' one too many times? Was he really subjected to death by a thousand paper cuts, and if so was it in homage to Georges Bataille or Taylor Swift?

News of Hattie Wyndham being turfed out of her own garden – expelled from Paradise, you might as well say – slowly filtered down to the guests, who exchanged grisly details gleaned from social media, like Panini stickers or Pokémon cards in the school playground. Apparently, an odoriferous white man with verdant green dreadlocks – claiming to be a latter-day Gerrard Winstanley, or even his reincarnation in some versions – had appeared at her front door very early one morning.[6] He announced that her garden (the subject of Hattie's latest opus) was being squatted in protest at the enclosure movement.

'Better late than never,' added the Green Man, as the members of his 'tribe' called him. 'All property is theft and you, Hattie, are a prime tea leaf.' He strongly advised her to join this unique experiment in anarcho-agrarianism before taking her round to see the encampment.

'Welcome to E-den,' the Green Man said. 'As you can see, your garden has now been reclaimed as common land. Soon, its boundaries will be the horizon.'

'Gosh!' said Hattie, surveying the tents and tepees pitched higgledy-piggledy all over her lovingly tended flower beds. 'Golly!' she added, thinking of all the energy she had expended; all that weeding, sowing, and pruning gone to seed. Some of the Donald Barthelme gnomes had already been damaged beyond repair.

'What were you expecting? Glamping? You've studied the history of radical gardens – now's the time to add

6 'Never trust a white man with dreadlocks,' said Blandine de Blancmange.

practice to theory.' He then went off on a tangent about sexual communism as a prelude to enticing her into his yurt – an offer which, strangely, she declined.[7]

At first, Hattie tried to ingratiate herself with the crusties by bringing them plenty of cups of tea and homemade biscuits. She attended their endless meetings, even taking part in all the votes, which was quite a commitment as they seemed to vote incessantly. She also used these occasions to advocate for the right to roam in the hope they would eventually take the hint and move on. 'The sedentary life is so bourgeois and sterile,' she assured them daily, 'you need pastures new, not this pasteurised existence; this stasis.' In the meantime, Hattie regaled the tribespeople with tales plucked from the garden's rich history.

'The mulberry tree,' she explained, full of wonder and pride, 'dates back to the reign of James I.'

One night, after ingesting too many magic mushrooms, a fire-eater inadvertently set the venerable tree alight. His fellow squatters began dancing around the flames, holding hands and singing, 'Here we go round the mulberry bush'. Hattie called the firefighters, but they were met with a barrage of compost and turnips from nearby allotments, as well as chants of 'I'm a fire starter, twisted fire starter'. Once the tree was burned to a cinder, the crusties torched the fire engine in a move one of them described as 'meta'.

'You must allow the tree to die,' the Green Man said, putting his arm around Hattie's shoulders. 'You've got to let it go. It's just part of the natural cycle of death and

7 'I can't believe he tried to pull that off,' his girlfriend later confided, laughing.

renewal.' He wiped a tear from her eye. 'Any chance of a biscuit?'

The next day, the tribespeople voted to bar Hattie and her husband from the garden, as they were now deemed 'a bit of a nuisance'. Following heated debates, a second ballot was held resulting in their wholesale expropriation, and the squatters promptly moved into their home. The last thing Hattie and her husband saw, as they were escorted out of their property, was an ominous slogan spray-painted across the front door: THE HACIENDA MUST BE RAISED TO THE GROUND. They walked away slowly, deliberating whether they had actually meant 'razed'.[8] Hattie was of the view that this was no spelling mistake: the author of the graffiti was clearly reaching for a notion akin to Robert Smithson's 'ruins in reverse' – buildings that 'rise into ruin' before actually being built.

'There are times when creation can only be achieved through pre-emptive destruction.'

'By Jove, I think you're right!' said her husband, full of admiration, and they went on, heads bowed in contemplation. The nearest hotel was quite some distance away, but they had all the time in the world now.

After the obligatory lamentations and crocodile tears, conversations turned to other topics. It was time for me to mingle.

8 This is reminiscent of Athelstan's reaction to the typo in Océane's text message at the end of the fourth chapter. Remember?

Chapter Thirteen
WHAT WE TALK ABOUT WHEN WE TALK ABOUT TALK

'I hate these parties.'

'Are you an author? Should I have heard of you?'

'Is that Giovanni Sfumato talking to Claire Iris?'

'Frankly, the best thing about her book is the erratum slip.'

'I know I hold a grudge against him, but can't remember why exactly.'

'Whenever a novel is described as "deeply humane", I reach for my gun.'

'Pastoral? I'm past everything, darling.'

'Mais enfin, vous nous racontez des salades, là, M. Mesclun!'

'It crept up on us and, before we knew it, it was Christmas every bloody day.'

'Is it kabuki or bukkake? I get confused.'

'Jean Baudrillard labours under the charming delusion that Jimi Hendrix is spelt Jimmy Hendricks.'

'Is it Nietzsche or nurture?'

'My methodology is simple. First, I copy someone else's book in longhand. Then, I copy what I've written down, but as my handwriting is illegible, I always end up with an entirely different text. A new one, written inadvertently.'

'Why do they produce so many misery memoirs?'

'I guess women are better at plumbing the depths and men are just better at plumbing.'

'Brett.'

'Sinclair or Anderson?'

'We must plan ahead going forward.'

'Our marketing strategy is robust.'

'It's not fit for purpose.'

'It is what it is.'

'But what is it?'

'I was the first book blogger, you know.'

'Did you see how Firmin's face lit up when she sneezed?'

'One lives in hope of finding an unexpected item in the bagging area.'

'A new agent wouldn't go amiss.'

'Manuella was saying earlier that she'd found something she'd never lost.'

'Well, I hope I never find what I'm looking for.'

'More diaristic diarrhoea, I suspect.'

'Anderson.'

'Lindsay or Sherwood?'

'*Une Chienne andalouse* is the sequel to *La France sans nuit*.'

'Who's that weird guy with the pipe?'

'Sometimes, the best way of saying something is not saying it.'

'Were those spots of blood on her riding breeches?'

'Longform journalism: two words that fill me with dread.'

'Where do you stand on creative non-fiction?'

'I hate these parties.'

'Are you an author? Should I know you?'

'Is that Francis Scopitone talking to Quentin Turpin-Goulet?'

'Ah! princesse, vous n'êtes pas Guermantes pour des prunes.'

'Oh, really, O'Reilly?'

'So annoying those people who say "brava" – we're not in Italy, people! Well, almost, but still.'

'Ah, Italy! Pizzas! Piazzas! Pizzazz!'

'It's always "bravo" in English, as in French. Why should congratulations be gendered all of a sudden?'

'It's total confusion on that front. I mean, isn't it sexist to call an actress an actor? As though her talent had to measure up to superior, supposedly objective, masculine standards in order to be taken seriously.'

'"Rest in power": another one that gets my goat.'

'Il a un nom de chèvre. Samuel Biquette, un truc comme ça.'

'Egon.'

'Schiele or Ronay?'

'"When you say my name," she said, "you retain nothing of me but my absence."'

'Not spots per se, perhaps, or even – upon closer inspection – spots at all, for that matter, which isn't to say, of course, that her breeches were ipso facto spotless. Far from it, in fact. Spot-free, yes, probably – *possibly* –

but not spotless, no, on account of those red flecks – or were they spots after all? – down the inside of her left thigh.'

'I hate these parties.'

'Are you an author? Should I have heard of you?'

'Is that Polly Semous talking to Anna Coluthon?'

'The whole point of his lengthy newsletters isn't to promote other writers, but to plug his own work right at the end, *l'air de rien,* as though it were merely an afterthought. The longer the newsletter, the more it's all about him, really. Deferred self-gratification. It's so transparent, it's hilarious!'

'Has Viv Albertine gone to bed?'

'Less snoozing, more schmoozing.'

'Doyle.'

'Rob?'

'No, Roddy.'

'Ha ha ha!'

'Funny how tattoos used to be the mark of the beast. Do you remember those skinheads, in the early eighties, who started getting their faces inked? It signalled they'd reached the point of no return – total alienation from society. Now, it's almost the opposite: you see people covered in tattoos, ten to one they're fucking accountants. It's become a sign of abject conformism.'

'I once tried to sniff glue with a UHU stick. I can smile about it now, but at the time it was terrible.'

'Is it a fox or a mole?'

'At some point Anne Carson and Lydia Davis must have merged. It's the only explanation.'

'I was the first book blogger, you know.'

'The English can't help turning everything into a pub quiz.'

'The only thing they believe in now is the NHS.'

'Is that Gary Oldman dancing to Gary Numan?'

'I only read books in translation.'

'J. K. Rowling and Sally Rooney share the same readers, who graduate quite naturally from *Harry Potter* to *Intermezzo*. Their books are marketed in the same way too, come to think of it.'

'Like many nefarious or absurd trends, this Christmas cult originated in the United States.'

'I hate these parties.'

'Are you an author? Should I know you?'

'Is that Félicien Marboeuf talking to Jacques Vaché?'

'There's no business like monkey business.'

'The Wombles have launched a campaign to get Wimbledon renamed Wombledon. They want to be recognised as a First Nations people.'

'Murdoch.'

'Rupert or Iris?'

'At what stage did she place her left foot on the milking stool? Was this before slipping on her rubber gloves?'

'"Nobody is present behind these words I speak."'

'Ben voyons, ils veulent noyer le poisson.'

'The weaker the story, the more convoluted it becomes. The plot thinnens.'

'Plots are for gardeners, anyway.'

'Oh, I really must tell you about László Krasznahorkai's pop-up mint garden before I forget.'

'Did you notice how Lily Samson and Sam Mills were holding hands?'

'Some blame those lazy fuckers who can't be bothered to take down their festive decorations, leaving them up all year round for all to see.'

'*Fly Fishing*: was that by J. R. Hartley or Richard Brautigan?'

'There's no such thing as a text. There are individual words and there are sentences. It's as simple as that.'

'Did she assume this position on practical or aesthetic grounds? Was it a bit of both? Did you read anything into it? If not, why not? Did you think, on reflection, that you should have done?'

'They fuck you up, your daughter and son. They may not mean to, but they do.'

'Gilbert.'

'And George or Sullivan?'

'I want my books to be read performatively.'

'And with these words she was gone! Would you believe it?'

'In Chiang Mai, you get more bang for your buck. In Bangkok, you get more cock for your bang. It's up to you.'

'Have you tasted the ham yet? It seems to have been curated rather than cured.'

'I was the first book blogger, you know.'

'Would you say that the adoption of this posture accounted (at least in part) for the presence of those flecks (or spots) down the inside of her left thigh? Was it, shall we say, a contributing factor?'

'C'est simple: si t'aimes un bouquin en France, il faut absolument écrire qu'il est subversif, jubilatoire et envoûtant. Point barre! Bien entendu, tu peux changer l'ordre, mais il faut toujours qu'il y ait ces trois trucs là. Tu vois, c'est vraiment pas sorcier.'

'Remember when queer meant taking it up the arse? Simpler times.'

'I hate these parties.'

'Are you a writer? Should I have heard of you?'

'Is that Tacita Rimini-Thompson talking to Félix Plotin?'

'If you spend your life thinking of death, you may spend your death thinking of life.'

'Lepiador? More snarky cunt than *Cutty Sark*, if you ask me.'

'When they publish my books over there, they change the spelling. When we publish theirs, we keep their spelling. I know it's mainly a financial issue, but this linguistic imperialism should be resisted at any cost. It's our soul we're losing.'

'Did you notice Lily's hand on Sam's arse? Or was it the other way round?'

'I knew immediately she was from a very privileged background when she said she was only interested in political art.'

'Others point to the growth of those TV channels that only broadcast festive movies. Imagine that: gorging on yuletide confections all year round! It's bound to rot your brain after a while. How could it not?'

'Green.'

'Henry?'

'No, with an E, I think.'

'Robert? Graham?'

'People who believe in evil are more likely to be evil.'

'That's Lacuna Wright over there – Sam Mills' personal assistant.'

'Was any cupping involved? Did your testes roll around in her hand like wine in a taster's palate? Was this before slipping on her rubber gloves?'

'A growing number of children refused to grow out of their belief in Santa Claus, then they grew up, and now you run the risk of being killed if you so much as cast doubt on his existence.'

'Awesome is the God who is not.'

'*The New York Times* described it as a parboiled thriller.'

'I think they're the very first bookshop not to sell any actual books – just totes and book-adjacent paraphernalia. It's a bold new concept. '

'Je suis émue.'

'Did she just say she was an emu?'

'Northern soul is the last refuge of the ageing punk.'

'It's always spelt "premiss" in the *TLS*. Always.'

'Dire? Geoff?'

'Tout le monde se plaint d'être "invisibilisé" de nos jours.'

'Alors qu'on devrait plutôt se plaindre du contraire, franchement.'

'In the future, everybody will be anonymous for fifteen minutes.'

'Did she apply a little pressure at any point, possibly towards the end? Did it remind you of the way she squeezes the bulb on her vintage atomiser? Did you reflect, however briefly, on the transformation of liquid into fine spray? Did you marvel, if only for a split second, at that small miracle? Did you picture her in a mist of musk and black silk stockings? Was this before slipping on her rubber gloves?'

'Swift.'

'Jonathan or Graham?'

'Taylor.'

'Their argument – and it's pretty watertight – is that you can't prove the existence of any other deity either.'

'Oh, it's on the tip of my tongue. Austrian dramatist. Name redolent of fried breaded meat.'

'Arthur Schnitzel?'

'I was the first book blogger, you know.'

'It's a discomfort read.'

'Apparently, there's another yacht heading towards us. It's all black and full of people dressed up as pirates.'

'I hate these parties.'

'Are you an author? Should I know you?'

'Is that Blandine de Blancmange talking to Theodore Stravinsky?'

'Those who are robbed of their childhood never grow up.'

'She always said her life was unforgettable, then she got dementia. The irony is heartrending.'

'What's your current word count?'

'You can overhear their music, they're so close now.'

'*You* know who she is: the author of *Sinéad Moonstomp*. Feel a bit sorry for her, to be honest. When you're Irish, everybody expects you to be the life and soul of the party. It's practically a patriotic duty.'

'She was born in Liechtenstein but self-identifies as Irish.'

'"Pirate Love". Who was that by again?'

'Anyone who uses the verb "to incentivise" is a cunt in my book. End of.'

'Johnny Thunders and the Heartbreakers.'

'Have you seen Raymonde Quenotte? She was here a minute ago.'

'Now it's "Jolly Roger".'

'Looks like Arthur Cravan is keen to impress Lily Samson.'

'Ah yes – Adam and the Ants. Let's take a shifty shufti at these pirates, shall we?'

'So, he was kidnapped by the terrorists and quizzed about his next book during the interrogation. They asked him all sorts of details. Really in-depth, granular stuff. They then said it was a shame he'd never get to write it, but that he should cheer up because ChatGPT had just done so on his behalf. Every cloud, etc. This guy comes in bearing a hefty manuscript. They let him read a few passages. He seemed both baffled and impressed. Then they shot him.'

'How do you know?'

'They posted it on TikTok. To add insult to injury, they mangled his name. He was mispronounced dead.'

'It's not publish-or-perish, it's publish-*and*-perish.'

'Ahoy!'

'I remember the braziers of brassieres with a certain fondness.'

'She published a book in which she argued that heteronormativity was a product of Western colonialism.

She soon started getting all these threats from various Jihadist groups.'

'What threats?'

'Well, you know – that they would flog her in public, push her off the roof of a building, stone her to death, burn her alive... The usual.'

'But what exactly do they object to?'

'They claim they've always been far more heteronormative than any decadent Western colonialist pussy.'

'He said he wanted to think outside the box, thereby demonstrating his incapacity to do so.'

'Nicole was sacked for selling drugs in school. She had dilated pupils.'

'He didn't have two penises to rub together at the time. Went to Paris to live a life of poetry.'

'They know "eponymous" is the correct word, but they write "titular" instead for fear of appearing elitist. How condescending can you get?'

'She meant *missile* not *missal,* although the two are often linked across the Pond.'

'Ahoy!'

'So he has a shoe fetish – well, so do all the women I know. They don't have a leg to stand on, if you ask me.'

'My take on identity politics is that it's the ultimate triumph of neoliberalism: freedom to choose taken to its logical conclusion. Everyone becomes their own little brand.'

'Did you witness the appearance of a pattern on her left thigh? Was it like a time-lapse of a newborn's features morphing, over the years, into a death mask? Was it at this juncture that you slipped on her rubber gloves?'

'Costello.'

'Elvis or Elizabeth?'

'My heart sinks whenever someone tells me they're starting a new Substack.'

'And what is your novel about?'

'It isn't *about* something; it is *that something itself*... Only kidding! It's about the daily life of a cleaning lady in the Champagne region, who spices up her mundane existence by taking on two lovers of either gender.'

'Sounds a bit binary if you don't mind me saying. What's the title?'

'It's called *Ménage à Troyes.*'

'I went to pieces.'

'Did you have nice weather?'

'Everything happens when nothing does.'

'Did you hurt yourself when you slipped on her rubber gloves?'

'I'm starting a new Substack.'

'I was the first book blogger, you know.'

'Ahoy!'

'I hate these pirates.'

'Are you an author? Should I know you?'

'This life writing trend is so morbid – more like death writing.'

'Is that Harold Brentwood talking to Chuck Valentine?'

'Verlaine.'

'Tom or Paul?'

'I sometimes think humanity is a vast wave, undulating.'

'None of us are getting out of here alive.'

'One way or another.'

'On est tous dans la même galère.'
'We're all in the same boat.'
'We're all at sea.'
'That ship has sailed.'
'Et vogue la galère!'

Chapter Fourteen
THE RAPTURE OF THE DEEP

Things were happening off-page.

I went out on to the swim platform, expecting to see the city lights shining in the dark like the eyes of innumerable cats, but the view was obscured by a big black yacht bobbing parallel to the *Argo,* almost flush with her. Lepiador's security agents followed me out, walkie-talkies all a-crackle. They observed the pirate-themed party through incongruous aviator sunglasses, awaiting orders. After a while, the bouncer *en chef* put his hand to his earpiece, flexing his bicep, listening in intently. In one fluid movement, he produced a handgun from the depths of his jacket, aimed it at the pirates, then slowly lifted his arm and fired a shot in the air, as though signalling the start of a race. Right on cue, the dark vessel retreated in the direction of the shore.

I went back in, but voices chanting 'Fifteen men on the dead man's chest – yo-ho-ho, and a bottle of rum!' could still be heard in the distance. It made my hair stand on end.

Girls wearing party dresses of gauze and silk glided like exotic flowers on a lake. Among them, dotted here and there, the odd pirate, who must have jumped on board unnoticed at some point. The *Argo* had been infiltrated.

A librarian-type was lurking at the far end of the main salon, smoking a pipe and sweating profusely. What was going on in that outsized scholarly head of his? Your guess is as good as mine. Here's mine. I fancy he was endeavouring to picture himself *à rebours*, as though he were another, but failing each time to make the imaginative leap. A blinding flash of bald patch – the kind he occasionally glimpsed on surveillance monitors – was all he could conjure up: Friedrich's Wanderer with rampant alopecia. He squinted at the floorboards, and slowly looked up as the world unfolded, leaving him behind. He was James Stewart in *Vertigo*; Roy Scheider in *Jaws*. He was the threshold he could never cross.

Now the librarian was surreptitiously staring at someone. I followed his eyeline, which led me straight to Ms Ipsum. Nothing exceptional about that: Loren always had plenty of admirers. What *was* surprising, however, is that the interest seemed to be mutual. I may have imagined this – so much was going on – but I had the distinct impression that furtive glances were being exchanged, as though in mute communication. With her golden eyeshadow, Loren appeared luminous, lit up from within. (Yes, I too was a smitten kitten!) When she noticed me observing her, she turned her back on the librarian and hailed a passing waiter. Like all the others, he was young and naked save for a bow tie.

'Where do you come from, sailor?'

'Derry, ma'am.'

She picked a cocktail from the tray balanced on the palm of his hand.

'Thank you.'

She smiled.

He lingered.

She smiled.

'Can I help you?'

'I've written a novel,' he whispered conspiratorially.

'Now you toddle along like a good little boy,' she said, patting his Derryère-Londonderryère. Her eyes lingered on his ebbing figure as it threaded its way through the clusters of champagne-flushed influencers and publishing tycoons. She swished her drink around in the glass, absentmindedly. The waiter seemed to sway to the cool clinking of the Zizek-shaped ice cubes. She swished some more.

Athelstan and Océane waved from across the room. Blandine touched her shoulder and smiled as she walked by, *en route* to Firmin. Arthur Cravan cracked a joke – a good one at that – and Lily laughed her head off. Archie West skulked in a corner hoping not to attract Cravan's attention. Manuella and Teddy were sprawled out on a sofa, which they shared with Lacuna, who, oblivious to all the snogging going on nearby, was busy fashioning a messy bun while perusing a little diary open on her lap. Loren swayed, ethereally, to one of her favourite pieces by Éliane Radigue, then[9] embarked upon a rather risqué slow

9 When 'Echo's Answer' by Broadcast came on (the *Maida Vale Sessions* version, 1996).

dance with Édouard Archinard during which she told him how much she had enjoyed his exhibition. He took this as licence to describe the different states of consciousness – all six of them – after which unconsciousness was the only state she truly aspired to. Loren excused herself when she began feeling the painter's erection against her thigh. The Ramens' gig was about to begin anyway.

While Baek Jun-hwa was out for the count, piercing screams came from the bridge deck. Thanks to my superior night vision and kinetic powers, I was the first to ascertain that the fracas originated from the hot tub, but what had happened therein only became clear once the lights came back on. Alice Lepiador and her bikini-clad besties[10] were jumping up and down around the Jacuzzi, covered in welts and toxic mucus. Visibly shaken, Mina Harpenden, the habitually indomitable editor, pointed at the jellyfish, suspended – eerily beautiful – in the water.

Stewards were still fishing out the gelatinous creatures when three things happened in quick succession: *jamais deux sans trois*, right? First, I caught sight of the unmistakable silhouette of Growltiger. Never a good omen, especially with tail on high. Then the black yacht returned with a vengeance, deliberately crashing into us. The *Argo* was soon overrun with hordes of rampaging pirates brandishing Jolly Rogers. Finally, a small explosive was detonated, blowing a hole in the hull and causing panic.

Stepping out of her shoes, Loren waded through the water in my direction, oblivious to the chaotic scenes going

10 Ninon Neenaw, Perrine Jouët, Philonie Demesdeux, Hernia Hamilton, and Ordalie de Nananaire.

on all around. A pink Sobranie (as yet unlit) dangling from her ruby lips, she picked me up – *Gurrhr!* – and petted me all the way to the galley, where she delicately deposited me on a marble worktop – *Mrkrgnao!* – before searching the numerous cupboards in pursuit of my high-end crunchies. Leaning against the wall, her left arm across her chest providing support for her right elbow, she watched me dining while leisurely smoking her pink cigarette, which (I now realised) matched her varnished toenails.

Chapter Fifteen
ENOUGH RIBENA TO INCARNADINE THE MULTITUDINOUS SEAS

Against the wine-dark sea, our flotilla of life rafts resembled a constellation fallen from heaven. Unless all our heads, spinning in unison, had contrived to turn the world upside down. I must confess that I too had imbibed too much, but there was no point in crying over spilt champagne. Talking of which, many guests had smuggled their drinks on board. Georges Davos even managed to spirit away a jeroboam of bubbly – you should have seen him, acting like the cat that got the cream. Boris Novichok was so royally – oligarchically – pissed, he was convinced he had seen a mermaid, the silly old soak!

People were raising their flutes of fizz and toasting the sinking *Argo*.[11] You could tell from the wistful look in their watery eyes that the yacht was not the only thing they were leaving behind, though. They were clinging on to something so elusive and evanescent – so intimate and trivial – as to

11 If I had a nickel for every reference to the *Titanic* that was made, I would be a very fat cat indeed.

be almost nothing. A secret message (unread) concealed in a crack in the wall on rue des Martyrs. Two sisters, possibly twins, waiting to be collected by their parents after a gig at the Electric Ballroom. A bike ride in the blazing August sun between two villages in Burgundy. Standing outside the gates of the Cité Internationale, watching a taxi disappear from view. A juicy-looking mouse hiding behind the dishwasher. Your son, aged five, running towards you as fast as he could, a smile of unadulterated joy on his face. Sobbing uncontrollably somewhere in the vicinity of St Mark's Place... All the images in their heads would vanish when they breathed their last. And so they held fast to the images in their spinning heads, as though sensing that suddenly, next summer, they would not be young any more. It was a sobering thought. We were beings in time, travelling inexorably towards the abode of the dead.[12] And then what? Where next, Columbus?

Everybody was texting everybody else to make sure they were safe. *We're in the raft behind yours. À plus. See you in a bit. À la guerre come à la guerre. Dunkirk spirit redux.* There was only one fairly large vessel – ours – and it was heaving. I dread to think what it was like on the other lifeboats. Anna Coluthon kept asking if all guests were accounted for. Some people shrugged, others groaned or exhaled impatiently; Victorine Gribiche gave her an anguished smile, which only made matters worse. Charon, who seemed to be in charge (although I noticed he was not wearing the regulation uniform of a *sapeur-pompier*) tried to reassure her. Someone muttered something about

12 Notice how I included myself there, despite still having eight lives to live.

the ecstasy of being in the world. It sounded like Karl Ove Knausgård, but when I looked round I saw a man with a straggly grey ponytail stretching theatrically, palms facing skywards, fingers intertwined. Monica Pittura and Julian Humbrol were conjuring up the ultimate Turner: a white incandescent surface, in their view. Evidently, Apolline de Ouf was tickled pink by some compliment N. E. Tchans had just paid her. Further along the chromatic spectrum, Hégésippe Turpin-Goulet (Quentin's elder brother) was busy turning puce as he harrumphed his way through a vein-popping diatribe against 'those fucking hermeneutic materialists'. Neither Perrine Jouët nor Ninon Neenaw knew what he was going on about. They looked up from their phones long enough to roll their eyes and sigh at the obsolescence of the elderly. He was beyond cancellation. Baz, one of The Ramens – commonly known as The Man with the Blue Guitar – serenaded Raymonde Quenotte. A few passengers joined in, singing snatches of the chorus. There was a ripple of excitement when news came in that the police had retrieved a pink scrunchie, which may, or may not, have belonged to the person who had planted the explosive device. Strangely, they had failed to locate the black superyacht. They could find the needle but not the haystack; the tree, not the forest. This realisation dampened spirits somewhat. Owing, I suspect, to a combination of booze and furball, Tacita Rimini-Thompson projectile vomited all over Francis Scopitone, who barely seemed to register. Up was simply the new down. The main thing was that the fun was not over. There was no escape route, and we were running out of places to hide, but the fun was not over. It would resume on some quay or beach – wherever we ended up. Who cared as long as we were reunited for all tomorrow's parties?

'Look at that ship of fools,' Charon said, referring to a dinghy slowly drifting away from all the other rafts.

'Navigation was always a difficult art,' said Teddy Huskinson, rubbing Manuella's back to warm her up.

The librarian leaned in towards Loren.

'Loose lips sink ships,' he whispered in her ear.

She remained inscrutable.

'What's its name?' he then enquired, pointing at me with his pipe.

'Beppo,' I said, but he could not speak cat.

'Beppo,' Loren confirmed in English.

I wondered if Ms Ipsum was taking such good care of me because she knew that my master had been kidnapped. Lepiador may already have walked the plank at this point. The next day his body, bloated like Robert Maxwell's, would be recovered, covered in black crabs.

Loren held me tight while she read an incoming email on her phone. It was from Adam Wandle.

Chapter Sixteen
VITA SUPERNOVA

Dear Loren,

Just a few thoughts following our last conversation...

Although nominally in December, the end of the year really occurs in early July, when schools break up for a two-month hiatus. By August, Paris looks eerily empty, in a way that London, for instance, rarely does. At times, it almost feels like the local population has been wiped out by a neutron bomb, leaving hordes of tourists roaming around a ghost town. Most of those who cannot afford to go away are relegated – out of sight, out of mind, and out of work – to the infamous *banlieues,* which, owing to some strange optical illusion, only become visible when they disappear in flames.

By the same token, it is September, and not January, which marks the true beginning of the year; a beginning that spells eternal recurrence rather than renaissance. *La rentrée* – the back-to-school season extended to the entire populace – never fails to remind me of Joey Kowalski, the narrator of Witold Gombrowicz's *Ferdydurke*, who, despite being thirty years old, is marched off to school as though caught playing truant. *La rentrée* is the bell that signals the end of playtime; the restoration that follows revolution. In an annual re-enactment of the *retour à la normale* after the carnival of May 1968, everybody returns to the old *train-train quotidien*: the daily grind of *métro, boulot, dodo* (commute, work, beddy-byes – an expression derived, as you may know, from a poem by Pierre Béarn). A vague sense that real life is elsewhere (as Rimbaud never quite put it) lingers awhile, before fading like suntans and memories of holiday romances.

What if we didn't go back?

What if we sailed off to the Blue Island instead?

Levons l'encre!

Adam

Chapter Seventeen
LE HARENG ROUGE

The elements were leading him a merry dance. The wind, in particular, was winding him up. He paused to remonstrate with his umbrella, which seemed to have developed a mind of its own since blowing inside out. Its erratic movements resembled those of a divination rod gone haywire. Buffeted on all sides, the man gripped the shaft with both hands, holding on for dear life. Oh, the gusto of those gusts! Loren pictured him soaring away like Mary Poppins – an unlikely prospect in view of his corpulence. Besides, the disjointed canopy lay presently in a puddle at his feet. The man gazed ruefully at the carnage of twisted ribs. Turning his chubby face skywards, he closed his eyes for a few seconds while the righteous rain streamed down his hirsute features. Ah, those rivers of rivulets! Whether he was communing with God, steeling himself for the next stage of his pilgrimage, or simply weathering the weather, Loren knew not. In fact, he was adrift on a vulva-shaped rowing boat in the middle of a fjord, sailing into darkness. The kind of absolute darkness where you can see the light, if only you look hard enough. And there it was, shimmering in the distance, and he was tingling all over and everything everywhere was growing luminous and numinous. He was alive. Right now, he was alive. Drenched – but alive. It was pouring and he was porous; part of everything. Never again would he take existence for granted. He resolved, there and then, to spurn the dead hand of stultifying routine and seek out the spiritual in the everyday. So he beat on, borne back ceaselessly onto the ground he had just covered, but eventually inching forwards through hard-won incremental triumphs. At a glacial pace, he thus contrived to travel the length of the bistro from whence Loren, transfixed, had observed the whole saga. This, she thought, is what happens when nothing happens. Nothing was happening before her very eyes.

No sooner was he out of sight than the man reappeared, making haste to the entrance with the wind now in his sails. 'A storm is blowing from Paradise,' he boomed jovially, closing the door behind him. No reaction. A lone voice in the wilderness. When he turned round he discovered, to his astonishment, that the establishment was almost empty despite the inclement climatic conditions and the full house in the hipster coffee shop next door. The sole customer, tapping away daintily at her MacBook Pro, was the epitome of effortless Gallic chic, which precluded her from being French, let alone Parisian. American, perhaps, or English, which would be even worse. Nation of philistines. The reviewers over there had never appreciated his plays. Did not understand them. He could not help noticing her long legs though. This too, he rationalised, fell within his purview. It was all part of his quest for the quotidian – his all-embracing remit. The rich tapestry of life. The wonderful everyday... Was that Stanley Cavell? Or Ikea? He could not remember. One of the two.

A lofty young fellow flitted in and out of the penumbra at the back. A waiter, no doubt – clearly intent on making him wait as long as possible. The man was having none of it, though. He slowly unwound his silk scarf – once an elaborate paisley affair; now a stringy, sodden mess – and started wringing the water out of it as if throttling a theatre critic. A vein throbbed in his temple; a puddle expanded at his feet. That would show him. Responding to this provocation, the aggrieved waiter loomed, cursing under his breath and wielding a large menu. He gestured towards a table, seemingly at random, before retreating into the shadows, leaving the menu behind like a ticking time bomb.

The man divested himself of his coat, which he hung on the back of the chair across the table, then sat down with the exalted mien of a holy fool. He suddenly got up again to examine the papers he had spotted on the bar – a copy of *L'Inhumanité* and the latest issue of *The End Times*, the international anglophone journal, whose headquarters, in Amsterdam, had been raided by the anti-terrorist squad. An old *Nice-Matin* too, which struck him as rather odd. He retreated to his seat, switching his attention to the large TV screen mounted on the brick wall.

A reporter, standing outside Shakespeare and Company, was piecing together the events which had led to the aborted abduction of a celebrated British author, now resident in the French capital. After attending a party thrown by Sylvia Whitman, she was approached by a man in a balaclava, who attempted to bundle her away in a car driven by an accomplice. The feisty novelist had managed to wrestle her assailant to the ground and taken flight, finding refuge among a cluster of distinguished guests including Marie Darrieussecq and Hari Kunzru. The story concluded with a close-up of the baseball cap the victim had been sporting – presumably in order to go about incognito – when she was accosted. Laying forlorn beside a Wallace fountain, it was cordoned off by red-and-white tape as though the true crime had consisted in donning the offending article in the first place. The reporter – now holding up an umbrella – stared at the camera with furrowed brow. She fumbled with her earpiece nervously, waiting for a signal. Back in the studio, the newsreader was enquiring if a connection could be made with the murders of Solange de la Turlute, Jonathan Titterington-Jones, the Marquis de Perlimpinpin, and Firmin Lepiador. The reporter, still visibly cue-less, remained silent, eyes narrowed in concentration, on the threshold of some revelation. The newsreader swivelled round in his chair and, with consummate professionalism, apologised for this technical glitch – *les aléas du direct* – before bringing us up to speed. The author's whereabouts were currently unknown, the baseball cap had gone missing; anyone who had seen a Simca 1000 in the Latin Quarter, on Thursday night, was invited to contact the police. Following a momentary pause during which he shuffled the papers on his desk, the newsreader segued into a related item concerning a spate of attacks on the publishing industry across the Channel. Shocking footage of a sensitivity reader, who had been tarred and feathered and then shackled to the railings on Mecklenburgh Square, was broadcast. The camera zoomed in on the sign hanging around his neck: 'Be kind' scrawled next to a smiley face.

Marimba. Less a ringtone than its Platonic ideal. The man picked up, cleared his throat, and started speaking in heavily-accented French. He was glad to be back in Paris. As always. What's not to like?... Okay then, sure: he agreed to join his interlocutor at Le Rostand later on. They could even go for a stroll in the Jardin du Luxembourg, weather permitting... Yes, just like Beckett... He was meeting her tomorrow at that little Japanese restaurant... Yes, on rue Monsieur-le-Prince... What wouldn't he do for the sake of sake, eh? Haha!... The critics, here, had really engaged with his new play... *À la recherche du pain perdu* in French... Very pleased with the translation, very pleased... That's right – Victorine Gribiche... *Le Monde* had described his work as a masterpiece, and who was he to argue, eh? Haha!... Yes... The guy said he had rarely seen so many spectators leave before the interval: it was *that* good! Put Edward Bond to shame. The final act, he wrote, was performed in front of a near-empty auditorium – an infallible barometer of a play's profundity in his eyes... People seldom gravitate towards gravitas, do they? Only the happy few, right?...

He had some reservations about one of the lead actors, though... Yes, that one! How did he guess? He laughed again, triggering a coughing fit, before resuming the conversation in a Scandinavian language. It was unclear whether he was still conversing with the same person.

Alexis Boyer, the winner of a cooking reality show, was being interviewed on television alongside the runner-up, Anaïs Chevalier. From her rearguard position, Loren contemplated the man's straggly grey ponytail with a mixture of pity and disgust. It put her in mind of roadkill. Now that his noisy phone call was over, she could get back to work, scouring Adam Wandle's collection of non-fiction in a bid to locate some quotations she wished to collate. They had all disappeared, though. Every single one. Could they have slipped out of the book? Might she have dreamt them up? Loren, it is true, had read the text so many times that the overly familiar words seemed to be printed in disappearing ink.

A deep intake of breath. Back to square one. The preface was called 'The Draft of the Medusa'...

Chapter Eighteen
THE DRAFT OF THE MEDUSA

This is not the book I wanted to write.

I thought I should warn you before you venture any further.

It is the least I can do.

As well as the most.

Dear Adam,

At long last, a contract! If all is in order, please sign the original and return it to me. The copy is for your files. You'll note that I've left several items blank: please estimate the final, printed length and fill that in; please fill in the date on which you plan to submit the final copy...

This letter (in front of me right now) is dated 14th September 1990. A few months prior, I had submitted a brief typescript to an American publisher of some repute – just on the off-chance. It was conceived on one of those early Macs, whose grey, Cold War aesthetic (ironic, given that the Eastern Bloc had just collapsed) was accentuated by my immoderate smoking. Yellowing around the edges, the computer sat squat on a desk lodged in a cosy alcove of our diminutive living room. I say *our* because I shared this bijou flat with V, my then girlfriend, whose penchant for al fresco frolics may have stemmed, in part, from claustrophobia. This desk was in fact nothing more than a table, and a very unremarkable one at that. I doubt whether it would ever have made it into Jill Krementz's celebrated compendium, published six years later, featuring stylish black-and-white portraits of prominent scribes at their escritoires.[13] Granted, my own lack of prominence would have been the main obstacle to inclusion, rather than the desk itself – however undistinguished it may have been.

Or would it?

After all, Stéphane Mallarmé believed that one 'can tell a great writer by the number of pages he does not publish' and I, who had published none, believed Stéphane Mallarmé. Ernest Hemingway – a very different kind of author, I'm sure you'll agree – argued, similarly, that the 'test of a book is how much good stuff you can throw away'. I inferred from this that a truly great book would be one in which there was *so much* 'good stuff' you could throw it *all* away. I soon came across Ulises Carrión's exhilarating observation that the 'most beautiful and perfect book in the world is a book with only blank pages, in the same way that the most complete language is that which lies beyond all that the words of a man can say'.[14] No matter that I did not recognise this

13 Jill Krementz, *The Writer's Desk*, Random House, 1996.
14 Ulises Carrión, *The New Art of Making Books*, 1975.

as something of a cliché or even fully appreciate what it meant; my mind was blown. I was in thrall to what Enrique Vila-Matas would call the 'literature of the No'.[15]

Writers who do not feel the need to publish in order to affirm or reaffirm their status *qua* writers. Writers for whom literature is the 'locus of a secret that should be preferred to the glory of making books'.[16] Writers who write in order to be able to stop writing. Writers whose decision to stop writing imparts 'an added power and authority to what was broken off; disavowal of the work becoming a new source of its validity, a certificate of unchallengeable seriousness'.[17] Writers who write in invisible ink. Writers of works whose potentiality never completely translates into actuality. Writers who seek out the untranslatable. Writers who think that words can do what they cannot say. Writers who believe in the existence of the books they have imagined but never composed. Writers whose books keep on writing themselves after completion. Writers who strive, quixotically, to bridge the gap between art and life. Writers who hold that every book should contain its counterbook. Writers who sense that every good novel is also an anti-novel. Writers who turn language against itself. Writers who can never finish their works. Writers who can never begin theirs. Writers who destroy their manuscripts and writers who are destroyed by them. Writers who take their time; writers who take their lives. Writers who may be as fictitious as the yarns they spin. Writers who vanish into their writing. Writers

---

15 Enrique Vila-Matas, *Bartleby & Co.*, 2000.
16 Maurice Blanchot, 'Joubert and Space', *The Book to Come*, 1959.
17 Susan Sontag, 'The Aesthetics of Silence', *Aspen* 5-6, 1967.

who vanish into thin air. Writers who haunted this book, which I wrote on the desk that was in fact a mere table. Plain. Bare, save for an overflowing ashtray and the Cold War Mac. A *tabula rasa.*

Once – in the small hours, just as I was about to nod off – I was visited by an epiphany. I know what you are thinking but, no, the word is not too strong. This was almost twenty years hence, in a different apartment. The living room overlooked the cemetery of Montmartre, which acted like a permanent *memento mori.* There are in fact two cemeteries in this area. The one that officially goes under the name of Cimetière de Montmartre is, naturally, the one that is not in Montmartre per se. This is doubtless designed to confuse tourists (just like boulevard Montmartre, which is even further away from its namesake). Jean-Martin Charcot, the Goncourt brothers, Francis Picabia, Jacques Rigaut, Stendhal as well as Émile Zola are all buried there, along with scores of others not mentioned – mainly through no fault of their own – in the book you are currently reading, which, lest we forget, is not the book I wanted to write. A recurring joke among residents (and there was a suspiciously high incidence of gallows humour) was that this was a street where one could rest in peace at night, the neighbours – across the road – being so frightfully quiet. Just as well as good ideas often come to me while I dip my toes in the shallows of slumber. On such occasions I am wont to rise promptly in order to scribble down whatever has occurred to me – be it a felicitous turn of phrase or a character's name – on the first scrap of paper that comes to hand. This time, however, I did not. The idea seemed so momentous that I was bound to remember it in the morning. It was a tale that was so simple, and yet so profound and all-encompassing, that it seemed almost inconceivable that no one had ever envisioned it before. I racked my brain – Dante? No; Shakespeare? No, etc. – drawing the implausible conclusion that no one, as far as I knew, ever had. I suddenly felt I had been singled out, in the grand tradition of Plato's Ion, to be the recipient of and conduit for this story of world-historical importance. My mind was still caressing its perfect contours when I woke up the next day. I recalled instantly how the story neatly encapsulated *everything* but could not for the life of me remember what it was. It had vanished like a dream vision rudely interrupted by some person on business from Porlock or Amazon. I sometimes wonder if other writers are visited nightly by this very same story only to forget it the following morning. Perhaps all of us are at some point. Perhaps the point of this story is to produce other stories, which we write while looking for the story we have forgotten. This may be the very source of all literature.

On the wall, above the table-cum-desk in our diminutive Parisian apartment, back in the early 1990s, I had blu-tacked a rather joyous picture of London ablaze during the Poll Tax riot. I would channel this incendiary image in the hope of writing my book into that state of incandescence, where it 'soars screaming like the phoenix, all its pages aflame'

(Bruno Schulz). In hindsight, I can see how more expedient, not to say expeditious, it would have been to print out all the pages I had typed up – the reams and reams of dreams –and burn the bloody lot in the fireplace.

A framed picture hung above the fireplace mantelpiece. It was a glorious sketch by the sculptor Antoine Bourdelle, ochre in hue and Greekish in inspiration. We were both very fond of it on account of its sensuous, sinuous lines and tantalising incompletion. Modernity, as George Steiner would point out, 'often prefers the sketch to the finished painting and prizes the draft, chaotic with corrections, to the published text'.[18] I was very modern in this regard: the more I proceeded towards the conclusion, the more it receded. The project soon took on a decidedly Shandyesque complexion. I even began referring to my work in regress as The Draft of the Medusa.

From my mother's in London, I had rung the editor, as requested in an earlier missive. The distance – especially in those days before email and smartphones – seemed to add gravitas to the occasion (as did the exorbitant cost of the call itself). I paced the dining room in an effort to calm down before plucking up the courage to dial the seemingly endless number, which I got wrong on first attempt. The editor was a kindly gentleman and scholar, with one of those improbable American names that conjures up wholesome frontier pursuits. To the accompaniment of intermittent static, I pictured him fighting off a big bear – bare-knuckle – against a wholly inappropriate background of cacti and tumbleweed. It turns out that my manuscript had really impressed him.

18 George Steiner, *Grammars of Creation*, 1991.

At first, he even tried to convince me to publish it in its present iteration, but relented as soon as he realised how unsatisfied I was with my work. He eventually granted me a one-year contract on the understanding that I would send in the revised version after six months, once I had effected a few cosmetic changes. Six months is plenty of time, he said, barely breaking sweat as he knocked the bear out cold.

Six years later – having repeatedly extended the deadline – I had to acknowledge that my book was not only unfinished, but probably unfinishable too. William H. Gass contends that Robert Musil polished *The Man Without Qualities* 'not to achieve a finish or a shine, but (like every perfectionist) to accomplish the inconclusive' and the same could be said of me back then.[19] What had been a blessing became a curse – a source of panic attacks and social anxiety. I stopped answering the publisher's letters. I shunned friends, who would inevitably ask me how the book was going, when it was going nowhere at a glacial pace. Even now I am exhausted at the mere thought of the smoke-filled days and nights I devoted to this book that never was. Ostensibly, it dealt with the life and work of a middling English novelist and playwright (dead), but in reality it was about many other things besides. So many other things. Always more things. I wanted my book to contain not only multitudes but *everything*. What I had in mind was more akin to Borges's 'total book' – that 'catalog of catalogs' rumoured to be lurking on some dusty shelf in the Library of Babel – or the volume, evoked by

19 William H. Gass, 'The Hovering Life', *The New York Review of Books*, 11 January 1996.

Wittgenstein, that would 'destroy all the other books in the world' (if it existed) rather than an academic monograph. *...please fill in the date on which you plan to submit the final copy...*

Can you wait until hell freezes over?

'If you meet your double, you should kill him.' This very useful piece of advice comes from Johan Grimonprez's film *Double Take* (2009), written by Tom McCarthy and based on a short story by Jorge Luis Borges. I once met my double but I am glad I did not kill him, nor him me. I was writing my doomed opus at my mother's in South London during the summer holidays and had decided to go for a walk and a smoke in the local park round the corner. In those days, the path leading into the park was bisected by railings. If you wanted to go to the pond, you took the right-hand side and if you wanted to go to the playground or the cricket pavilion you took the left-hand side. My doppelgänger (the word means double walker in German) was coming towards me on the other side of the railings. He was on the right-hand side, which of course was left to him: I was coming; he was going. We walked past each other, then stopped in our tracks and turned round at the same time. We faced each other – I myself and he himself – in shocked silence for a few seconds before turning round again and walking on. I have never seen him since that day. If I did, I would ask him what it is like being me and if, by any chance, he had written the book I wanted to write all those years ago. The phantom book that haunts the following pages.

Chapter Nineteen
A MESSAGE FROM THE RUNOUT GROOVE

The man with the ponytail opened the large menu in front of him, absent-mindedly. He was thinking of a desert island; of coral, treasure, and footprints in the sand. Suddenly, it dawned on him that this so-called menu was not fit for purpose. It was worthless; indeed, it was wordless save for the name of the café – LE HARENG ROUGE – in all-caps Helvetica Neue, and what use was that? The contrast between size and lack of content was most disquieting. There was nothing, and far too much of it. Leafing through the barren pages felt like drowning in blank space. He was being emptied out; eviscerated. He needed food. Fast. Fast food. An omelette, a *croque*, anything – he was wasting away. So he dived under the table to make sure he had not dropped a loose sheet containing vital culinary information, but only found a few stray quotations from some non-fiction book. He looked up in dismay just as the prodigal waiter emerged, carrying a bucket and mop, *en route*, no doubt, to the piddling puddle he had produced at the entrance. The man held his arm aloft in such an emphatic way that the waiter could not have failed to notice as he flounced by, impervious. You almost expected a taxi to pull up outside. The waiter then proceeded to prove he was a past master at passing the man's table while avoiding eye contact and ignoring his pleas, please, please... He did so repeatedly and on the flimsiest of excuses – a stray glass here, a strewn napkin there – sometimes brazenly brushing against his table or running his fingers along its brass edge as he went about his urgent business. He finally consented to stop when the man stood up, ready to collar him. Before the latter had had time to raise the issue of the menu, the waiter enquired if *Monsieur* had made his choice, immediately vanishing again in order 'to give *Monsieur* a few more minutes'. He was struggling to keep a straight face. The man sat down with a sigh, conceding defeat. Shortly thereafter, he got up, collected his coat, and shuffled to the exit. Paris had already knocked the stuffing out of him. Loren felt a little sorry for the poor playwright despite that wretched ponytail.

Two old-timers – dressed like the Corsican mafiosi who once lorded it over the local demi-monde – hovered outside. They signalled to the waiter that they wished to sit on the terrace now that the sun was shining. He rushed out to wipe down the seats and tables with a grey cloth, soon returning with two espressos and two small glasses of tap water. The men, already deep in conversation, dismissed him with a cursory nod of the head.

Loren recognised these habitués. Their presence provided a smokescreen for some of the more subversive meetings held at Le Hareng Rouge. Bola Bola, the flamboyant landlady, had once told her as much while under the influence. These former mobsters were now retired – *rangés des voitures*, she had said – but kept all sorts of useful connections with the police. No longer untouchable, they were still shrouded in a cloak of semi-invisibility that extended to the entire bistro whenever they patronised it. The cops seemed to turn a blind eye to whatever went on inside, so long as these old dudes were sitting outside, shooting the breeze instead of gang rivals. They acted like a force field, which is why – she concluded with a theatrical wink – they were always plied with free drinks. At this juncture someone put 'C'est la ouate' on the vintage Wurlitzer jukebox. It must have been Djamel, the waiter, or Michel, the landlady's husband, as no one else was there. Bola Bola got up and got down, down and dirty on the improvised dance floor, then spun round with the unexpected grace of a Disney hippotamus, right on cue as Caroline Loeb sang *'elle balance son cul avec indolence'*, waggling her behind in front of Loren like a swaying galleon. No sooner was the dancing over than Michel emerged from behind the bar to top up their drinks and join them for a chat. The two women were already three sheets to the wind: he had some serious catching up to do.

With a haunted look on her face, Loren began recounting a dream she had had the night before, unless (as she pointed out, immediately qualifying her statement) it was the dream that had had her. She added that she had been feeling eerily oneiric – insubstantial, ethereal – ever since, as though not fully awake. Would she ever feel fully awake again? Her head was spinning from all the wine.

In the dream, Loren comes upon a forest with a notice at its entrance saying OURS. This message strikes her as so generous, so deeply humane, that it brings tears to her eyes. She ventures forth amid the lush foliage, her faith in mankind fully restored. She skips coltishly, her heart at one with nature; her head buzzing with all manner of arborescent and rhizomatic schemes. A grizzly bear appears out of nowhere. She recognises it from Adam Wandle's preface. She runs for her life. It dawns on her that the notice was in fact a warning written in French. She looks round and discovers, with relief, that the bear – *l'ours* – now on its hind legs, is stuck behind a screen and can proceed no further. As the screen fades to black, the word FIN appears. She expects the dream, along with the film, to draw to a close, but a fin suddenly punctures the screen as a great white shark breaks surface. The celluloid then starts consuming itself under the heat of the projector. It bubbles and crackles, curling upwards until there is nothing left but blinding light.

'That's it – that's my dream.'

'I pity your psychoanalyst!' Bola Bola laughed.

'So do I. Anyway, enough of me. Where did you two meet?'

'At Chez Moune, you know, rue Pigalle, when it was still a proper dyke club,' said Michel, pouring himself another glass of alligoté. 'I was called Michèle in those days and Bola Bola went under the name of Bolo Bolo. He was a successful *transformiste,* who performed in some of Montmartre's finest cabarets. I couldn't keep my eyes off him: he was the most beautiful woman I'd ever seen. Of course, I had no idea he was a drag artist. His stage name was Sarrasine, a dead giveaway, but I didn't get the reference back then. So I bought her – him – a drink and we immediately hit it off. A few months later we were married. Then we both transitioned. My husband became my wife...'.

'And my wife became my husband,' said Bola Bola, beaming. 'We bought this café and lived happily ever after.'

A man breezed in. He was inordinately tall – even taller than Athelstan or Will Self. A humungous human. He was also unfeasibly floppy-haired, like a foppish young Wyndham Lewis on a flying visit to Brideshead Castle. Loren was immediately struck by the contrast between his delicate, almost effeminate features – he may have been wearing make-up – and his hands. Big lumberjack hands that could be balled into mighty fists. Presumably.

'Have you met Arthur, the pugilist poet?' Michel said. 'Or is it the other way round?'

'For me, writing is boxing by another means.' He bowed in Loren's direction. 'And vice-versa.' There was a mischievous glint in his eye.

'I spotted you in Antibes over the summer. Le Blue Lady pub? I also remember you from the party on the yacht – the night Firmin was murdered. You were talking to Lily Samson.'

'Ah, Lily!' he sighed lasciviously. 'Lily, Lily, Lily...'

'I kept wondering who this handsome giant was.'

'Let me introduce myself: Arthur Cravan, *pour vous servir.*' He gently kissed her hand. 'My reputation usually precedes me. I'm a shameless self-publicist with no self to publicise.'

'What do you mean?'

'Let's just say that my negative capability borders on personality disorder.' He flashed her a carnivorous smile. 'I'm afflicted with a fatal plurality.'

'Arthur is just too bad to be true,' Bola Bola interjected. 'Last time he gave a talk here, he wore nothing but a butcher's apron and concluded proceedings by mooning the audience.'

'Can't believe I missed that,' Loren blurted, a trifle too enthusiastically. She did not want to appear too keen.

'It's largely Arthur's fake-painting trafficking that bankrolls our struggle,' Michel explained.

'Your struggle?'

'Better not ask too many questions,' Arthur snapped. 'Sometimes ignorance is bliss. Loose lips sink ships.'

'It's okay,' Bola Bola interceded, eager to defuse the sudden tension. 'She's writing a book on Adam.'

'So you're one of us then!' Arthur said, visibly relieved. 'I could tell you a thing or two about Adam. Lord Biro! We go way back, way back.' He was flirting again but an aura of danger still hung in the air. It was a potent combination. 'First things first, though – the books.'

'Come,' Bola Bola said, 'I'll show you something.'

She led the way into a small backroom lined from floor to ceiling with overflowing bookshelves. Arthur followed, folding himself in half as he stepped through the alcove. Loren observed him, mesmerised. He appeared larger than life: a colossus in a petty, petty world.

As Michel sifted through the volumes Arthur had brought in two suitcases, Bola Bola explained that they collected banned books as an act of resistance. 'Everything you see here,' she said with a sweeping gesture, 'is currently banned somewhere in the world.'

'We also keep unexpurgated editions of titles that have been bowdlerised to reflect society's current values,' Arthur said. 'This is of the utmost importance, not only for artistic reasons – literature being beyond good and evil – but also because we cannot allow the past to be rewritten. That should be the preserve of Stalinists and Holocaust deniers.'

'The trustafarians who campaign to erase all racial slurs from old books are frequently the descendants of the slave owners whose statues they topple,' Bola Bola continued. 'Sooner or later, these people will revert to type, they always do, and when they do – when they can no longer tell their keffiyeh from their djembe – they'll be able to deny the very existence of the oppression their privilege stems from. The posh cunts are just covering their tracks, basically.'

'In my experience these young militants are very idealistic and genuine, however privileged they may be,' Loren objected.

'The impotence of being earnest,' Arthur joked. 'Most of them are, you're quite right, but they're led by an invisible hand to promote an end which wasn't part of their original intention.' He paused before adding, 'And that end justifies our means'.

Michel played some more records on the jukebox, mainly French singles from the eighties that Loren was unfamiliar with. She knew this was not Adam's style of music, that he probably loathed most of these songs, but she enjoyed thinking he would have heard them in the background, while eating his breakfast croissant in a café or browsing the shelves down the supermarket. There are two soundtracks to our lives: the personal one we lovingly curate and the collective one that is like the air we breathe. She felt she was breathing in the same air as young Adam, blowing in from a time long before she was even born.

Bola Bola started dancing again, a glass of Aperol spritz glowing neon orange in her hand – the landlady turned alchemist. Arthur sang *'Le monde est bleu comme toi'* along with Étienne Daho. Sitting down next to Loren, he whispered something in her ear that she did not quite catch. Something about travelling together to the Blue Island.

'You better watch out, Loren,' Bola Bola warned. 'He's the last of the famous international playboys.' Arthur grinned. 'By the way, I meant to ask: is that weedy tweedy twerp – the bigwig literary agent who always reeks of cigars and aftershave – pressing charges?'

'Unlikely now,' Arthur said, leaning back with his hands locked behind his head.

'Hang on – do you mean Archie West? *You're* the big brute who assaulted him and stole his wife?'

'Borrowed. Don't get me wrong: Effie is a lovely lady but she's a bit vanilla, no offence.' He turned towards Loren, pressing his palm firmly against the small of her back. 'So we've heard all about this little altercation, have we?'

'Poor Archie told me,' she said, a little breathless. 'Apparently...' They kissed. 'You gave him...' Another kiss. 'A damn good thrashing.'

They were devouring each other.

Chapter Twenty
DR MARTENS' BOUNCING SOULS

It didn't hit me at first. Not straight away, it didn't. For a few long seconds there, the world was freeze-framed. I half expected to see tumbleweed blow by. All around, people emitted muffled sounds, as if sporting ball-gags under water. Seemingly swathed in cotton wool, they spoke in slow motion, their syllables hideously elongated like limbs on the rack. I distinctly recall being put in mind of an unravelling audio cassette, or one of those avant-garde sound poems that were all the rage back in the day.

And then it hit me.

Hard.

Really hard.

Repeatedly.

To describe the pain as excruciating just wouldn't do it justice. It was unspeakable, full stop. What I *can* attempt to convey, however – to a certain degree, at least, though not, alas, to the third – is the unrelenting nature of the whole episode. I was stunned. Dumbfounded. Gobsmacked. At a loss for words. Mouth agog, screaming on mute. Bent triple, pissing bleeding blood. Pummelled into that liminal zone beyond which no representation is possible. With the benefit of hindsight, I see it as a crash course in transgression, no less. Nothing would ever be the same again. Not quite. Not for me. Uh-uh.

Blown was my mind.

Rocked were my foundations.

Shaken was my core.

Topsy-turvy was my world.

Over tit was my arse.

And then it hit me again.

Hard.

Really hard.

Really, really hard.

Repeatedly.

Repeatedly.

Repeatedly.

Repeatedly...

I blame it on Effie. Effing Effie and her fucking iffy frock. A brown flower-print number, the kind usually modelled by ladies of a certain age. Ladies who have long ceased to turn heads. Ladies who are fading away inexorably. Ladies who are almost invisible already. Ladies who, even as we speak, are being cut out of the equation with tiny toenail scissors. Slowly. Surely. Snip, snip – snip. But draped around Effie's nubility, it became impossibly erotic, as though the breath of life had suddenly been pumped into a long deflated blow-up doll. As though all the old biddies in their flower-print dresses were in bloom again, having magically recovered their pertness of yore. As though our very planet were a tight pair of bouncy buttocks and the whole wide universe had a massive hard-on.

Hard.

Really hard.

Rock-hard.

Rock on.

Blowing mellow bellows from below, a bracing breeze sported with the hem. Effie even had to hold it down on occasion, lending her an air of charming vulnerability. Despite this precaution, and after a great deal of hemming and hawing, the flimsy material finally resolved to flare up, possibly in answer to the prayers of all those who had slowed down to admire the young lady's graceful sway. Time almost came to a standstill as the dress made its giddy ascent in the manner of a Big Dipper inching up the steepest of slopes. I half expected to see tumbleweed blow by. Then suddenly – amid a cacophony of catcalls, wolf whistles, and screeching tyres – the world went into overdrive. Effie gasped in surprise, looking back instinctively to see how many oglers would be going home with a spring in their proverbial and diaphanous black lace on their minds. As she did so, I couldn't help but notice the imaginary ejaculates from a dozen passers-by glistening in her hair like so many constellations of icicles. It was hard not to really.

Really hard.

Really, really hard.

The heat was well and truly on. You could almost feel the sap rising as Effie strutted by. Men for miles around were picking up illicit frequencies; pricking up their ears at the sound of her heels in the distance. I endeavoured to throw them off the scent by accelerating or crossing the road at regular intervals, but to no avail. I knew I would bump into him eventually, or rather that he would bump into me. He was out there somewhere – everywhere – whoever he may be. It was just a matter of time now and now was the time. He loomed up, he loomed large, hurtling towards me with tragic inevitability. There was no way I could avoid him. In fact, he veered slightly to the right to ensure we were on a collision course. It was fight or flight. It was lose face and face loss. It was too fucking late.

Effie didn't notice anything at first. She pursued her monologue, looking straight ahead as he rammed into me, only pulling up when I remonstrated with my assailant. This, of course, was the cue he had been waiting for. I was playing right into his big lumberjack hands, which he balled into mighty fists before felling me like a sapling. Effie screamed while I attempted to regain verticality by means of the wall. Paying no heed to the abuse that was being hurled his way, he slowly removed his jacket and folded it rather fastidiously. By the time he had finished rolling up his shirtsleeves, Effie had run out of expletives or patience. I noticed how she rolled her eyes in desperation as I finally staggered to my feet, still puffing and panting, only to hear that I was going to be taught a bloody good lesson in front of my wife. And then he hit me again. Hard. Really hard.

Repeatedly. He decked me, then he floored me, then he pulled me up again and decked me some more. At first I was under the cosh, but I soon became conversant with the sentence that was being executed with such surgical precision. I could even distinguish the nuances of each blow. It was like learning a new language.

Taking on the demeanour of an impartial spectator at a boxing match, Effie stepped back to embrace the whole scene. She appeared more open-minded now, wanted to hear him out. She was hedging her bets: let the best man win. At one point – a couple of cheeky jabs followed by a cracking right cross – she even started seeing his, which he put across so eloquently, so forcefully. After all, he was only being fair. Firm but fair. So fair and so firm. Hard, really hard. With her arms folded across her bosom, she looked down upon me, sighing and shaking her head, as though thinking, on reflection, that a good lesson would indeed do me the world of good. She was bowing to the inevitable, submitting to a superior force and silently urging me to do likewise, to let go. All resistance was futile: I had this coming all along and now it had come, and that was that. It was in the order of things to put things in order. It felt right. It even felt good, so good. Hard, so hard. The wicked gleam in her eye proved she was now baying for blood. Baying, obeying some primitive urge. Harder, really harder.

After an uppercut and left hook had left me on my knees again, begging for mercy, he slipped his jacket back on and bitch-slapped me to the ground. Blinking through the streaming blood, I caught a glimpse of my wife's expensive black panties as she stepped over me to join him. They walked off into the sunset, hand in hand.

Chapter Twenty-One
PETIT GUIGNOL

De Niro and Al Pacino, as Loren had nicknamed them, were ogling some model-types emerging from the museum across the road, where a photoshoot must have just ended. Joyous shrieks of children at play emanated from the primary school playground a little further along, to their right. A woman stormed by, leaving a fragrant slipstream in her wake. Her heels sounded like gunshots, such was her wrath. She almost collided with a delivery driver carrying a rectangular cardboard box. The box was so big, he had to peer round the side to see where he was going. When he reached the two Corsicans, he put the box down and produced a folded piece of paper from his pocket.

'Cité Chaptal? C'est l'impasse juste en face,' one of them said.

He thanked them, picked up his load, crossed the road cautiously and walked to the yellow building at the far end of the blind alley, where he rang the doorbell. A woman opened almost immediately.

'Bonjour Madame. C'est bien le Théâtre du Grand Guignol?'

'Autrefois, oui, mais il n'existe plus depuis bien longtemps. Une bonne soixantaine d'années, je dirais. Au bas mot. Votre colis est très en retard, dites-moi!' She smiled, stepping out to point at the inscription above the door: INTERNATIONAL VISUAL THEATRE.

The delivery driver eyed her with suspicion.

'C'est bien la cité Chaptal ici?'

'Oui.'

'Et on est bien au numéro 7?'

'Oui.'

'Et c'est bien un théâtre?'

'Oui.'

'Le colis est donc bien pour vous, Madame,' he concluded emphatically, handing her his phone for signature. *'Allez, bonne journée,'* he said, eager to move on to his next destination.

Isabelle turned round and asked Lorenzo, in sign language, if he could lend her a hand. A bespectacled young man with dark curly hair appeared. He carried the box inside, placing it on the table. They took turns trying to remove the lid, then joined forces, with Lorenzo gripping the tilted box and Isabelle pulling, as though engaging in a tug of war. The lid finally came loose and something flew out, but they paid it no heed at first.

Lorenzo did the unboxing.

He stepped back in awe – it seemed too perfect, far too beautiful.

Isabelle studied the terracotta pot with greater analytical detachment than her young colleague, who left the room.

She assumed the assemblage was part of an upcoming production or exhibition. Some kind of controversial prop. A *contra naturam* coupling. A desperate yoking together of disparate elements. A sewing machine and an umbrella on a dissecting table kind of scenario. Putting two and two together, as she had been taught in school – *thèse, antithèse, synthèse* – would be of no avail in this instance.

Her eyes flitted from the basil to the head. Never could they be reconciled, but neither could they ever be separated again. There was irrefutable evidence of commingling, strands of lustrous hair and glossy leaves having become irrevocably intertwined. The head was now partly vegetal, as if Arcimboldo had presided over its makeover. Was not wax already composed of organic components, anyway? Some kinship may well have been there all along.

The installation also had a definite *memento mori* quality about it. *Thou too will wilt,* head whispered to plant, but there was life still in this still life. This stilled life. Although her eyes were shut, the woman did not appear to be asleep. Isabelle fancied she had been frozen in an instant of delirious delight – static, ecstatic. She was attempting to feel more intensely by losing sight of the visible world.

Poppycock! This was no invitation to a beheading. The head was like one of those Romantic follies that come ready ruined. It had never been severed. There was no acephalous body out there, roaming Marly forest with a dagger in one hand, a burning heart in the other, and a skull covering its cunt. No, this lady had never bitten her lip to stifle cries of pleasure – she had never lost her head. Her ageless visage was so lifelike that Isabelle felt compelled to touch the basil in order to confirm it was as real as the face was fake. She recalled the fresh flowers concealed among the artificial ones in Nabokov's *Ada*. Real flowers pretending to be fake flowers pretending to be real flowers. She had read somewhere that the word mimesis derives from mimosa. How apt.

As a little girl, Isabelle had loved nothing more than going to see the waxworks at the Musée Grévin with her parents and siblings. Her favourite tableau was the reproduction of David's *The Death of Marat*, with the beturbaned revolutionary leader collapsed sideways – towards the visitor – in his bathtub, having just been slain by Charlotte Corday. What she had found so thrilling was that both the bath and the knife were authentic: real flowers concealed among the fakes; the original nestled in a copy of a copy. In Munch's more recent rendition, which she had come across online, Charlotte Corday stands beside her prone victim. In a strange departure from tradition, and indeed historical accuracy, she is depicted stark naked. She stands stock still as though petrified by the enormity of her action; so still in fact that her head, beneath a fetching thatch of blonde hair, appears to be throbbing like a sex toy.

Isabelle was then transported back to that day – in the mid- to late-nineties – when she was driving down a narrow street in the Sentier district. An entire building was being gutted. The plan was clearly to erase almost everything except the elegant façade. Traffic had come to a standstill, affording her the time to observe demolition workers casting showroom dummies out of the gaping windows. Countless naked ladies, and a few men, diving headlong into large skips, which obstructed the pavement, obliging pedestrians to circumnavigate them by stepping onto the road. Just as the gridlock started easing, and Isabelle readied herself to move forwards, a mannequin fell right in front of her car. She alighted with the intention of moving it out of the way, only to realise it was a human body lying in a pool of blood. Drivers in the vehicles behind began honking impatiently. Death is but an inconvenience on the road of life; an obstacle to be swiftly swept aside. Isabelle felt nauseous as she did whenever commuters complained that the metro or RER was held up for a few minutes due to an *accident grâve de voyageur* – a common euphemism for suicide. How inconsiderate to top oneself during the rush hour! In subsequent years, she would often wonder if the woman had jumped or been pushed, and why she was naked like Munch's Charlotte Corday.

Isabelle's fingertips glided from the fragrant leaves to the face's smooth surface, which she caressed abstractedly until the wax caved in, revealing human flesh underneath: a real severed head covered in wax.

At the very instant when she got through to the police, Isabelle spotted the baseball cap on the floor. It had rolled over to the door as though trying to escape.

Chapter Twenty-Two
THE TWO MAGGOTS

The playwright with the ponytail was now heading towards Anvers, having elected to walk to Barbès, where he would ride Line 4 all the way to Odéon, instead of catching the metro at Pigalle. He thought of Victorine Gribiche as he approached La Fourmi. They had met there on several occasions when she was translating his work. The playwright had fond memories of her garrulous jollity and concise skirts. He reached Barbès just as Djamel, the waiter at Le Hareng Rouge, was about to transfer a flat white from tray to table, eager to impress his favourite customer with newly-acquired barista skills. The artwork on the frothy surface was a variation on the classic rosette pattern. Loren recognised this image, but could not identify the original. Its title was on the tip of her raspberry tongue.

She was still racking her brains when Tim Selkirk shuffled in. He waved at Djamel, ordered a double espresso, kissed Loren on both cheeks, and flopped down in the chair facing her. Ginger hair aside, he reminded her of the poet Robert Desnos, with those heavy lidded eyes he was currently rubbing. Today, he looked shattered. More than usual.

They saw each other regularly at Le Hareng Rouge, either by happenstance or because Loren wanted to quiz him about Adam Wandle as part of her research. Between 1993 and 2003, the decade that spanned most of their thirties, the two men had lived in the same building on rue de Tournon, near the Senate and the Jardin du Luxembourg. They both rented overpriced *chambres de bonne* – glorified garrets local estate agents had the audacity to pass off as modern studio apartments. This being an 18th century listed building, there was no lift, which often proved challenging as they were both heavy smokers and binge drinkers in those days.

The people who lived on the floors below were guillotine dodgers of various stripes. Living, Tim remarked, was probably the wrong word. 'As for living,' he declaimed, quoting a play by Villiers de l'Isle-Adam, 'our servants will do that for us'! These neighbours were such snobs, they did not even deign to respond when you greeted them on the marble staircase. They just walked on, up or down, staring straight ahead – straight through you – as though moving in rarefied circles where you – us, we – simply did not exist. Initially, Tim assumed that the building was home to an inordinate number of deaf people, but when he realised what was going on, he began casting aspersions – behind their backs but loud enough to be heard – usually *enculé de ta mère* for a man and *grosse pute* or a variation thereof (*sale pute*, etc.) for a woman; both if required. When they turned round, outraged, he would blank them out, condemning them in turn to non-existence, as though *he* lived on a higher plane – which, of course, he did, spatially speaking.

Adam's closest neighbour on the sixth floor was their local hero. He was a failed artist in his late fifties, originally from Tangiers, who had long stopped paying rent and was slowly turning into a tramp. His tiny room was cluttered with the hideous styrofoam sculptures he produced and trawled around the local galleries. It broke Adam's heart to see him return each time carrying all the pieces he had set out with. There was no lavatory in his flat: he had to use the collective one at the end of the narrow corridor. At night, though, he just opened the window and relieved himself into the private garden below, which belonged to a high-ranking American diplomat. Adam smiled whenever he heard the shrieks of posh partygoers, in their expensive frocks or dinner jackets, being pissed on from a great height. Unfortunately, the bailiffs broke into his room one day and locked him out – an eviction which seemed to symbolise the end of an era. The antiquarian bookshops of Saint-Germain-des-Prés were all closing down one by one. Le Saint-Claude café vanished overnight. Soon, an Armani emporium would replace the Drugstore Publicis, where Serge Gainsbourg bought his Cuban cigars and the terrorist Carlos once threw a grenade.

The next tenant was an untenable tenor from Madrid, who could have sprung from Rosemary Tonks' quirky imagination. He would crank up his music at full volume, nightly, and sing over the top *à tue-tête.* Adam tried to reason with him, explaining that he needed to sleep because he had to go to work because, you know, he had to earn a living. The titled Spaniard retorted that he was entitled, nay duty bound, to rehearse whenever the Muse visited him. He finally left, along with his nocturnal Muse, after nine months, by which time Adam had developed a strong aversion to opera. He was replaced by a student of sorts, who slept all day and smoked pot all night with a group of boisterous friends. It was amazing how many wankers could cram into such a small space and how they could all exist in a state of permanent hilarity despite being utterly witless.

The third floor was inhabited by a von Trapp type – a professional musician, who cycled around with a permanent scowl on his face that expressed his rejection (bicycles excepted) of all things modern, starting, no doubt, with the Reformation. He had sired multiple daughters – his long-suffering spouse was hardly ever to be seen – whom he drilled military-fashion. They all filed out each year for the *Fête de la musique,* on 21st June, performed a little recital next to the newspaper kiosk on square Francis Poulenc, then marched back in again. *Trois p'tits tours et puis s'en vont.* You could imagine them committing suicide – quietly, without fuss, one by one – like in the Jeffrey Eugenides novel.

The only person who seemed decent enough in the building was an ageing dandy, who lived alone with his eccentric mother and doused himself in lavender cologne. Tim and Adam nicknamed him Robert de Montesquiou, after the aesthete who served as a model for both Huysmans's des Esseintes and Proust's Charlus. Mother and son sometimes took a taxi in the small hours to go dancing at L'Insolite, where the old lady revelled in the attention showered on her by all the pretty boys. *I was the only woman there,* she once said, a little incredulous.

Loren suddenly felt low-magnitude tremors between her thighs, like the aftershocks in the wake of an earthquake. A lusty young Adam had come to her in her sleep, making her come, and now it was all coming back. In the dream, Adam was fucking a blonde woman behind a tarpaulin that covered the entire façade of a building. Flashback snapshots of the woman's hands pulling down Adam's jeans and boxers in one swift movement, then slowly guiding his cock deep inside her. The shocking paleness of Adam's buttocks contrasting with scarlet nail varnish. The woman's head tilting back against the wall, her face squeegeed as in a Gerhard Richter portrait. Loren knew who she was, though.

V had been Adam's girlfriend between 1987 and 1991, when he still lived on rue Didot in the fourteenth *arrondissement,* before his move to the sixth. She was mentioned, along with her proclivity for al fresco sex, in the non-fiction volume that was currently open on the table in front of her.

Loren, cheeks flushed, closed the book. Once more, she was moved to broach the subject of Adam's sentimental life, which she could not help finding endlessly fascinating and was still struggling to get a handle on. She was unsure how much space she should devote to it, and how important it really was, anyway. She did not want to be accused of prurience. Tim reassured her. He was of the view that this aspect of Adam's life had a great deal of bearing upon his writing. In fact, it was crucial. He often cited 'Sweet Fanny Adams', a short section of *The Blue Island,* which could still be found knocking around on dusty old websites despite the author's attempts to erase all traces of it. Read 'Sweet Fanny Adams', he would say – it's all in there.

'We can only desire – really desire – what we do not possess, right? This is true of all of us, of course, but it's absolutely key in his case,' Tim argued. 'As you know, Adam was wrenched from his mother at the age of five and he's never fully recovered. The pain he felt growing up is unspeakable and yet he must speak it, but all he can do is speak *from* it. There is no outside.'

'Yes, I see what you mean,' Loren said.

'This trauma is the only thing that feels authentic to him. He has a vague recollection of what happened just before the separation and remembers, of course, what happened thereafter, but the event itself is missing. It's been wiped from his memory's hard drive – it was just too damn painful to assimilate.'

'So, nothing to him is more real than this lacuna.'

'Exactly. You know what Borges said: "God lurks in the gaps". Well, it's all in the gaps, in the blanks with Lord Biro – the divine gaps. As a kid, Adam was obsessed with history, particularly the French Revolution and Napoleonic period. He had this feeling that people in the past were heroic and idealistic, a far cry from the vulgarity and stupidity he observed in the playground. Feeling alienated from his peers, he took refuge in a mythical past in his head. When people addressed him, they didn't realise that, in parallel, he was conducting a mute conversation with historical figures!'

'How has this affected his relationships?'

'Well, as you know, he finds social interaction challenging. He's okay one-on-one with people he already knows, but otherwise he really struggles.'

'And with women, more particularly?'

'He tends to associate them with absence and loss. Before a relationship has even truly begun, he's already envisaging the inevitable break-up, which of course he engineers. It's a classic case of repetition compulsion. When we were young, he would often refer to Denis de Rougemont's idea that there can be no desire in the absence of obstacles; that desire is ultimately desire *for* the obstacle. What struck me most is that Adam's love affairs were always pitched at a hysterical level of intensity. They were all-consuming. He needed to vanish into them. They were a means of escape from the self – a form of self-immolation, of sacrifice.'

'A form of suicide?'

'Definitely.'

'Can you give me a specific example?'

'Yes. The reason he moved into that studio apartment, on rue de Tournon, is that he'd fallen in love with this beautiful Italian girl he barely knew. She was called S and lived in the neighbourhood. His feelings for her were so overwhelming that they took over his entire life. He would spend all his days off at Les Deux Magots, from where he could observe the grand entrance to her building. It wasn't stalking: he never actually spotted her and he always told me he wouldn't have done anything if he had. Wouldn't have spoken to her. He just had to be there. Roland Barthes defines the lover as the one who waits: *je suis celui qui attend*. Well, that was him. He was waiting for Godot knows what S had crystallised. It was completely insane, of course, but also strangely beautiful. It had an epic quality. On Sundays I'd often drop by and we'd read the books sections in the British broadsheets together. We called ourselves the Two Maggots!'

'What happened to S?'

'I think she's some kind of diplomat now... I must confess that I disliked her intensely. She and her aristocratic friends used to mock their fellow students who had to work as cashiers to fund their studies. I'll never forget that. And now they're all at the head of NGOs, bemoaning Western imperialism, crying their humanitarian crocodile tears. They make me fucking sick. I also remember that she used to go through these phases where she'd hallucinate that people had rats on their heads. Adam eventually sent her a letter and they started dating. They even lived together, rue de Tournon, for a short while. Of course, it quickly went tits up... You really should read "Sweet Fanny Adams", even though it's an early piece and very much of its time. Some of the first readers took it at face value, missing the satire of toxic masculinity. Anyway, as I said, it's all in there.'

And Loren read the story on her laptop.

Chapter Twenty-Three
SWEET FANNY ADAMS

Granted, it could have been an airport, say, or any other point of departure for that matter, not necessarily a railway station. Then again, I would not want you to go thinking that his choice had been totally arbitrary, although he was, admittedly, no stranger to acts of random behaviour. It did not *have* to be an overcrowded railway station, but it sort of made sense somehow.

It's like this: your train is due to leave any minute now. You look up from your book or paper – if you are reading, that is, but I think we can safely assume that you, *mon semblable, mon frère,* are reading at least one or the other, possibly even both, one after the other, or, better still, simultaneously. You check the time on your wristwatch – the kind that they advertise in *The Economist* and suchlike periodicals, something Swiss or German with knobs on (the more, the merrier) which exudes manly sophistication. Just as the Red Sea parted for Moses, the door slides open, blissfully pneumatic, to reveal a stunning apparition in a comely knicker-skimming skirt: entrancing entrance. Being the proud possessor of a Y chromosome, your eyes make a beeline for her A-line, zooming in on silken thighs, NordicTrack-toned. While she faffs about with her umbrella (which will be left behind, of course, accidentally-on purpose), you are at leisure to divide her putative weight in kilograms by her hypothetical height in metres squared, thus reaching the satisfactory conclusion that the young woman's Body Mass Index slots into the ideal 18 to 20 range. She click-clicks her way towards the only vacant space (which just so happens to be facing you) aloft a pair of chichi cha-cha heels, whereupon she takes a pew. As she crosses her legs with a hushed swish whoosh, the bright young ~~thong~~ thing hitches up her skirt a notch, pinching the flimsy fabric on either side of broad hips between manicured thumb and forefinger. At this juncture – when you are about to abandon wife and children, sail the seven seas, or commit genocide because men cannot help acting on impulse – you notice that those are tear- and not rain-drops irrigating her tanned, yet still unblemished, features. Ever the gentleman, or simply embarrassed, you interrupt your ornithological study and peer out of the window which, being in dire need of a good clean, forces you to squint in the most unsightly fashion. *Now* is when it happens. For a few split nanoseconds, another train pulling into the station tricks you into believing your train is pulling out.

Jamie Curren – 33, caucasian, 5'6", thinning on top – viewed this sensation as a perfect metaphor of his stumbling through life like a sleepwalker on a treadmill, a pet hamster on a wheel, or a commuter on the Circle Line. Hence the choice of a railway station over any other point of departure. But which one? Paris offered *un embarras de choix*.

Gare de l'Est was a definite no-no for some obscure reason. Gare d'Austerlitz was likewise ruled out: Jamie, you see, had a passion for Waterloo Station. Since childhood, he had conceived of Austerlitz as a sort of counter- or even anti-Waterloo; it was enemy territory. This still left Gare de Lyon, built in the grandiose style – probably the most pleasing, aesthetically. Gare Saint-Lazare, caught between the red-light district and the posh department stores, scored a few brownie points. Proust's *lycée* was close by, as well as the Opéra Garnier (a fine example of architectural eclecticism) and, more importantly, Marks & Spencer with its large lingerie section, where Jamie often indulged in a little lingering among the petticoats and suspender belts. There was also Gare Montparnasse, where the illustrious Muses hung out, free and easy, lustrous locks flailing the air. They rode around like BMX bandits astride expensive Dutch bicycles sporting a saucy look on their faces and precious little else. The area never failed to remind him of that time when he micturated on the tomb of Jean-Paul Sartre after burying his late goldfish (Botty, short for Botticelli) in the shadow of Baudelaire's corpse. Such fond memories.

In the end, however, he had plumped for Gare du Nord, which houses the Eurostar terminal. Jamie's grasp of French had greatly improved over the past twelve months, but he was looking for a lady who spoke the old mother tongue. Besides, the word *terminal* had a certain ring to it – the finality of a full stop.

The air hung heavy with Chaucerian expletives; dropped aitches were strewn about his feet. Here and there, love thugs sprouting Hoxton fins were reading red-tops from back to front. The odd diamond geezer was getting twatted while his missus flaunted the latest erogenous zones. In the distance, a posse of blue-rinsed senior citizens could be seen giving a spirited rendition of the hokey cokey. A good vibe was being had by one and all. *If I should die,* Jamie muttered*, think only this of me: that there's some corner of a foreign railway station that is forever In-ger-land.* And there she was.

Sweet Fanny Adams.

Sweet Fanny Adams and no mistake.

Although he had never seen her before, he recognised her at once, and once he had recognised her, he realised he would never see her again. After all, not being there was what she was all about; it was the essence of her being, her being Fanny Adams and all that.

As he walked towards the bench where she was sitting pretty, Jamie missed her already. Missed her bad.

'How do you do?'

The imperfect stranger looked up from her small gilt-edged missal, flashing him a baking-soda smile, all cocky like. 'How do I do what?

Their eyes met, pairing off at first sight. The earth moved, orbiting at half a kilometre per second around her celestial globes – a couple of scalloped cupfuls with peek-a-boo trimmings – in what can only be described as a new Copernican revolution. For the first time since Mrs Curren's belaboured parturition, when he was eventually thrown (*geworfen*) into the world, Jamie did not feel at the wrong place at the wrong time: he was back in the bountiful bosom of Mummy Nature. As if to celebrate this return to the much-maligned Ptolemaic system, a gaggle of gurgling putti glided overhead to the strains of syrupy muzak and departing trains. All in all, it was an auspicious overture, fraught with the promise of premise.

'Jamie,' said Jamie, extending his right arm.

'Margherita,' said Margherita, giving it a hearty shake.

Still reeling from that initial blinding smile – let alone the handshake – he struggled to regain his composure.

'Have you read *The Leaning Tower of Pizzas* by N. E. Tchans?'

'Is that the one which ends with an epic battle between gangs of pre-pubescent herberts bouncing around on orange space hoppers?'

'Yes.'

'No, but I read a review at the time.'

'Well, it's all about this bloke, who comes from Italy and settles down in South London, where he falls in love with a girl called Margherita.'

She was fiddling with her umbrella, a faraway look on her face.

'Like you, like.'

'Oh, I see, yes. Sorry, I was miles away.'

'I know: that's the attraction,' he sighed *sotto voce*, before getting a grip on himself. 'Anyway, you should check it out some time – if you're into lolloping lollipop ladies, lesbians from Lisbon, the romance of ice-cream vans, that kind of thing.'

'Sounds right up my street.'

'I see it as a contemporary footnote to Dante.'

'Talking of contemporary feet, mine are killing me.'

'Dying on our footnotes are we? One footnote in the grave, eh? How long have you got left?'

'Long enough to grab a bite to eat – or so says my chiropodist.'

'I think there's an Italian just round the corner that might tickle your fancy.'

'Sounds great. I feel like a pizza.'

'I'm not surprised, love, with a name like that.'

Jamie caught a fleeting glimpse of the dark, gaping twilight zone between Margherita's parted thighs as she uncrossed her legs to get up. That topsy-turvy Bermuda Triangle betwixt skirt and stocking exerted a gravitational pull of such magnitude that he was sucked in, there and then, never to re-emerge. He picked up her bulky suitcase, *l'air de rien,* but in his mind's X-ray eye he could see her neatly-packed unmentionables. He was big on smalls, was old Jamie Curren.

'Heavy, isn't it?'

'It's a burden I feel I've been carrying all my life.' He turned to face her, dead serious. 'This may sound absurd, but you are the hollowness inside. At last, I have found my sense of loss.'

'I'm flattered,' she said in Estuarine undertones, blushing a little. Her dimpled cheeks resembled two squashed cherry tomatoes, only bigger. 'I always like to be of assistance to strangers.'

'After you,' said Jamie, bowing theatrically while showing the way with her suitcase, like a truncheon-toting *gendarme* stopping the traffic for pedestrians. He could not help noticing the shaft of light that fell on Margherita's bottom – proof positive that the sun shone out of her behind – before leaving the station, hot on her high heels.

They repaired to a Greekish spoon, which Margherita praised on account of its 'atmosphere'.

'Looks great,' she gushed, surveying the menu in the window, 'I feel like a cocktail'.

'I'm not surprised, love, with a name like that.'

The walls were festooned with fairy lights, garlands of garlic, and pictures of Asma Assad, the Syrian President's trophy wife. The waiters were all male to a man. It soon transpired that none of them was actually Italian, having been born and bred, through no fault of their own, on the wrong side of Thessaloniki. ('Oh, that's a shame, isn't it?' cooed Margherita, detaching each word as though dismembering some wingèd insect.) The chef, a diminutive Algerian with an endearing paunch, had a Saddam Hussein moustache going on and a nice line in knock-knock jokes. The toilets were typically Turkish.

Having taken in the scenery, Jamie proceeded to pour out his heart and a couple of cheap, albeit cheerless, bottles of retsina. Whining and dining *in medias res.*

'We are all post-Denis de Rougemont.'

'Couldn't agwee maw,' said Marwghewita, making a mental note never again to shpeak wiv her mouf full.

Frankly, she did not have a clue what he was going on about.

'We are one of the first generations to know full well that love doesn't last, and yet we cling to the ideal like a protective blanket.'

She turned up her already-*retroussé* nose. How more *retroussé* can it get? he wondered.

'Maybe it's just me. The whole thing's very Oedipal, I know.' Jamie cringed at his attempt to laugh it off.

'I could mother you, free of charge, if you think that might help.'

'I'd rather not if it's all the same with you,' he replied rather primly, 'but thanks for the offer. Might even take you up on it some other time. Except' – Jamie paused for effect – 'there won't be another time.' He sighed, baleful, into his bowlful of miniature bow ties, topped up their glasses, and cleared his throat. 'Love stories are like fairy tales...'

'Aren't they just.'

'...in that we know the end from the start. Only it's not *and they lived happily ever after*, is it?'

Tears welled up in her belladonna eyes.

'You know, someone should really write a different kind of love story for the new millenium. It would start with the foregone conclusion and work its way back towards the unknown: how it all started in the first place.'

'Will you write this new-fangled romance?'

'I'm writing the first pages even as we speak – with your assistance, of course.'

'I like to be of assistance.' She smiled a wet smile.

'Shall we call it a day then?'

'Call it what you like. Your book, your call... So that's it then, is it?'

'Yes. In our beginning is our end.'

Margherita seemed in a hell of a hurry all of a sudden; even her nose was running. *Where is it running to?* he wondered. *To by-corners Byzantine, I'll be bound, and wondrous Wherevers, to the end of the earth, at the end of its tether.* Then he shrugged – to himself and at it all – because it did not really matter any more, it really did not. Whatever: yeah, right.

It was raining when Margherita stepped out of the restaurant. Jamie watched her amber umbrella disappear from view, a Belisha beacon of hope on a dimmer switch. He scribbled a few words on the paper tablecloth. *D'elle, il ne reste que ses tagliatelles.*

The door slides open – which is where you came in. You assess her golden-delicious breasts as though picking apples on a market stall. You think that a man should never trust a woman who offers him an apple, let alone two. You think that this woman's tits are perfectly identical, for Christ's sake. Like bookends.

God knows what happens next. God – and you.

Chapter Twenty-Four
QUIET DAYS IN NOISY

Looking up from the laptop, I raised my eyebrows as far as they would go. Tim did not take umbrage. He was lost in the remembrance of things past. A strange phrase, don't you think? It seems to imply that you can also remember things future, which is actually quite fitting now that we locate modernity in the past. 'Sweet Fanny Adams,' he explained, gazing into the far-near, was written at Le Tournon, the little café on their doorstep. You turned right as you exited the building, walked up a few yards in the direction of the Senate – past the antiquarian bookshop that was so select it only opened by appointment – and there you were. He trotted two digits across the table, as though stepping back in time. The modest establishment's heyday was well and truly over by the time they began frequenting it. On reflection, 'patronised' might be a better choice of verb, he said, given their youthful condescension. They had no idea the café had ever had such a thing as a heyday. What was it like? Nondescript would be an apt description, he ventured after a short pause, although, to be fair, the place was not without its endearing little quirks and discreet provincial charm.

Le Tournon's main claim to fame was that Joseph Roth had drunk himself to death on the premises. One page, one pastis: more than a mantra, it was a manifesto, whereby the porous borders between drinking and writing flowed into each other, becoming almost indistinguishable. In the manner of surtitles at the opera, a plaque affixed to the wall indicated the table where Roth worked on *The Legend of the Holy Drinker* and eventually collapsed. The sour-faced landlady, a likely martyr to dyspepsia, disapproved of this tribute to a foreign Jewish dipsomaniac. You know the portly matrons who serve as foils for Groucho Marx? She looked just like that, Tim said, but with a strong *accent du Midi*. Her creepy, florid-complexioned husband would rhapsodise about young women's tight little arses – *Ah, les p'tits culs, les p'tits culs!* – as soon as the old battleaxe was at a safe distance. He had a rheumy roaming eye for M, the unfeasibly French waitress, who in turn had a bit of a crush on Adam, himself in a relationship with A by now.

Louis Barthomé-Saint-André's murals – depicting scenes from the nearby Luxembourg Garden – set Le Tournon apart from similar old-school watering holes in the area. The American novelist William Gardner Smith had once described them as hideous. Tim only came across this information much later, though. He did not rate the murals as artworks either, but believed this judgement was a little harsh. For one, he rather enjoyed their brash energy. He also appreciated the way they brought the outdoors indoors. This, he argued, was in keeping with the spirit of Parisian parks, most of which are designed to endow the exterior with interior urbanity. *'Il n'y a pas de hors-texte,'* he deadpanned. The paintings tampered with one's sense of time as well as space. They were peopled with characters from another age, most of whom would have been dead, Tim surmised, by the 1990s – had they ever existed. They reminded him of one of the most haunting passages in Albert Cossery's *Men God Forgot*: the description of a crude fresco representing a sailing boat on the Nile – motionless, frozen in time – steadfastly refusing to move on.

The Egyptian writer moved from his native Cairo to Paris in 1945, soon becoming a fixture of bohemian Saint-Germain-des-Prés. Durrell, Genet, Giacometti, Gréco, Miller, Queneau, Sartre, Tzara, and Vian all ranked among his friends. Accompanied by Camus, he cruised the streets of the Latin Quarter, soon acquiring something of a reputation as a Levantine lover. He claimed to have had more than 3000 female conquests in his life, which, if true, would place him in Simenon's priapic super league. Upon hearing this, I raised a very arch eyebrow; Tim smiled. Time stood still, he continued, as soon as Cossery settled in Paris. He checked into a small room in a hotel called La Louisiane[20] (France's answer to the Hotel Chelsea, something like that) remaining there, living off handouts and meagre publishing rights, until his death. The writer despised hackwork – work *tout court*, for that matter

20 Jean-Paul Sartre resided there during the war. It provided the backdrop to Miles Davis and Juliette Gréco's idyll, and is depicted in Lucian Freud's *Hotel Bedroom* (1954).

– often producing a single, perfectly-honed sentence a week, which accounted for his financial woes. His last novel (only a slim volume) was fifteen years in the making! When he died, the French Culture Minister described him as a 'prince', although he owned little more than the clogs he had just popped. In his books (and you must read his books, he insisted) holy hooligans jump through the eyes of needles, hashish-smoke halos raffishly askew, with the ease of biblical camels: those who lack or reject material wealth gain access to a heightened state of consciousness.

Cossery would get up at midday, dress in his habitual dandified fashion, and make his way to Brasserie Lipp for a spot of lunch. From there, he usually repaired to the Café de Flore, across the road, where Tim often observed him casting an Olympian eye over the passers-by milling about outside. Then it was time for his all-important siesta. Repeat *ad infinitum*.

During these years, Tim, his partner (and now wife) Saskia, Adam, and his Serbian girlfriend A, all lived just up the road from La Louisiane. Whenever they got home in the small hours – usually a little worse for wear – they would tread lightly as they passed the hotel, their muted conversation turning to the Voltaire of the Nile, whom they pictured asleep, mummified in his diminutive mausoleum. It was a comforting thought, Tim said, like a sailing boat that will never sail away.

Le Tournon was usually very quiet, even at lunchtime. There was a steady turnover of working-class customers, often in their *bleu de travail*, who had a quick drink and chat standing at the shiny zinc bar, where prices were cheaper. Those who could afford table service were mainly people who worked, in some capacity, at the Senate. It was also a conveniently discreet spot, where Senators – almost all of them men – could meet their mistresses, typically *grandes blondes* straight out of Jean Echenoz's eponymous novel.[21]

Around 2000, Adam started posting pictures of Le Tournon in *3:AM Magazine,* claiming it was the Parisian headquarters of the so-called Offbeat group of writers to which he belonged. It was a joke more than anything else. A kind of prank. He relished the idea of a young American hipster making the pilgrimage to this hotbed of avant-garde activity, only to find, well, Le Tournon! Little did he know that the café actually had an illustrious cultural history. After the war, it was the meeting place of African-American writers such as James Baldwin or Chester Himes. Duke Ellington and his orchestra even made their European debut there. In the fifties, you could bump into Scottish émigré Alexander Trocchi and other contributors to *Merlin,* his influential literary journal. George Plimpton and the entire *Paris Review* team held their editorial meetings there...

Tim began looking over his shoulder at regular intervals. Never a good sign. He had lowered his voice, so as not to be overheard, although Le Hareng Rouge was empty apart from us. I could see Djamel outside, laughing with De Niro and Al Pacino. When paranoia settled in, as it invariably did, Tim would suddenly spring up at some point and disappear without so much as a by-your-leave,

21 *Les Grandes Blondes,* 1995.

so I quizzed him about some of their other local haunts to keep the conversation flowing. Well, he said, there was the cheap Chinese restaurant across the road, where Adam often went with S in their early rue de Tournon days. They always ordered *un porc sauce aigre douce* (for him), *un méli-mélo vapeur* (for her), and *deux riz cantonnais* (one each) and usually had the place to themselves. Jean-Edern Hallier – the controversial writer, who had co-founded *Tel Quel* and masterminded his own kidnapping by a fake revolutionary commando – came in on one occasion when Tim was also present. He spent a long time conferring with the moon-faced waitress before taking a seat. He looked quite impressive due to his stature and blindness, the latter feature lending him a seer-like quality. Much later, they would discover that Roland Barthes had also been a habitué of the *petit chinois de la rue de Tournon*, as he called it.

Had he mentioned Marcello Mastroianni? The Italian film star used to live on the same street, which becomes rue de Seine once you cross Saint-Sulpice on the way down. Mastroianni and Adam had their morning coffee at Le Mandarin, a café on boulevard Saint-Germain, which no longer exists today. They were both creatures of habit, always sitting in the exact same spot. They never spoke; not in so many words, but Mastroianni often silently acknowledged Adam's presence, gratifying him with a glance or half-smile as he walked past his table. After all, they were often the only customers there. No sooner had the venerable actor been served, than a strange performance, straight out of *commedia dell'arte*, would begin. One of the waiters stood at the entrance, on the lookout for Mastroianni's partner, film director Anna Maria Tatò. When she finally loomed into view – often accompanied by a retinue of well-heeled Italian friends – the waiter gave a discreet signal to his colleagues, who would whisk away the actor's glass and ashtray. Another waiter would spray a few squirts of air freshener to ensure that Marcello's partner did not suspect he was still a heavy smoker, while yet another produced a fresh cup of coffee to ensure she did not suspect he was still a heavy drinker. One of Mastroianni's friends once applauded the *garçons'* performance, shouting '*Bravo! Bravo!*' (in Italian) just as Mrs Tatò walked in, right on cue.

Bola Bola and Michel returned from running some errands and joined us, which seemed to calm Tim down for a while, although I noticed his left eye was twitching a little. They reminisced about some of the eccentric characters whose paths they frequently crossed back in the day. Michel immediately mentioned Ali Akbar, who started selling newspapers on the streets of the Latin Quarter in the early seventies[22], freshly arrived from Pakistan. Everybody knew him as 'Ça y est' because he always shouted *'Ça y est! Ça y est!'* – his version of *Read all about it!* – as a prelude to some far-fetched fabricated headline designed to put a smile on your face and a few francs in his palm. Remember the time he announced Jean-Marie Le Pen had converted to Islam? We all laughed.

There was also that weirdo who asked passers-by if they liked poetry, Bola Bola said. Everybody always ignored him, Tim added. Poor thing. He wandered, he roved;

22 1973, to be precise.

he shuffled, he roamed; he pounded, he expounded, he strode and he strolled. Perry Pathetic, Adam called him, this peripatetic poet, who paced the streets of the Left Bank, flogging his verse to all and sundry. 'My work I have costed,' he told whoever he accosted, 'and I'll spin you a rhyme, if you slip me a dime,' or words to that effect. Then one day he stopped asking the same question over and over again, as though he had suddenly found the answer and fallen silent as a result. From then on, his walking did the talking; it had no rhyme nor reason – he was poetry in motion.

And what about Arnaud Gobillot? Remember him? He was renowned for spending an inordinate amount of time in the Café de Flore with neatly stacked sheets of paper and an expensive-looking fountain pen in front of him. He practically lived there. People spoke of him in hushed tones. Look, they would whisper, that's Gobillot over there. Rumour had it he was hard at work on a *magnum opus* of world-historical importance – his *Grand Oeuvre*. Names like Musil, Proust, and Joyce were bandied about in his vicinity. Literary stars such as Philippe Sollers always made a point of saluting him with the utmost reverence. They admired, and even envied, the strength with which he resisted the sirens of publication. Arnaud Gobillot was playing the long game. It was posterity or nothing with him: he was already conversant with eternity. When he died, however, it became apparent that he had never written anything beyond a few letters and shopping lists, neither of great literary merit. To this day, Michel explained, some are convinced that a monumental manuscript is stashed away somewhere. They await its inevitable discovery and eventual publication like the Second Coming. They too are biding their time.

Somehow, the conversation meandered all the way to Noisy, where Adam disappeared for a few years following his marriage and the birth of his son. He always called it 'Noisy' for short, so that no one never knew for sure whether he meant Noisy-le-Grand or Noisy-le-Sec (it was, in fact, the latter). This put me in mind of Sostène Zanzibar and his Schrödinger's flat – that interzone or grey area, where he poetically dwells. Meanwhile, Tim was looking increasingly agitated. Both eyes were twitching now and his right foot was tapping out some tachycardic rhythm involving his whole leg. Tap-tap-tapping. Saskia had told me all about the episode when he had truly lost the plot. We're still living in the wreckage of that incident, she had said, and the memory of that word – *wreckage* – resonated mysteriously as I peered blankly into my empty cup of coffee. Wreckage upon wreckage.

Chapter Twenty-Five
FORTY TIDDLY WINKS

He found it difficult to get up of a morning because he found it difficult to wake up of a morning. The waking-up problem lay in the fact that he did not want to.

Some people cannot go to sleep for fear of passing away in their slumber. Not him, though. Unconsciousness was a state he positively aspired to, and often contrived to reach – through artificial means – whenever nature would not take its course, which, truth be told, was more often than not these days.

Others can just doze off as soon as their heads hit the pillow. Not Tim, though. He needed knocking out flat by dint of drinking himself into a stupor. Otherwise, he was condemned to toss and turn till dawn at the thought of Time's wingèd chariot hurrying near: Chitty Chitty Bang Bang you're dead!

Instinctively, Tim would tune into the hypnotic ticking of his wristwatch on the bedside table. Like a clock in a crocodile, it grew closer by the minute until the din became truly deafening. Now, he just knocks back another stiff one and waits for the effect to kick in. The clockodial starts melting, Dali-stylee. The ticking gradually fades into a teeny-tiny tinny background backbeat. Soon it is drowned out by Saskia's sonorous snoring. Forty tiddly winks.

Tim is back in class wearing his old school uniform. He cannot see himself wearing it, but a dormant sensation of itchy acrylic chafing skinny white-boy skin is rudely awakened. A remembered forgotten land of man-made fabrics.

That morning after, he emerged more dead than alive from his customary semi-coma.

A boot had been stamping on his face – for ever. Nothing else could account for the excruciating pain. Straight away, Tim spotted the tell-tale stigmata: skull resonating like a flushing toilet bowl, snail's trail of saliva smeared across right cheek; dried-up mucus encrusting limp upper lip having seeped nightly from cavernous nostrils. To think that these were the very same orifices through which the breath of life had once been breathed! It did not bear thinking about.

Behold the tiny tots sitting two by two behind dinky desks, all chubby chops and tuck-shop tums, bless them.

As a dog returneth to its vomit, so he looked back and noticed a saline snowfall of dandruff liberally sprinkled all over the black pillowcase. God knows how much of his mortal coil ended up in the hoover on a weekly basis – it was a slow shuffling off. Dust bunnies thou *art*, Tim, and unto dust bunnies shalt thou return along with every creepy-crawly that creepeth and crawleth upon the earth. He yawned: a putrid, piscine stench issued forth from the cesspool of his mouth, as though he had spent the night snogging a siren in the snot-green sea.

In pursuit of a good blushing, Miss Ramsay wags an incarnadined digit at some dumpling demon cherub. A few vigorous wags are enough to finger-paint him the colour of her nail varnish. Having achieved the desired chromatic merger, she surveys row upon row of wonky ties and concertinaed tights and sees that it is good. Oh, of course, there are socks to pull up, crinkly smirks to wipe off, curly-wurly minds to straighten out and what-not. But she can tell by the smarmy look on their faces that nobody else has forgotten to bring their apple as specified, quite audibly and in plain English, on Thursday last at nine o'clock sharp. To drive the point home, had not she chalked the instructions up there on the blackboard for all to see? The writing was on the wall, for Christ's sake! In fancy curlicue letters.

And it came to pass that Tim came to piss. Fishing Moby Dick out of his boxers was a daily battle, a classic struggle between Man and Beast, the outcome of which seemed most uncertain. In the sweat of thy face shalt thou toil in the toilet.

'A-pples,' she hisses as she click-clicks past Adam, sh-shaking her head from side to side and tut-tutting for added effect, 'The lesson of the day is: a-pples.' (She has a good mind to expel him, cast him into the wilderness.)

After faffing around his nether-nether regions, Tim gave in to what was, by any standard, a formidable, and indeed enviable, gravity-defying pull. A skyscraping tumescence and no mistake. Oh yes, it was at times like this – when up was the only way – that one grasped the true meaning of transcendence. Casting all remnants of dignity to the wind, he dropped his kecks around his ankles, and braced himself for the daunting challenge that still lay ahead. They were both bollock naked, the man and his manhood, and were not ashamed.

'Don't let me catch anybody eating during the lesson,' she roars, 'or that body will have hell to pay.' Miss Ramsay paces the classroom, handing out the odd pre-emptive clip round the proverbial earhole.

He stepped back, psyching himself up, mentally gauging distances like a top athlete, stood on tiptoe, took aim and – there she blows! A sudden spurt of steamy, spumy liquid came pissing down onto the lid, which Saskia would insist on using as a lavatorial fig leaf. Tim tensed his pubococcygeus to stop the flow by way of a damage-limitation exercise. Still effing and blinding, he micturated in the sink, mopped up the spillage with wads of pink toilet paper; was out of there like a flush in the pan.

Miss Ramsay's is the mother of all fuck-off apples. Genetically modified by a Dr Frankenstein multinational, it squats obscenely on the desk, complete in its ur-ness, replete in its rotundity – surfing on surfeit. And it puts the fear of God in the tiny tots, who, for some reason, are now hitting puberty.

Somehow Tim stumbled into the kitchen, morning glory at half-mast dripping all over the shop. Upon thy belly shalt thou go. His mind was void and without form. His joints felt rusty – a Tin Woodman in dire need of lubrication. Like some right divvynity, he fumbled for the switch (*fiat lux!*) and went to pick a mug from the tree in the midst of the table. It was a toss-up between James Joyce and Gromit. Predictably enough, given his habitual matutinal regression, he plumped for the reassuring cosiness of the latter.

The apples are drawn, quartered, dissected, and analysed, right down to the very last pip. Mission accomplished, class dismissed. They can stuff their freckly faces now, for all she cares.

Tim stood before the work surface, scratching his balls, contemplating yesterday's dirty dishes, waiting for the boil to kettle. Over to the right, the leftover soup, primordial-looking in its present enforced-gazpacho incarnation. Click: tea for Tim. He chose to pour in the milk last, although he did not make a religion of it. In these small matters, as in others, Tim liked to exercise his free will.

Shifting all her weight on one cheek, Eve dislodges her wayward panties by plucking the elastic like a harp string – smack! In so doing, she bares her gleaming pearlies. Tim can smell her fragrant bubblegum breath, passion-fruit flavoured. He will write an ode to that west wind with his Magnetic Poetry Kit as soon as he gets a refrigerator of his own. Eve's wide-open mouth is moist and warm. Tim's wily willy will worm itself willy-nilly into the moist warmth of Eve's yum-yum mouth. Her glossed lips quiver over the polished surface of the apple. She dribbles a little, giggles a lot, and finally puts it down.

Tim was out of joints. Paranoia was slowly taking hold of him. He switched on the radio to catch the news, feeling relieved when he relived the expected sense of *dejà entendu*. As always, *Today* sounded like yesterday or the day before. Different but the same in a same-difference kind of way. Two female critics were discussing a cutting-edge novel, which was causing some sort of sensation. If you hadn't heard of *E-Den*, it was like, *Hello-o, where have you been for the past seven days?*

'It's very gritty.'

'Well, he spares us no details, if that's what you mean.'

'It's very nitty-gritty.'

As per usual, the reception was crispy-bacon crackly, but simply hearing the presenter's voice, in between sonorous slurps, microwaved the cockles of his little heart.

Row upon row of crisp, unblemished apples looking sorry for themselves. The word 'pristine' springs to mind. It's all sinking in, like a body falling down its own precipice. The tree, the not-eating thereof. Tim's classmates, their placid, bovine features. His head spins. His heart pounds. Tim looks round the classroom. We all don't know nothing, he wants to scream, and we all don't bloody care. The words, however, remain stuck in his throat. Pause. They don't know they don't know, do they? He knows. He alone. He. Alone. Panic.

Scientists were flocking in droves to Azerbaijan, where supercentenarians were thick on the ground. Many of them still reared their sheep. In fact, the sheep seemed to be blessed with exceptionally long lifespans too. The BBC correspondent evoked a couple who could remember the October revolution. Professor Gordon Bennett dismissed the notion of 'genetic predisposition', adducing his attempts to rejuvenate elderly mice, which had met – he was pleased to say – with a degree of success. Then it was the turn of Jessica Saunders, a gerontologist, whose voice had a very angular – almost Vorticist – quality. She briefly interviewed Bryan Johnson, the tech entrepreneur, who is spending millions trying to roll back his biological age with a view to achieving immortality. Death, he argued, is optional. 'The question, therefore, isn't so much why some people enjoy exceptionally long lifespans,' Ms Saunders concluded, 'but why they should ever die at all.' Tim winked at the battered transistor radio. He was a bit of a winker, was old Tim.

Scattergun impact of killer heels marching towards the window. She looks up with heaving bosom, erect nipples standing to attention beneath tight lab coat. A plane hovers above the playground tree.

One cuppa, of course, was grossly inadequate, especially after getting trolleyed in such a reckless fashion. He needed three or four at the best of times to feel halfway awake. What he knew – he alone, for some inexplicable reason – was simply too much to bear. As a result, Tim no longer rose from the half-dead: he went through life like a somnambulist. This is how he found himself in the bathless bathroom, face to face with a vaguely-familiar figure he could not quite place.

Juicy fruit hang heavy from the branches of the playground tree. Dewy drops glisten metaphysically on the juicy fruit that hang heavy from the branches of the playground tree. Eve wants to climb up the well-hung playground tree. Eve wants to dip the tip of her tongue in the saccharine stickiness of the angel come. Look, look, the apples are crying!

Rooted to the suppurating spot, downright rotting upright, Tim grinned ever so painfully at the imperfect stranger, who was likewise wreathed in smiles, pushing up daisies. In times past, he would probably have squinted disdainfully at the random combination of atoms through a lorgnette. Instead, he unscrewed his plastic optics, slicing them in half, and dipped a rigid digit deep into the tear-filled, gouged-out sockets. Left, then right. Putting the lenses in orbit brought about a bout of briny blinking. They looked like circular, ocular shellfish, but felt like spiky sea urchins.

Miss Ramsay is still gazing up into the heavens, marmalade hair cascading down her back. 'Sod this for a skylark!' she murmurs.

No sooner had his eyes stopped their stroboscopic lashing than high resolution replaced the impressionistic blur. Tim could now recognise the crow's feet, which had been gaining ground at an alarming rate since John Major's general election victory and the release of Suede's first single. A river of rivulets branched out symmetrically on either side of his once sacred temples, producing a groovy, deltoid-etching effect. His complexion reminded him of a ruddy red-pencil drawing by one of the lesser masters. He stood staring at this receding hair- and life-line as though it were a grizzly road accident. 'I'm the chosen one,' he said by way of introduction, 'can'tcha fuckin' see?'

Dappled-shadow camouflage war-dances upon Miss Ramsay's follicular waterfall; it's a jolly kind of jig. 'Mark my words' – she warns jabbing the air with a menstrual fingernail – 'the day cometh that shall burn as an oven.'

There was a handy timing device on Tim's electric toothbrush. You got two minutes flat of serious rotation before a little green light came on indicating that your time was up. With toothpaste dribbling down the hairs of his chinny-chin-chin, he drew back the plastic curtain and glanced at the waterproof fish clock hanging from the shower head. Jeeeesus Christ!

She notices four shadowy figures beyond the plane, silhouetted against the sun of righteousness. Four ghostly figures beyond the pale, skimming candyfloss clouds on e-scooters.

'If thou wilt, thou canst make me clean,' said Tim to the yellow plastic duckling in the chipped polka dot soap dish. He repeated his plea until the yellow plastic duckling told him to cleanse first that *which is* within. 'Sure,' he said, 'but after such knowledge, what forgiveness?' Tim often ended up mourning absolution midway through his morning ablution.

Miss Ramsay's serpentine locks start coiling and recoiling in anticipation of a summery execution.

He stepped gingerly into the bedroom, a sodden towel wrapped round his waist, mumbling something about this duck being a quack. Saskia's black stockings lay legless on the rug. He quickly averted his eyes, so as not to reawaken The Beast at this crucial stage in his grooming routine. As he closed the front door behind him, reeking of Escape by Calvin Klein, Tim felt there was something odd about the apple logo on his PowerBook. He could have sworn that the bitten-off chunk on the right-hand side was missing. Surely, it could not have grown back. No time to check.

An apple falls in slow motion from the playground tree: Tim sees its reflection in the apple of her eye.

The hound in the flat opposite started howling as it did every morning. Cerberus, as they called it, lived at number sixty-six. Whenever he walked by, Tim felt like adding the third, missing six with a chunky black marker pen. All he ever found at the bottom of his briefcase was a tiny stump of a pencil that had almost been sharpened into non-existence.

Glass, shattered; damage, collateral; moans, despair, guts, gore, everywhere, everywhere. 'C'est rien, chéri. T'as encore fait un cauchemar. Allez, rendors-toi'*: Saskia's soothing tones. She wanks him back to sleep. It is not the most professional of wanks, but it certainly does the trick. Next thing he knows, Saskia is trying to wake him up. She is less successful in this endeavour than in the former. She is also far less soothing:* 'Allez, debout, tu vas être en retard si ça continue. C'est toujours la même chose, fais chier à la fin.' *Sitting up in bed, she watches him emerge more dead than alive from his customary semi-coma.*

The night before, it came to pass that Tim dreamed The Dream. Tim dreamed The Dream the night before it came to pass.

Whenever he could reasonably expect his descent to start grinding to a halt, another flight of steps appeared out of nowhere and the ground floor receded again. He would never get to the bottom: it was symbolic, they knew he understood symbolism; they were fucking with his brain, that's what they were doing; they wanted him to jump, they did, over the banister and into the bottomless pit.

He eventually crossed the cobbled courtyard and opened the heavy blue door with the panting lion's head poking its tongue out at passers-by on the other side. Rattling his car keys in his khakis, he walked towards the battered old banger – a Cinquecento straight out of the quattrocento. Thing is, it was not there any more. The car to the keys had vanished, as though erased by Robert Rauschenberg during the night.

Tim stood in the vacant space left by his car, like a phantom limb. He was on the horns of a devilish dilemma. If he did not call Saskia straight away, well, frankly, his life just would not be worth living. If he did call her, however, she would order him to go to the police station. Tim would then have to explain why that was simply out of the question. Sure, he would be convincing: what kind of nitwit would choose to nick *our* car in a street full of Bentleys and BMWs? But she would remain unconvinced. He would be moving: the prophet that hath a dream, let him tell a dream, and Tim would tell her his dream all over again. But she would remain unmoved. He would be argumentative; she would pick an argument. He would remain calm; she would drum her nails on the table. He would be gentle; she would threaten him with the spatula or, worse still, the chopping board.

Tim walked to the Sorbonne, trying to work out how late he would be for his lecture on Milton. As he pontificated on autopilot, he recalled that vain, inglorious paper he had published in *Études Anglaises* at the beginning of his academic career. The thrust of his argument had been that Adam and Eve were, in effect, committing suicide when they partook of the forbidden fruit. It had made quite a stir in the English Department at the time. Little did he know, of course, that, contrary to popular belief, Adam and Eve had never eaten of the tree at all. He still did not know why today; why was beside the point – the tree may have been fruitless for all he knew. Now he firmly believed that their eyes were never opened, and that they were therefore never as gods, knowing good and evil. If all this ran counter to received wisdom, it was precisely because no wisdom had been received in the first place.

Tim was walking back home when, lo and behold, he spotted his car in the very same spot where he had parked it the day before. Inside, there was a letter which, loosely translated, went something like this: it was an emergency – a matter of life and death – we're awfully sorry, please accept these two tickets to the opera in compensation. Saskia, who believed in noble bandits and absolutely adored the opera (*'J'a-dore l'opéra!'*), thought it was a very romantic story. She whooped. She squealed. She even cried. She cried some more when she found out that the apartment had been burgled in their absence.

Tim went straight for the bottle. This time, they were just poking and prying; trying to find out if he had any proof. It was only the beginning. They would not leave him alone. They were closing in on him. After all, he had stumbled upon the greatest genocide in the history of humanity. The genocide of humanity itself.

He knocked back another stiff one and waited for the effect to kick in.

Forty tiddly winks.

Chapter Twenty-Six
FALLING INTO FANCY FRAGMENTS

Where were you – if anywhere – on the night of 5th December 1986?

I was lying low. As low as I was high as they hunted high and low. I was the lowest of the low in the witching hour. Held my peace in the war zone; kept my ear to the ground. I felt the rumbling of the motorbikes in the bowels of the earth, approaching, then receding, then looping round, getting dangerously close again – too close for comfort, certainly, whenever batons were struck against the corrugated iron or scraped across it, making me flinch and close my eyes – and finally growing more and more distant. And so it was that distance grew until, eventually, I realised I could no longer hear the engines at all. There were no more running footsteps either, if memory serves, or screams in the distance; no more ambulance sirens. Just me and my fear and the fullness of solitude shockingly laid bare. Just me, in my second-hand overcoat, lying face down under a roadworks hut, petrified and all alone. Just me.

As predicted, Tim had suddenly vanished. Shortly thereafter, Michel disappeared into the kitchen to rustle up a couple of omelettes for De Niro and Al Pacino (on the house, *bien sûr*). Bola Bola retired behind the counter, where she leafed languidly through the latest issue of *Télé Z,* instead of doing the accounts. Maya made a brief appearance, exchanging a few words with Djamel before leaving a pile of colourful leaflets advertising her next gig on a pedestal table at the entrance. Meanwhile, having lunched at an Italian on rue Monsieur-le-Prince, the man with the ponytail walked past the plaque commemorating the spot where, in the early hours of 6th December 1986, Malik Oussekine was battered to death.

At some point, tomorrow had become today – it must have done or I would not be here, now, writing this – but trying to pinpoint when exactly would be a pointless exercise, and indeed a waste of time, mine as well as yours, my wristwatch having stopped. Ironically, or perhaps fittingly, the opening line of Proust's In Search of Lost Time *wound its way round the elegant clock face like a spiral staircase to oblivion. While I was not looking, and could not see because I could not be seen, you see, Time had come to a standstill. The end of history. Three years before Francis Fukuyama. Since this is not chronicled in any history books, you will just have to take my word for it.*

Simultaneously, as though by telepathy, Loren clicked on the file pertaining to the 1986 student strike. It contained all the pictures taken when they had visited the scene of the crime together. Adam was astonished that he could not recall the exact location of his hideout. Admittedly, the incident had occurred at night, almost forty years earlier. Besides, he had been running for his life. But still. He always expected to experience that flash of recognition – *Ah, that's where it was! That's where I was!* – but it never materialised.

The past few weeks had been a feverish blur of frenzied agitation building up, or so I thought, to a messianic climax. The now of nows, when I would coincide with the world and myself, and feel truly alive at last. This is probably what some Communards were hoping to achieve when, in 1871, they started firing shots at sundry Parisian clocks – literally killing time as opposed to my enforced Beckettian biding. In the event it was a non-event – neither revolution nor revelation came to pass – unless, of course, the non-event was *the event. Jorge Luis Borges suggests that the 'aesthetic phenomenon' is nothing but 'this imminence of a revelation which does not occur', and who am I to argue?*

The most likely spot, he said, was at the intersection of rue Racine and rue Monsieur-le-Prince. Or further along, he later added, as they headed back towards Odéon, in the recess above the steep steps[23] leading down to rue de l'École-de-Médecine. That was another possibility, he said,

23 These steps are on rue Antoine Dubois.

before dismissing it after pacing up and down and looking round with a quizzical mien.

I crawled out from under my hideout, and began the long march home, all the way to Pigalle, now that the coast was clear. The following morning I would learn, on the radio, that a young man – Malik Oussekine – had been killed by the voltigeurs *just a few metres from where I was holed up. Some of the screams I heard were probably his.*

Loren asked many questions about the student occupation of the Sorbonne. Not without a certain amount of pride, Adam pointed out it was the first (and, as far as he knew, the last) time this had happened since *les événements* of May 1968. In Homeric terms, he recounted the episode when a far-right professor let in a group of tooled-up fascist stormtroopers through a back door. Following a brief but bruising altercation, the invaders were repelled.

The voltigeurs *– a police motorcycle unit created in response to the 1968 riots – had been deployed in order to transform a peaceful student movement (that was largely supported by public opinion) into a violent one, thus triggering a cycle of disorder and repression. Behind the driver sat a truncheon-toting thug, whose mission it was to hit anything that moved. The first time I ever saw them, I was having a coffee, one evening, with a fellow Sorbonne student in a small café (that no longer exists) on boulevard Saint-Michel. We watched as the motorcyclists* *lined up across the boulevard, wondering what on earth they were up to.*

In the jubilant aftermath, someone played 'White Riot' on a little cassette player. Joe Strummer would have been so chuffed, Adam observed. The occupation came to an end when it was broken up by the riot police. That same night was when it happened.

There had been a demonstration in the afternoon, but the Latin Quarter was now occupied by people who were eating out or going to the cinema. Suddenly, the motorcyclists charged in unison, attacking indiscriminately all those they encountered, including an elderly couple who – unbelievably – were knocked to the ground and battered senseless. The motorcyclists pursued those who fled on to the pavement and even, in some cases, into the buildings where they sought refuge. The owner of our café promptly locked the door, to prevent the police from coming in: the windows of his establishment were soon smeared with the blood of those who had remained outside. This terrifying and shameful event was not reported in the press as no journalists were present at the time. We contacted Le Monde, Libération, *and the AFP news agency, but to no avail. It was as though nothing had happened. The counterrevolution would not be televised.*

After the strike, they launched a student magazine called *Le Temps Révolu.* The title was chosen by opening *Zarathustra* at random until they stumbled upon something they liked the sound of. Editorial meetings were held at a Greek student's flat. He was called Costas, and had fled his homeland in order to escape military service. According to rumours, he had been a kind of Cohn-Bendit figure back home. (Adam still has the copy of Bourdieu's *La Distinction* he lent him. A sticker on the back indicates it was purchased in November 1984.) All in all, two issues were produced, which they sold half-heartedly on Place de la Sorbonne. In the first one – by far the best – a girl called Myriam had written an intriguing review of *Bad Blood* – a film which, for Adam, came to embody the spirit of 86, despite never having seen it. (Unless, of course, it was for that very reason.) Myriam was one of at least two girlfriends Costas was sleeping with, although not (as far as he knew) simultaneously. He had absolutely no idea what the other one was called, although he could still vaguely conjure up her tomboyish features and *coupe au carré*. The last time he bumped into Myriam and Costas, they were scrutinising pictures from *Down By Law* and *Stranger Than Paradise* outside an arthouse cinema — possibly the same one those pensioners had left before being assaulted by the police.

The second, and last time, I came face to face with the voltigeurs, *I was walking down boulevard Saint-Michel with a couple of friends following our eviction from the Sorbonne. As soon as I saw the motorbikes on the horizon, I told them to run for their lives. They did not understand because we were doing nothing wrong, but I knew what was about to happen, so I ran as fast as I could and my friends followed me after a moment's hesitation and we could hear the motorbikes behind us, catching up, and we turned a corner and then possibly another and I dived under a roadworks hut. A few minutes later batons were being struck against the walls of my hideout.*

The file also contained a short text written by Adam, but you know that, having just read it.

Chapter Twenty-Seven
WORDS FOR LOST

The man with the ponytail took rue Racine on his left. His heart skipped a beat when he spotted the neoclassical columns of Théâtre de l'Odéon in the distance. He crossed over onto Place de l'Europe, narrowly avoiding a laundry van that stopped abruptly outside Hôtel Michelet Odéon. Still cursing under his breath, he contemplated the colourful banners hanging from the theatre's façade advertising several plays, including – crucially – *À la recherche du pain perdu*. He took a few pictures with his phone camera, turned round and essayed a selfie. Not bad, he thought. He then ambled up rue Corneille with its arches *en enfilade*. Black railings resembling spears with gilded pointed heads denied access to the gallery running round the theatre above street level. The man knew that one of the arches – used by staff members to access their workplace through a side entrance – was devoid of railings. As he reached this opening, three figures wearing balaclavas jumped down from the gallery, obstructing his passage. Sensing something whizzing towards him *a tergo*, he looked round and saw two other figures in balaclavas riding an e-scooter on the pavement. The passenger, who towered above the driver, sported angel wings and brandished a large pair of scissors – snip, snip, snip. A scuffle ensued. The next thing he knew, the scooter was speeding away, ahead of him. *J'ai attrapé la queue du Mickey*, the passenger shrieked, holding his ponytail aloft like a scalp or a severed head.

Chapter Twenty-Eight
LONG STORY SHORT

Of course, that's it! Loren, who had ordered another flat white, suddenly realised what the rosette pattern reminded her of: *Angelus Novus,* Paul Klee's famous artwork, which Walter Benjamin identified as the angel of history. She looked up. A young woman marched past the café, almost colliding with a courier carrying a large cardboard box. The heels of her brown boots sounded like gunshots. She crossed the road, checked the time on her phone, and loitered awhile outside the primary school, smoking a cigarette. She had the air of someone who thought she was late but turned out to be early. Loren opened a file named '1973' and clicked on the class picture. The teacher, standing on the left (not far from little Adam, sitting in the second row), looked remarkably like this woman. It was uncanny. Was she a teacher too? Loren wondered. Did she view history as a chain of events, or as a single catastrophe?

Chapter Twenty-Nine
THE POETICS OF NON-SPACE: AN INSTRUCTION MANUAL

I live on a trap street. One of those fictitious roads cartographers add to their maps in order to confound plagiarists. Have I confounded you now that you have found me? Found me here, of all places – a nonexistent one. Do you feel trapped, or should I say cornered, in my snug little cul-de-sac?

Never place a foot outside the operator area. Make sure you do not get pinned or crushed. Watch your hands at all times.

I was watching you down there from up here, walking up and down. Watching you all along doing it all wrong. Cocking it up for fifty odd years – drifting. You couldn't see me, but I was shaking my head. Shaking my head slowly. At you. Shaking my head while brushing my hair. Brushing my hair at you. Slowly.

Pull up your socks. Buck up your ideas. Sit up straight. Wash your hands at all times.

I had a good mind to go down – give you a piece of it. Put an end to this nonsense right there and then. Nip it in the bud.

The display shows the code for a detected event requiring service: contact your supervisor at once.

I felt the urge to walk at a brisk pace. Dramatically. Arms folded over my breasts. Majestically. A body in motion. Alarmingly. Producing a fragrant slipstream for the two men outside the café. Sitting idly. Weaponising my boots to make them look up while stirring their dinky espressos. Distractedly. Creating a bit of a stir. Assuredly. Causing minor spillages in their saucers. Saucily.

Beware, the power unit will swing wide in the opposite direction.

Would you sense me slicing the air like a rent in the fabric of time? Would you turn round as I breathed 'Shit's about to get real' down the back of your neck? Would I wag my finger before marching you from whence I came? Would I have to drag you, kicking and screaming, past the café with the two Corsicans stirring their dinky espressos? Alas, these are but idle musings. Corners cannot be cut in such a reckless fashion. I must bide my time up here, like a spider in its web, while you lose yourself in the nooks and crannies of streets grown uncanny.

Rotate the top of the twist grip in the direction you wish to travel.

I summoned you by text, citing unfinished business – making a point of leaving no wriggle room regarding time and place. I knew you'd appreciate the gesture. Naturally it came as a shock, but deep down you felt blessed I hadn't forgotten; relieved that the chase was over at last. Could I still be of this world? You tried to work it out but mental arithmetics was never your forte. Could I be AI-generated? Some kind of ghost? How on earth had I – *if indeed it really was I* – got your number? None of it made any sense, yet everything seemed to slot back into place. It was as though a great weight had suddenly been lifted from your shoulders. This, Adam, is how one feels when one cannot sink any lower.

Tilt forwards or backwards for the required angle.

Having hit rock bottom, you opened the window and just stared into space. The whole universe had slowed down to a leisurely pace, now that you were resigned to it. Everything seemed right. Necessary, even. Lest you forget: I am the woman who stilled the world. You'd just fall apart without me.

Know the distance it takes to stop before you start.

The metro came to a standstill. (At this juncture I started drumming my fingernails on the dining-room table, providing a tense backbeat to your excursion.) The lights went out and the driver explained, over the tannoy, that the power cut was due to the presence of trespassers on the line. The kind of people who fail to recognise that they will always be on the wrong side of the tracks, however many times they cross them. Besides a few bewildered tourists – who had probably strayed too far north – no one seemed in the least surprised.

If you wish to interrupt the process, press the cancel button.

With the lights back on, the metro resumed its journey. You plucked the freesheet that was poking out of the folding seat next to yours, intent on using it as a prop. *Que faisaient les employés de leur journée alors que le musée avait été vidé de ses oeuvres?* A passenger alighted at the next stop. Despite your best efforts, you couldn't help but notice a large black shape lying on the platform. Out of the corner of your eye, through the open doors. *Dans son rapport public annuel publié mercredi, la Cour des comptes épingle la gestion de l'ancien musée national des Arts et Traditions populaires (MNATP), dans le XVIe.* Another chthonic denizen. Drug-addled, no doubt, or mentally ill – possibly both. *L'endroit a fermé en 2005, mais le ministère de la Culture y a maintenu jusqu'en 2011 une centaine d'employés, 'dont l'activité était des plus réduites'.* Still, how on earth could he sleep with trainloads of commuters trundling through his bedroom every few minutes? Was he playing dead or dead serious? Filthy blanket or body bag?

Wash it inside and out with soap and water, using the brush provided.

As you exited – via a flight of steps, along a corridor, up an escalator, through automatic doors, up a second flight of steps into the sunlight – you squinted over your left shoulder at the cinema across the road. Sandwiched between a cheap chain *brasserie* and a McDonald's, L'Atlas is one of the last porn fleapits in town. An all-caps CINE X neon sign drives the point home. You can just about recall when such establishments spread through the neighbourhood – between the release of *Emmanuelle* and the rise of VHS – like a bad case of the clap. Endless downmarket iterations of Sylvia Kristel and Bruce Lee – the poor man's sex and violence. The titles were often so absurd that they veered into surreal territory (not that you'd heard of surrealism despite living only a few minutes away from André Breton's apartment). *Coupe-toi les ongles et passe-moi le beurre* was a classic in this respect (although I rather suspect you didn't get the reference to *Last Tango in Paris* which, to be fair, mitigates the title's utter stupidity). You spotted it on Place de Clichy (where *Journey to the End of the Night* begins; not that you would have been cognizant of this either). I know because I was on the same bus as you. You pretended not to see me. I knew you had, though, as you went bright red. It was standing-room only when I boarded the bus; you were ensconced at the back with your father. At each stop passengers got off and I was able to inch up the aisle in my brown boots. The closer I got, the more you blushed. You reached your destination before I reached you, but you have always wondered what would have happened. The scenario plays out again and again in your twisted daydreams and sweetest nightmares. Alfred Hitchcock claimed that 'sitting outside the headmaster's office' had taught him all he knew about 'suspense and fear'. Brace yourself, Adam. You are sitting outside the headmistress's office. I am about to open the door. I am shortening the longing.

Learn your ABC. Mind your P's and Q's. Dot the i's and cross the t's.

In their heyday, adult cinemas were mainly frequented by people who couldn't afford the services of the numerous *filles de joie* working in the area. L'Atlas's patrons today are different. They go there to fuck, not to watch cheesy vintage porn. At least, that's what you've heard and you like the idea: real life trumping its representation. You are also attracted to the enigmatic painting above the entrance. It depicts a topless, semi-recumbent woman in suspenders, white stockings, and a skimpy baby-blue slip. Her hairdo and features remind you from afar of Dorothea Tanning in that famous self-portrait. Its title momentarily eludes you. (I'm shaking my head again.) The artist's remit was obviously to go for a sci-fi sexploitation vibe vaguely reminiscent of *Barbarella.* A huge full moon looms up behind the young woman, itself set against the infinity of space dotted with the odd planet here and there. Some of these, like Mars, are recognisable, but most are generic. Atlas, one presumes, is holding up Planet Earth on which the Tanning lookalike is proudly showcasing her tits. This, of course, is a common, but most regrettable, misconception: it is in fact the sky that the Greek Titan was condemned to hold up on his shoulders. You wonder what you will be condemned to as you make your way across Place Pigalle.

The suction power can be adjusted by using the airflow control on the hose handle.

There is a recess on the right-hand side of the Folies Pigalle nightclub, where the last old-school *péripatéticienne* still plied her trade only a few years ago. She looked both ancient and timeless, putting you in mind of Walter Pater's description of Mona Lisa: 'like the vampire, she has been dead many times, and learned the secrets of the grave'. Dressed in black from head to toe, she would emerge from her gloomy cavity – like a spider out of a dark corner – whenever a potential punter walked by. The last time you saw her, her face was ravaged by what looked like bubonic plague. Baudelaire would have appreciated this touch. You couldn't help thinking that she must have introduced a substantial discount owing to this disfigurement. She soon disappeared altogether. As you near the corner of rue Pigalle and rue de Douai, you think of another relic from the early seventies, who worked well into her seventies, at number sixty-five. She embodied a strange inversion that occurred in the wake of the sexual revolution: *les p'tites femmes de Pigalle* – as Serge Lama called them in his 1973 hit – became increasingly mumsy and schoolmarmish, while many civilian women started dressing like streetwalkers. There's a lesson in there somewhere. Towards the end of her long career, the hoary old whore, as she called herself cheerily, confided that her clients were now so old they could barely get up the stairs, let alone get it up. She has disappeared too, presumed dead. The street corners of Pigalle are all haunted.

This appliance is for indoor use only. Do not store in wet places.

You are now on rue Chaptal. The street where I live should be the second on the left, shortly after rue Henner. You can't find it. You backtrack when you hit rue Blanche and start messing around with your phone. You bump into a child with a weird pudding-basin haircut. Worse still, the street has now vanished altogether from Google Maps. You start feeling dizzy. You think of the sex workers who would approach you when you were no more than ten or eleven, on your way to school, with your *cartable* on your back. They'd say, *'Tu viens, chéri?'* in the softest of voices and you'd blush like you did that time on the bus. Two men are drinking espressos outside Le Hareng Rouge. They look like gangsters in a film. Some kids have emerged from the school across the road, chanting curiously old-fashioned political slogans. One of them reminds you of yourself at the same age. Your head is spinning. You can hear the deafening sound of fingernails drumming on a table nearby. You go bright red. Same colour as the fingernails. The boy with the weird pudding-basin haircut bumps into you again and you fall in front of the gangsters sipping their espressos. The drumming stops abruptly.

Keep an eye on the power supply cable and obstructions along the way. Press the release button to adjust the length of the telescopic tube.

I shall leave you there, young man, to reflect upon what you've done – or rather what you haven't. Where you went wrong. Why you never got a handle on life; could never make head nor tail of it. I mean, did it even occur to you to read the instructions at any point? Did you ever open your copy of the manual? Anyway, you'll hear me pottering about in the background. Doing *stuff.* Things that need to be done. After all, I can't dilly-dally all day. Daily. I'm a busy woman, me. Busy, busy, busy. I shall make as much noise as possible, like a little girl trying on her mother's shoes. Talking of which, I'm removing my brown boots. And now my filmy white blouse. I'm wriggling out of my tight skirt. Stepping out of it. I'm walking about in my underwear. Bet you're picturing it baby blue and white like the Tanning lookalike – am I right? Well, I'm not saying because that would be telling. Just sketching out. Intimating the intimate. Are you panting in the corner you painted yourself into? You hear me switch on the vacuum cleaner. I'm cleaning the vacuum. In my mysterious underwear. I leave the room. There is even more room now. More vacuum to hoover up. It's a conundrum – a woman's work is never done. I'm in the kitchen. Pouring myself a glass of wine. A cheeky rosé I bought on rue Lepic. You hear the music from the transistor radio. It's the end of 'La bonne du curé' by Annie Cordy followed by Ninno Ferrer's 'Le sud'. You can hear water coming from somewhere else and Michel Sardou singing 'Le France' as I carry the radio into the bathroom. I'm running a bath. Bubbles galore. Earrings by the soap dish on the washbasin. Glass on the tub's rim. Foam on the stem. Candles. The works. I close the door. I remove my underwear. The mirror is all steamed up. Frankly, I'm not surprised. I pick up my copy of *Ferdydurke*. You recognise a song by Carlos – the singer, not the terrorist, silly – but can't recall the title or make out the lyrics. I open the door and take the transistor back into the kitchen. I return for the empty glass I forgot. They're playing Joe Dassin's 'L'été indien'. I tilt the glass back and poke my tongue inside to receive the last drop of wine. Pour myself a second one – don't mind if I do. A different kind of music is now emanating from the kitchen. It's the sound of a girl band produced by Phil Spector underwater. The sound of Ann Quin drowning. A few droplets run down the length of my back. I'm rummaging through my knicker drawer, swaying to the music, a towel draped around my long hair. All women are secret mermaids. I return to the living room, where you are still standing in the corner; in the corner standing still. I sit down to put on some black silk stockings, then stand up to fasten them to the suspender belts. If only you stepped back a little, you'd be able to see a shadow play on the wall, like the prisoners in Plato's Cave. A moving cave painting. Moving, of course, is strictly forbidden: no reverse striptease for you, you naughty boy! I step into a pair of high heels and walk back to the bedroom, switching off the radio on my way. I return, a few minutes later, wearing a semi-fitted dress with three-quarter-length sleeves and a bold print designed to make a statement in the office – which in my case is a classroom. Your classroom. Our classroom. I sit down to paint my nails. I cross my legs so you can hear the whisper of my stockings under my dress.

The air intake should be lined up with the notch in the motor unit.

Ah, there goes the school bell! I open the window: you can see rue Chaptal from here if you crane your neck. That's me down there, at the entrance. That bold print on my dress really is making a statement, isn't it? And you can just tell I'm wearing stockings, even at this distance. It's nice to make an effort. So rare these days. The two men across the road haven't failed to notice. They keep staring while stirring their cafés con lech. Further along the street there's a gang of six or seven diminutive hooligans, chanting the same slogan over and over again. And – *quelle surprise!* – there you are in their midst. '*Debré, salaud, le peuple aura ta peau.*' You've no idea who Debré is or what *ratapo* means, for that matter, and I'm adding an extra thirty minutes to your corner time, young man. That'll teach you to chant political slogans in public. It's 1973. You're not even eight, for crying out loud! Picasso has just died and you've all been doing these cubist-style doodles – trying to outweird one another. I tell you that whatever shit you make up, it will always resemble something that already exists in the world. This doesn't go down too well. Some of you are looking positively depressed. I also inform you that the late Spanish artist once declared that it had taken him just four years to paint like Raphael but a lifetime to paint like a child. There's a lesson in there, I say. You all look at me nonplussed. To be honest, I'm not sure either how this relates to the utter crap you've all produced. Perhaps you're already passed it at eight. Maybe that's what it is. As J. M. Barrie writes, 'Two is the beginning of the end'.

Tighten the nut by hand until the surface is properly adjusted.

How do you dwell in your little corner? There was a spider there the other day, you know. In that very same spot. I won't lie to you: it was massive. I walked past it several times, as it had somehow managed to blend in with the surroundings. A true corner dweller. It reminded me of one of Francesca Woodman's long exposures, where the artist merges with the wallpaper. The spider had absented itself by becoming the corner it was cornered in. *Tu es l'espace où tu es.* I was most impressed and endeavoured to live up to the arachnid's cunning. It was the least I could do. I flattered it by feigning ignorance of its sinister presence, reached for the first suitable object to hand – a copy of *The Poetics of Space* – and flattened the abomination so many times that legs were flying in all directions. 'That most sordid of all havens, the corner, deserves to be examined,' writes Bachelard in that now somewhat battered book. You focus on the modulations of my voice; the sound of my high heels on the creaking floorboards. 'But life in corners, and the universe itself withdrawn into a corner with the daydreamer, is a subject about which poets will have more to tell us.' Breathe deeper, daydreamer. I wonder if you are picturing me walking towards you as my voice grows louder and then walking away as it fades? 'They will not hesitate to give this daydream all its reality.' Can you detect that I'm holding up the paperback in one hand while the other rests elegantly on my hip? You see, a corner is both a dead end and a gateway. A negation of the world that leads to the rise of a new one, which – although imaginary – has its own reality and power to alter the real world. Does the angle between two walls have a happy ending?

Use paper that is commensurate with the quality of the product. Choose a clean, readable sans-serif font. Provide plenty of white space.

You've been staring at that white wall for hours on end. You must know it by heart. Every scuff and scratch. Leonardo da Vinci advised artists to find inspiration in the marks on walls. These, he claimed, would furnish them with an 'abundance of designs and subjects perfectly new'. Max Ernst swore by this method. He was Dorothea Tanning's lover and then husband. There's no such thing as a white wall. I put the book down, sensing that your attention is wandering – drifting. When I look up, you've vanished. According to Bachelard, 'all corners are haunted, if not inhabited'. I walk over to the corner you're haunting and examine the wall, in search of inspiration. There's a faint crack I've never noticed before. I trace its trajectory with my painted forefinger. You'd just fall apart without me.

Switch off the appliance. Remove the plug from the mains supply and rewind the power cable.

Chapter Thirty
WHAT THE BUTLER NEVER SAW

(The dinner party / living room)

The doorbell rings. Blandine de Blancmange is about to get up, but her husband, Odilon, puts his hand on her shoulder. He absents himself. It is a process. The living room is so vast that his egress takes on an epic quality, as in a film by Antonioni. The two women eavesdrop on the two male voices in the hall. They exchange a knowing glance: they have recognised the first guest. Hégésippe Turpin-Goulet strides in, all limbs outstretched. He kisses Blandine on both cheeks, holds her at arm's length to take in her elaborate outfit. He lets go and she gives him a twirl. Now it is Loren's turn. She does not twirl. He looks crestfallen but tries to hide it. Odilon appears in the doorframe. He mouths something, pointing frantically towards the lengthy corridor leading to the kitchen. Blandine excuses herself. Hégésippe scrutinises the books on the shelves while engaging in amiable small talk. He runs his forefinger along their spines until it alights on *Je suis la Femme Bigorneau.*

'Ah, *Bigorneau*! Such an important novel for people of my generation.'

He opens the tattered tome, which is dedicated to Odilon; smiles at the squiggly chicken-scratch script, then slides the book back on the shelf. He sees himself reading it, totally engrossed, sitting cross-legged on the stone floor in the occupied Sorbonne during the student strike, back in 1986. All he remembers clearly is the ecstatic climax, when the protagonist – a young female writer given to extravagant mystical visions – perishes of spontaneous combustion triggered by her incendiary prose.

'I trust Zanzibar won't be joining us tonight,' he sighs.

'No, he was sectioned at Sainte-Anne during the summer. I paid him a visit yesterday: he was heavily sedated and delirious half the time.'

She does not mention the letter Sostène gave her in which he describes a recurring dream that has been haunting him of late. It involves Loren. Her face is smudged, 'as though by Francis Bacon's thumb' but he knows it is Loren. She stands motionless, bolt upright in a pair of high-heeled shoes, looking straight ahead, then slowly hitches up her pleated miniskirt, under which she is naked, to reveal a burning bush. Sostène holds out his hands, as you might do in front of a camp fire on a cold winter's night, but the skirt comes down, like a curtain at the end of a play. '*La Femme Bigorneau, c'est moi,*' she says in mellifluous yet robotic tones – the kind used for airport announcements. A faint enigmatic smile plays upon her lips.

The letter was splattered with dried semen stains.

'It really won't be the same without old Zanzibar. I don't think he's ever missed one of these dinner parties.'

Hégésippe walks to a long table laden with crudités, canapés, and all manner of finger food: devilled quail eggs, cod cured in vine leaves, honey and chilli sweet potatoes... He helps himself to a generous handful of Jerusalem artichoke crisps.

'What you English call *amuse-bouche,* we call *amuse-gueule.* We're not so polite,' he remarks with his mouth full. '*Oh, génial! Des Apéricubes!...* You had a bit of a *ménage à trois* going on with Zanzibar and Meuniaire if I'm not mistaken. It was the talk of the town.'

'You make it sound like a French farce,' says Loren, sensing this is retribution for refusing to flirt. 'I shagged both of them, not that it's any business of yours, but I did so sequentially.'

'So no threesome then?'

'No. I'm sorry to disappoint. The configuration was triangular, though, if that's any consolation. It was a textbook case of mimetic desire. The fact that I'd slept with Sostène obviously spiced things up for Théodule – he probably felt he was cuckolding his great rival. They were both one-night stands but they became obsessed and started stalking me and, through me, each other. I remember one time, at Gare du Nord when I was going back to London to see my parents: Théodule was watching Sostène watching me travel up the escalator to the Eurostar terminal. I was on the phone and pretended not to see them.'

Chapter Thirty-One
ANGEL AT A 35 DEGREE ANGLE

Imperious, impervious, girl on the escalator going up, pulling her case behind her like a lapdog on a lead, going up. Nifty, shifty, eyeing up girl going up; naughty, haughty, hoity-toity.

Did she condescend to look down upon you as she went up, angel at a 35 degree angle? Did she acknowledge your existence, as she plucked celestial chords on her flyaway hair and breathed honeyed tones down her cellular phone? Did she fuck. No: your eyes did not meet. You looked at me looking at you looking at her looking up, all high and mighty, pulling her case behind her behind like a slave on a lead, soaring up – she mighty high, you mighty sore. Looked at me, you did, with your chastised eyes, all hot and bothered, hot, hot under the collar, your face a slapped arse.

Chapter Thirty-Two
AND THE ANGEL SAW THE ASS

(The dinner party / living room)

Blandine reappears. She beckons with one hand, shushes with the other. Loren exits, an inquisitive look on her face. Odilon smiles at them as they walk by. *He* knows. The doorbell rings: Mina Harpenden, followed by Francis Scopitone and Tacita Rimini-Thompson. Odilon is about to close the front door when Giovanni Sfumato and Claire Iris emerge from the dimly-lit art deco lift. Kisses and pleasantries are exchanged; coats and scarves removed and hung up in the vestibule.

In the living room, Hégésippe attempts to peel off the foil encasing a little cube of cheese. It is ever so fiddly and in no way as straightforward as it sounds. In fact, it is fiendishly difficult: a Herculean task of Lilliputian proportions that proves well-nigh impossible to accomplish. The tiny red strip is most recalcitrant. Most recalcitrant indeed. Infuriatingly so. Hégésippe is all thumbs. Flummoxed, he curses under his breath. Foiled again. No matter. He tries once more. Fails again. Fails better.

Odilon puts a record on the stereo. *This is the end of every song that we sing.* The new arrivals are greeted by Robert Smith's rather majestic melancholy hymn to ultimacy. A fitting choice.

Meanwhile, the two women tiptoe down the endless corridor with its treacherous floorboards. When they finally reach their destination, Blandine spins round, forefinger crossed over puckered lips. Struggling not to burst out laughing, she steps aside to let her friend go by. The door is ajar. Loren pushes it a little further, peeks in and gasps audibly. They flee, shrieking like schoolgirls. They are two bowling balls rolling down the narrow corridor – on a collision course with the ten-pin guests now encumbering the hallway. Blandine head-butts Ninon Neenaw, whose sharp elbow angles into Anna Coluthon, whose nose bleeds so profusely that Archie West faints, his prone body a booby trap for Perrine Jouët as she strides confidently through the front door Odilon has deliberately left wide open. Loren simply stumbles into the arms of Georges Davos, who, as a recent divorcee fancies his chances, but Perrine accidentally yanks his trousers down in a bid to decelerate her headlong plunge into the void. Donatienne, who has just walked up the four flights of stairs as part of her fitness regimen, stops in her tracks when she catches sight of her ex-husband standing in public with his slacks around his ankles. Océane and Athelstan rush to pick up Perrine, who is still draped over Archie. Archie gradually comes to. Manuella and Teddy try to convince him that he has not been attacked by anyone, let alone Arthur Cravan, but Archie is having none of it. *I saw him, I tell you – saw him with my very own eyes. It was him,* he raves, *he's back...*

Oblivious to all the brouhaha, Donatienne hands Blandine a little gift in a dainty paper bag from Le Bon Marché. *C'est rien, tu sais.* It is a blouse. Blandine seems delighted, kisses her on both cheeks. *Fallait pas.* She walks to the vestibule. Donatienne calls her back. She removes a sticker from the cellophane wrapper – S for small – and slaps it on Georges's Y-fronts as she walks by without even making eye contact. Ordalie de Nananaire giggles. Vaping in front of an open window, she vanishes intermittently in a puff of smoke.

Odilon shepherds everyone into the living room, the lame and the blind drunk. He puts on the latest Nick Cave. Hégésippe, who is chatting to Francis by the bookshelves, holds up a copy of *And the Ass Saw the Angel.* They were just talking about Nick Cave, he says. *Ça alors!* Their conversation then turns to coincidences – whether they exist or not.

'What is Alexis Boyer doing?' Victorine Gribiche is eager to meet the handsome young celebrity chef Blandine has managed to recruit for this year's dinner party.

'You mean who,' says Loren. 'You know Anaïs Chevalier?'

'Wasn't she the runner-up on the show?'

'Indeed she was.'

'Well?'

'Well, I just saw Alexis doing her on Blandine's kitchen table.' She points in the general direction of the corridor.

'He has the most gorgeous backside, with these cute little dimples.' She awards it a chef's kiss. 'Frankly, I can't think of anything else right now.'

They move over to the table. Loren passes her a plate, and Victorine helps herself to the food on offer. She tries a little bit of everything. Loren's evocation of Alexis and his buns of steel has given her quite an appetite. So fair and so firm. Hard, really hard.

Tacita sidles up to her. What are you working on?' she whispers.

'Tacita! You made me jump! No need to whisper – it's not a state secret, you know! I'm translating a novel by N. E. Tchans called *Corydon in Croydon*.'

'Intriguing title.'

'Yes. I'm not quite sure what to do with it, to be honest. I mean, *Corydon à Croydon* is perfectly adequate, especially as Chans alludes to Gide on a couple of occasions.[24] Then again, nobody's heard of Croydon over here.'

'But Croydon offers a shopping experience nonpareil! The French really don't know what they're missing.' Tacita laughs. 'What's it about?'

'It's about a guy who, driven by a morbid obsession with Captain Sensible, suddenly decides to up sticks and move to South London, having lived in the sticks all his life.'

'Tim – my husband – is a big fan of the Captain,' says Saskia Selkirk.

'Isn't he here?' Loren asks, scanning the room.

'He was meant to come, but you know how unpredictable and eccentric he is.'

'*I* don't,' Tacita says.

24 Loren is referring to André Gide's controversial *Corydon*, 1924.

'Where do I even start? Let me give you one example. We've been living in Paris for decades, but he's never set eyes on the Eiffel Tower. I mean, he's probably seen it out of the corner of his eye on occasion – it's almost impossible not to – but he's never looked at it directly. Not deliberately.'

'Guy de Maupassant, who thought the Eiffel Tower was an abominable blot on the cityscape, used to dine there regularly,' Tacita says, 'because it was pretty much the only spot in Paris where you could avoid it.'

'That's funny! Tim has no aesthetic objections, as far as I know. He's just convinced his experience of Paris would cease to be authentic – that he would suddenly be reduced to the level of a glorified tourist.'

'That *is* a little odd,' Tacita concedes.

The doorbell rings. A baby cries in the hallway. Loren goes to meet the proud parents – Crispin and Millicent Beaufort – who are also this year's guests of honour. Fashionably late, thinks Loren, as Théodule Meuniaire emerges from Ordalie's candyfloss-scented cloud of smoke.

'Salut Loren, ça va? Des nouvelles de Sostène?'

Animated by animus, he cuts to the quick. His tone is deceptively casual, but Loren is not taken in. The hatchet has not been buried. The rivalry goes on...

Chapter Thirty-Three
CELESTEVILLE'S BURNING

Sostène Zanzibar was not feeling himself that day; someone else was. A journalist from an English paper. Name of Loren. Loren Ipsum. Something along those lines. The interview had gone remarkably well. Such probing questions. Very stimulating, very in-depth. There was no denying that Ms Ipsum was thoroughly a young woman. Hang on, cross that out. Was a thorough young woman. Very thorough indeed.

In a bid to impress her host, she had taken up gesticulation with all the fervour of a new convert. It was a joy to behold. Her impeccably-manicured hands would suddenly flutter away from the warmth of her lap, describing graceful ellipses as if trying to conjure up words that could not possibly exist. Ever. In any language. *Even French.*

Yet Loren had struggled to comprehend the answers to some (if not most) of her questions. The fact that the former bore little (if any) relation to the latter did not help. Neither did Zanzibar's scattergun delivery nor his baffling habit of peppering his sentences with arcane references to Heidegger and Blanchot. Whenever he switched to pidgin English, he sounded like Jacques Derrida dubbed by Inspector Clouseau, which proved an even greater source of confusion, frankly.

At one point, the ink ran out of her biro, whereupon Zanzibar produced a pencil from his inside pocket with a little flourish. 'Men,' he said, 'alwez ave two penceuls.' He almost winked, but thought better of it.

*

Published in late 1986, *Je suis la Femme Bigorneau* was a *succès de scandale* which took the literary establishment by storm; a *cause célèbre* that turned Zanzibar into the *enfant terrible* of French letters overnight. Like Leos Carax's film *Bad Blood*, also released at the end of that year, it seemed to capture the zeitgeist, polarising opinion along a generational fault line. Louis Pauwels, editor of *Le Figaro Magazine*, claimed the novella was a perfect illustration of the 'mental AIDS' afflicting the nation's youth. 'Makes Schopenhauer sound positively chipper,' wrote Josyanne Savigneau in her full-page rave review for *Le Monde*. 'The kind of book that exists on the slippery cusp between pure genius and utter gibberish,' wrote a critic at *Le Matin de Paris*. 'Bof!' Philippe Sollers is reported to have said, when sounded on the subject, mid-*pied de porc farci grillé*, at Brasserie Lipp. Zanzibar was all over the gossip columns too. He dated Béatrice Dalle (who had recently starred in *Betty Blue*), wrote a song for Étienne Daho, appeared in a video with Les Rita Mitsouko (playing the glockenspiel), spent his nights at the ultra hip Bains Douches nightclub and was headbutted by Jean d'Ormesson on prime-time TV during *Apostrophes*, the highly influential literary talk show. His parents – René and Monique – told *Actuel* that they had always known, deep down, that Sostène was special. *'On sentait bien qu'il allait devenir artiste ou écrivain,'* said his mum. *'C'était vraiment un chieur,'* his father concurred. They confided that they had done their level best to make him as miserable as possible throughout his childhood, so as to provide him with a lifetime of neuroses that would feed his future creative endeavours. *'N'empêche qu'on a drôlement bien réussi notre coup,'* said René, beaming with paternal pride: it was the gift that keeps giving. Zanzibar, however, was overwhelmed by his new-found notoriety. Béatrice Dalle soon left him and he started dabbling in too many drugs. Rumour has it that he could drink the likes of Antoine Blondin, Serge Gainsbourg or Alain Pacadis under the table (all three of them on one occasion, if certain reports are to be believed). His next four books were minor bestsellers, and one of them was even turned into a film with Juliette Binoche (*La Bonniche*, 1991), but Zanzibar was never able to replicate the impact of *Bigorneau*, which he always likened to his seminal first orgasm (1979). Each new novel resembled an increasingly faded photocopy of the original blueprint, giving rise to what Sam Jordison described in *The Guardian* as 'a sense of perpetual *déjà vu* on a dimmer switch'. *Bref*, his work seemed condemned to a gradual, but irreversible, running down; a depletion of vital energy that implied a dismal future of erectile dysfunction, hair loss, and growing inertia.

*

The journalist's black Moleskin notebook lay open, face down, on the coffee table. After an hour or so, weighty topics had been dropped in favour of increasingly flirtatious small talk. Zanzibar got up to refill her glass and, instinctively, she got up too and now they were kissing, deep and slow, their tongues going round and round and round like the ground bass number in the background, and he gently lifted up her summer frock as the melody soared over the looping bassline, and their bodies were grinding, their tongues intertwining, her head spinning, and she found herself reclining in a Le Corbusier-style chaise longue. *'J'aime quand ça s'incarne,'* she whispered, drawing him hither with her long legs that he now sported nonchalantly over his shoulders. Leaning on her forearms, she tilted her head back, closed her eyes and bit her lower lip. A slow intake of breath – like a deep drag on a Gitane – subsided into a faint, low-pitched moan, not dissimilar to the sound a puppy makes when kicked.

'Thanks,' she said, upon leaving. Zanzibar stared at the outstretched hand last seen clasping his erect penis. 'For having me?' she added by way of explanation, but the high-rising terminal transformed her statement into a question. A final probing question that she left dangling like one of Pat Butcher's earrings as she departed with a toss of hair and rustle of chiffon. She was marching past Erwin the cat, who – curled up on a beanbag – did not even bother to look up. She was making her way down the transparent spiral staircase that seemed to be wound around nothing. Zanzibar just stood there, in the doorway, buffeted by the fragrant breeze she had generated. With closed eyes, he breathed in a lungful of her absence and just stood there. He just stood there, caught in her slipstream. Winded, he just stood there. He just stood there. *'Putain!'* he muttered, finally closing the door.

*

The presidential candidate emerged from the sea to spontaneous cries of *'Vive la République!'*. She was naked save for a tricolour sash – *'Un rien m'habille'* – that bisected the perkiest pair of Delacrucian tits to have ever stalked Le Touquet Plage. *'Tu vois, là,'* said a young father to his son, *'ce sont les deux mammelles de la France.'* As he pointed, tears welled up in his grateful eyes. Everything would be all right now. *Everything.* The crowd parted and Mme Royal glided by. Majestically. Regally. Eponymously... Photographers had a field day, fireworks were let off, babies were brandished, a brass band struck up the national anthem and, just when he was about to get an eyeful, Zanzibar found himself back home in his bathroom. He was standing in front of the mirror, trying to remove his contact lenses, which (as he would discover after plucking out an eyeball) he had forgotten to put in. The eye he was now staring at, and that stared back at him intermittently as he rolled it around in the palm of his hand, resembled a large white egg with a black dot inside – or rather the drawing of a white egg. The black dot alone contained more atoms than all the *penceuls* in the world.

*

Zanzibar was seated at one of the little round tables dotting the semicircle of cobbled stones outside the Théâtre de l'Europe. He had opted for the last row, furthest away from the road, with the steps leading up to the theatre right behind him. He was the only one there now, a couple of German tourists having just departed. The sun was shining; birds were chirping in the nearby Luxembourg Garden: summer was in the air. A waiter – as stylish as he was young – brought over an espresso and a glass of water, which he placed gingerly beside Zanzibar's copy of *Le Monde*. They had devoted a whole page to *l'affaire Zanzibar*. It was all over the papers, blogs, social networks, podcasts, and news bulletins – both radio and television, local and national. There was no escaping it, and that was precisely why he was seated at one of the little round tables dotting the semicircle of cobbled stones outside the Théâtre de l'Europe.

A 58 bus turned into rue de l'Odéon. Zanzibar followed its slow progress past the clothes shop where the original Shakespeare and Company once stood. It stopped outside the pharmacy at the other end, on the other side, where an attractive woman he vaguely recognised – but could not quite place – alighted, before walking back in his direction. As she crossed the road, he recognised the one-night stand graphologist who, a few months back, had publicly pooh-poohed his cunnilingus technique, describing the result as a series of 'indecipherable chicken-scratch squiggles'. Name of Amélie. Or possibly Émilie. Something along those lines. It was she too, he now realised, who had played the part of the presidential candidate in that strange dream that haunted him still. Thankfully, she had not noticed Zanzibar and picked a table in the second row, next to an olive tree in a square metal pot. With an uncanny sense of apropos, she ordered a kir royal. No sooner had the waiter scuttled away than she proceeded to hitch up her maxi dress until vast swathes of thigh were exposed to the warm rays. She completed this preprandial routine by crossing her legs and lowering, visor-style, the designer sunglasses that had been perched on her head, like a tiara. Zanzibar's beady eyes darted from the rear view of the graphologist to the restaurant facing him on the left, back to the graphologist's signature legs, and on to the Flammarion building facing him on the right. He repeated this circuit many times with meticulous, almost obsessive care, until the person he was waiting for finally emerged from the building.

Théodule Meuniaire was a thirtysomething publishing whizz-kid with rock star good looks, who – it was an open secret – was largely responsible for reviving Zanzibar's flagging career. He lingered awhile outside Flammarion, talking to someone on his mobile, seemingly in a foreign tongue (possibly *franglais* or Globish), then walked over to his car (an Aston Martin DB5) that was parked only a few metres away. He opened the door, removed his jacket and hung it on a hook inside. Before closing the door, he hooted twice in brief succession while looking over at the pavement café. He waved. Zanzibar quickly unfolded his paper and hid behind it. Peering over his copy of *Le Monde,* he saw the graphologist lift up her sunglasses with one hand and wave back with the other. A broad smile had now lit up her face. She sprinkled a few coins on the table and skipped across the road to join her date. They kissed like models in a Doisneau picture and walked, hand in hand, to La Méditerranée, the posh restaurant with its blue exterior and original Cocteau decorations inside. Once they had disappeared from view, Zanzibar called the waiter and whispered something in his ear. *'Bien entendu, Monsieur, au-cun problème,'* he said. Zanzibar got up and ran over to examine the Aston Martin. Loren's horn-rimmed glasses (which, as he recalled, she had removed just before shaking her hair loose) taunted him from the leather dashboard, where they had been conspicuously displayed. With closed eyes, he breathed in a lungful of absence and just stood there. He just stood there, in front of the Aston Martin with the horn-rimmed glasses on the leather dashboard. For a minute or so, he just stood there. He just stood there. *'Putain!'* he muttered, before making his way back.

The waiter smiled at him and Zanzibar felt obliged to order another espresso. He checked his emails on his iPhone, then glanced at the latest tweets, most of which revolved around *l'affaire*. After a brief recap, the article in

Le Monde focused on the TV show, to be broadcast live that very evening, during which a confrontation between Meuniaire and himself was to take place. Whether it would or not was a moot point, not least because the programme consisted of a series of announcements for nominally forthcoming – but, in reality, constantly deferred – features, followed by lengthy commercial breaks, themselves followed by further announcements, and so on until the closing credits. Although quite taken with the concept of a show that was for ever in the process of becoming, Zanzibar had no intention whatsoever of being party to this travesty. He was equally determined to ensure his rival did not make it to the studio either, and that was – more precisely – why he was seated at one of the little round tables dotting the semicircle of cobbled stones outside the Théâtre de l'Europe.

He looked up, squinting into the sun, just in time to see Meuniaire and the graphologist glide past in the Aston Martin.

Putain!

*

In 1992, having finally acknowledged that there was little lead in his *penceul* left, Sostène Zanzibar embarked on an ill-fated prequel to Genesis. Although this grandiose project would occupy him for the best part of two decades, we have precious little to show for it. A few meagre excerpts appeared at irregular intervals in obscure Japanese style magazines, whose prohibitive cover prices were inversely proportional to their confidential circulation. The rest of this 'work in regress,' as he liked to describe it, was destroyed. One night, in November 2009, the author deleted the computer files containing the typescript and burned all the printouts he had archived over the years. According to legend, he then took a taxi to Denfert-Rochereau, uncovered a manhole and disappeared down the Catacombs, where he spent the following fortnight listening to the same album over and over again on a battered old ghetto blaster believed to have once belonged to Don Letts.

Franco-Swiss all-girl band Les Péronelles (think Shangri-Las meet Slits) always maintained that they had rounded off their first (and last) album (*Trois fois rien*, 1983) with a hidden track. 'L'Arlésienne' was so well hidden, however, that no one had ever found it. With time, it became the Holy Grail of Franco-Swiss rock criticism. An early issue of *Les Inrockuptibles* contained a six-page feature ('A l'écoute de l'inouï') devoted to this unheard melody. It included interviews with the producer and sound engineer as well as cultural luminaries such as Patrick Eudeline, Gérard Genette, Jean Baudrillard, John Cage, and assorted roadies.

Listening to this ten-minute stretch of silence over and over again was a Zen-like experience at first. Soon, though, Zanzibar was able to recognise, and even anticipate, every hum, hiss, and crackle on the track: its teeny-tiny tinny tinnitus quality. The song had to be concealed *behind*, or perhaps even *within*, this silence that was not quite silence. It had to. He even thought he could sense its presence in the same, almost physical way one is always aware of being observed. It was just out of earshot; a mere whisper away.

By the middle of the second week, a melody had emerged from the static and wormed itself into his eardrums. It was the sound of music leaking from a commuter's headphones on public transport. It was the sound of a distant party carried on the wind of time, ebbing and flowing. It was the sound of mythical monsters plumbing the murky depths of ancient oceans. It was the sound of half a dozen rashers sizzling away like nobody's business in Loren's big fuck-off frying pan. Above all, it was the sound of a wannabe troglodyte slowly going out of his mind.

By the end of the second week, the melody had disappeared. It had never been there in the first place; not really. Zanzibar, now at his wit's end, had a rare eureka moment. The ghost track was not concealed *behind,* or even *within,* the silence – it was that silence itself. He had been listening to it all along, or rather he had not: all along, he had been listening *into* it for something else. There was, however, nothing else: no *behind* or *within*; no depth or beyond. Zanzibar had finally acceded to a heightened sense of hearing. He was now firmly convinced that this recording of real silence – silence that was not quite silence – constituted, *en soi,* some kind of irreducible message. Communication stripped back to its bare essentials; atomised – *degré zéro.*

The author's discovery could not but chime with his long-standing interest in the many-worlds interpretation of quantum mechanics. Whenever he wrestled with the blank page and the blank page won, Zanzibar would shrug it off as being of little import since it meant, ipso facto, that another version of himself was scribbling away in some parallel universe. Although this explanation was offered in jest, the author started thinking of his alter ego – hard at work on The Great Novel *he* was not working on – with increasing regularity. Some would say that these thoughts even blossomed into a beautiful, full-blown obsession.

In the early days, Zanzibar had tried his hand at *creatio ex nihilo*. Did not work. He then had a go at recreating the world within a whopping great *Gesamtkuntswerk*. This proved equally unfruitful. The words he used to conjure things up simply recorded their absence, instead of preserving them for all eternity: *Evanescence, ou la naissance d'Eva* (1992) expressed nothing but itself – if that. Writing *something*, as opposed to writing *about* something, seemed to be the way forwards – or rather backwards, since it implied rediscovering some prelapsarian language that merged with the reality of things. *Chemin faisant*, as he strived to bridge the gap between signifier and signified, Zanzibar also hoped to recapture some of that old magic which had inspired *Bigorneau* back in the day. A *soupçon* of oomph. *Un peu de* welly. In the event, he did neither. Every single volume he ever published had thus been an approximate translation – and ultimately a failed instantiation – of the ideal book in his head. Were his novels, then, simply intimations or imitations of his other self's works: dim echoes, pale copies? Were they inferior versions of the masterpieces his doppelgänger could come up with given half the chance? Zanzibar thought long and hard about all this, finally electing to stop writing in order to let his more talented likeness – whom he pictured as slightly taller and better-looking than himself – get on with it.

Flammarion ruthlessly exploited Zanzibar's disappearance by encouraging the hypothesis of a suicide. Meuniaire claimed on television that this, *après tout*, would only be in keeping with his 'fundamentally nihilistic outlook'. Vaché and Rigaut were frequently invoked by literary journalists in support of this argument. As a result, Zanzibar's back catalogue flew off the shelves, with *Bigorneau* topping the bestseller lists once again. Of course, the second stage of this cunning marketing strategy – i.e. cashing in on Zanzibar's miraculous reappearance by bringing out a new book asap – was jeopardised by the author's decision to down *penceuls*. Meuniaire was promptly dispatched to resolve this delicate problem. As expected, Zanzibar adopted a hardline position (*'C'est une question de principe, un-point-c'est-tout!'*) but proved far more amenable as soon as Flammarion threatened legal action. A compromise was finally thrashed out between the two parties, down at Les Deux Magots, where many a bottle of Perrier-Jouët was downed, almost *cul sec*.

Zanzibar, who had always tried and failed to convey the inadequacy of words with words, came up with the concept of a novel printed in disappearing ink. Once read, each word would vanish for ever, the full text living on in people's minds – retold, reinterpreted, reinvented... *'Novels can't be set in stone,'* he said, a little worse for wear. He climbed on the table and, punching the air, began chanting, *'Li-bé-rez le texte! Li-bé-rez le texte!'* After a few phone calls, Meuniaire put a damper on proceedings: the project was too complex to pull off from a technical point of view, and would be far too costly anyway. So it was back to the drawing board. *'Une autre bouteille, s'il vous plaît!'* They finally decided that Zanzibar would write an entire novel in longhand, using disappearing ink, and that Flammarion would publish a facsimile of the manuscript – blank page after blank page. *'Garçon, une autre bouteille!'* What better way to say something without saying it? *'Allez hop, on fête ça, une autre bouteille!'* What better way to express the idea that the writer has nothing to express? *'Vous nous remettrez la même chose.'* In between hiccoughs, Zanzibar explained that his blank book would – somehow – retain traces of the novel that had once graced them. He then spoke confusedly of palimpsests, and the tradition of erasure in contemporary poetry; the word *biffure* was used thrice. When he started claiming that the absent text would be a kind of manifestation, *en creux*, of The Great Novel his other self was composing in a parallel universe, Meuniaire decided to call it a day.

It was probably that night, as he walked home to clear his head, that he resolved to publish *Le Roman invisible* under his own name. Two grown men – intellectuals! French ones at that! – claiming rights to a blank book was bound to hit the headlines. It also made Meuniaire shitloads of money as *Le Roman invisible* became the must-have accessory of that *rentrée littéraire*. Suddenly, it was not only *subversif* and *jubilatoire* (two adjectives which, by law, must feature in all French book reviews) but also *incontournable* and, paradoxically, everywhere to be seen. The fact that it doubled up as a handy memo pad turned it into a top seller in the run-up to Christmas too. With the royalties, Meuniaire treated himself to a luxury yacht worthy of a Russian oligarch. He called her *Author Ship*.

*

A laundry van stopped outside the Michelet Odéon hotel. The words *Maison Binger* were painted on the side in quaint curlicue letters. A young man in a crisp beige uniform jumped out, leaving the door wide open. Zanzibar made a wild dash for it. The keys were in the ignition; the driver was talking to a pretty receptionist: the race was on.

The van picked up speed, crushing the asphalt beneath its burning wheels, like a shirt-collar under a Morphy Richards. Meuniaire's Aston Martin was still only a dot in the distance, but it was growing bigger by the second. It contained more atoms than all the *penceuls* in the world. Soon, those atoms would be spilled all over the leather dashboard and horn-rimmed glasses like chicken-scratch squiggles. Zanzibar was already living in the future. He could see it all, now, with blinding clarity. The shattered glass. The chromium twisted into the shape of Byzantine rings. The gory action painting on the tarmac. The charred corpses in their chariot of fire. He was hunched over the steering wheel, headbutting the windshield, laughing manically; whooping and hollering, with the wind in his combover and imaginary music blaring away in his ears. Four cars now separated him from his prey. He was closing in.

Just as he was about to go for the kill, the Aston Martin lurched into the outside lane. A sudden but steady – and, indeed, uninterrupted – flow of traffic prevented Zanzibar from giving chase. This being Paris, no one saw fit to let him go: steaming ahead was a woman's prerogative and a man's virility test. To make matters worse, the cars in his lane had now ground to a halt in what seemed like the mother of all tailbacks. Those on the left-hand side, however, continued to race past, as though taking part in a dry run for Le Mans. Watching them whizz by made him a little drowsy after a while. Feeling his eyes glaze over, he stretched, and noticed two large white eggs with black dots inside. The eyes belonged to the Michelin Man, who was towering above him benignly from a billboard.

Zanzibar fell asleep and was transported back to the tiny village in Burgundy, where he spent his summer holidays as a child. His grandparents' house with the dark-green shutters and, across the road, the plot of land where his grandfather grew tomatoes and carrots and beans. Halfway up the hill, you passed a water pump that looked like an obscene squat robot with a chunky, phallic-looking spout. It bore the inscriptions POMPES LEMAIRE and TOURNEZ LENTEMENT (although there was no water in it) and it was green, but a lighter shade than the shutters. On the same side, further up, you came across a little convenience store – the only one for miles.

People used to go there to make and receive telephone calls. At the other end of the village, there was a big barn, and on the door of this big barn was an advertisement with the Michelin Man. It was already old and faded by the early seventies.

Going back there, he thought, now waking up and rubbing his eyes, would be a little like visiting the setting of his past following the detonation of a neutron bomb. Zanzibar looked up at the hoarding again, and it was at this juncture that he realised that there was no driver in the car in front. And none in the one in front of that. And so on. *Putain!*

Night was beginning to fall. He wondered how long it would take to drive back to the past, and if the Michelin Man would still be waiting for him.

Chapter Thirty-Four
APRÈS LA LETTRE

(The dinner party / living room)

When Claude François died, electrocuted in his bathroom in 1978, malicious rumours began to spread: the French pop star had been pleasuring himself with a vibrator rather than fiddling with a loose light bulb. Théodule envisions him in the guise of David's Marat, but with Cloclo's characteristic blond moptop instead of a turban. The image is incongruous. It makes no sense. Why on earth would he have been using an electric sex toy in the first place, and in the bath of all places? How do such preposterous urban legends take hold?

As he makes his way across the living room – it is quite a trek – Théodule ponders these vexed questions, fully aware that gossiping guests are whispering sibilants in his wake. His first encounter with Loren is recounted time and time again, by the mouth for the ear. There is no escaping this eternal rehashing of their origin story: it will not be hushed. From party to party, glamorous women in evening gowns glance at him, giggling. They go shh, shh behind his back...

Chapter Thirty-Five
FIFTY SHADES OF GREY MATTER

Théodule Meuniaire was not one to be shushed lightly. He exuded natural authority. It was in his stature, posture, and ancestry; the cut of his suits and crispness of his shirts. It was in the thickness of his hair, the size of his yacht, the knobs on his timepiece and, above all, the bulge in his trousers. The latter was never openly acknowledged: like an eclipse, it could not be observed directly. The bulge was a given; its hegemonic presence always lurking in the background, just out of sight. It hummed in unison with the air conditioning, an integral part of the ambient music of the corporate world.

Théodule Meuniaire was not one to be shushed lightly. Chiselled of chop, shiny of shoe, and stripy of sock, he lorded it over board meetings with a patrician sense of entitlement everyone agreed he was entitled to. With his property portfolio, gold cuff links, and vintage sports cars, he fancied himself as an enlightened despot, although he would never have put it in such terms. He was a stickler for democracy, and a great believer in robust debate, only imposing his own views once his colleagues had had ample opportunity to put forward theirs.

No, Théodule Meuniaire really was not one to be shushed lightly. In fact, he was not one to be shushed at all, but shushed he had been, and nothing would ever be the same again. *Nothing!*

Granted, it was not the loudest of shushes, not by a long chalk or any stretch of the imagination. More of a hush, really, if that. In truth, half a hush would probably cover it. And then some. A librarian's shush caught in a shell.

Yet this curt exhalation – this ill wind of change – had reverberated around the round table like a violence without measure. Meuniaire played it over and over again in his mind, and each time it sounded more like a guillotine: shh!

He began to wonder if it had not just been a loud sniffle, a muffled sneeze, or even a mere figment of his imagination. Incredulous, he made another attempt to get a word in edgeways, but Ms Ipsum motioned him to hold his peace once more. The look of utter disbelief on his face was something to behold. He felt like Nicolae Ceaușescu when his balcony speech was rudely interrupted by chanting. He was Saddam Hussein's statue in Fiords Square, just before its toppling.

'*Madame*, your debut novel is an undisputed triumph,' he said, 'but that's no excuse for...'

Loren raised a finger to her lips before resuming her conversation with Victorine Gribiche, her translator and friend. Still in full flow, she unbuttoned her blouse and cupped a breast out of her scalloped brassiere. She let it defy gravity for a few instants, while leafing through the typescript before her.

'Hang on, hang on... Ah, here's the passage!' she said. Without even really looking, she reached out and placed her hand on the back of Meuniaire's head, slowly bringing him level with her exposed mammary gland. Holding him tight by the scruff of the neck, she smeared his mouth across her nipple, and round and round and round the areola area. Thus embosomed, he had no other option but to suckle at her teat. He did so greedily, like a piglet, and soon closed his eyes.

'There, there,' she whispered, running her fingers through his mane of hair, 'all better now. Loren is here. Shh... Shh... Right. Where were were? Ah yes, that passage on page 289...'

Chapter Thirty-Six
ONLY DISCONNECT

(The dinner party / kitchen)

Standing on the long-suffering kitchen table, diminutive Maya belts out her repertoire while Anaïs improvises experimental dance moves in a style vaguely reminiscent of Isadora Duncan.

C'est l'artiste, c'est le bohème
Qui, sans souper, rime rêveur
Un sonnet à celle qu'il aime,
Trompant l'estomac par le coeur.

Maya has a weekly residency at Le Hareng Rouge, where she embodies an anarcho-feminist character of her own invention called Paloma Maximov, *pétroleuse et poète*. Against a makeshift backdrop depicting the Moulin Rouge and *vieux Montmartre*, Paloma recounts her experience of the Paris Commune, interspersing argotic soliloquy with rabble-rousing revolutionary hymns. The moment when she brandishes a black flag is usually met with wild whoops of joy and a standing ovation.

C'est à crédit qu'il fait ripaille,
Qu'il loge et qu'il a des habits.
C'est la canaille, et bien j'en suis!

If her set is a hit with regulars, who like to sing along, the landlords are far more reserved. Michel teases Maya mercilessly, arguing that anarchist ideas were already outdated ('stillborn') in the 19th century. The whole history of anarchism, he reckons, is a convoluted – essentially pointless, albeit sometimes beautiful – rearguard action. According to Bola Bola, human society itself – whatever political shape it may take – is inherently oppressive. An anarchist society is simply one in which the coercive nature of the social contract is concealed behind endless meetings, where local busybodies ('tossers') hold forth on recycling bins or refuse collection. Refuse their rubbish, she counsels! All things considered, Bola Bola would much rather delegate such decisions, so that more time may be devoted to creative pursuits.[25] Michel concurs. If it's freedom you really want, you've got to break the social contract itself. Having said that, the very notion of freedom is liable to become a form of slavery; a conceptual prison people are afraid to break free from. He remembers a creepy leftist militant who used to skulk around the entrance to his lycée in the hope of grooming youngsters like him into the fanatical red guards of tomorrow. *Tu penses*

25 Such as reading *Télé Z*, no doubt.

quoi de la révolution? was his opening gambit. Michel saw no difference between him and the religious nutters, who lurked likewise at the entrance. They all believed in a perfect future – Year Zero, *le Grand Soir*, the Second Coming, etc. – which invariably harked back to some idyllic prelapsarian past. Being born again is precisely that: being born *again*; being borne back. With a neat sleight of hand, they distracted you from the miracle of what is, pointing to the verity behind the veil or the authentic self deep within that can only be revealed by the right product or belief system – *because you're worth it.* Enemies of beauty, the lot of them, incapable as they are of actually seeing anything through their ideological blinkers! Michel would then go off on one against the virtue-signalling abomination called *l'écriture inclusive* which, besides being binary and stemming from a misunderstanding of French grammar, epitomises the utilitarian indoctrination of language that is the very antithesis of literature. Maya was never quite sure whether they were taking the piss or not.

Chapter Thirty-Seven
OUT TO LUNCH

Lucien Brissonneau was expecting to hear fireworks in the distance. With a little luck, he might even see one or two, illuminating the sky with the white radiance of Eternity. Any minute now, he thought, any minute now... *Que dalle!...* Surely, it was time. A new year. A fresh start. A second chance. Redemption. He fished around in his satchel, finally locating his phone. 23:59. Here we go. Commencing countdown, engines on. 10 - 9 - 8 - 7 - 6 - 5 - 4 - 3 - 2 - 1... HAPPY NEW YEAR! Throughout the land, people would be embracing, kissing, drinking, and drinking some more. He recalled how his father always used to open the front door on the stroke of midnight: out with the old, in with the new... Something did not seem quite right. Not a single message. Not one. Never had he felt so lonely on this planet. It was at this point, when he was beginning to feel sorry for himself, that he noticed the date on his screen: WED 32. How was this possible? Had January been postponed? Had he accidentally cancelled the future?

Things had started innocently enough, as they so often do. Lucien woke up, exhausted and – *Fuck it!* – decided to call in sick. It was not a complete lie: he really was sick and tired of his job. Besides, the office would be almost empty, he rationalised, and the workload minimal. Then again, this could make his absence all the more conspicuous. Most of his colleagues had been away on holiday since before Christmas. He started wondering whether his performance over the phone had been convincing enough. Had he succeeded in conjuring up the right ratio of hoarseness to coughing, or had he overdone it? The phone was a notoriously slippery medium. Lucien reassured himself by arguing that he was, in fact, doing the company a favour by forfeiting the extra pay he would have earned in exchange for minimal exertion on his part. Thus becalmed, he went back to sleep.

It was gone midday when he woke up again, feeling elated as he used to on those rare occasions when he had mustered enough courage to bunk off school. The sun was shining and, although it looked bitterly cold outside, he fell prey to an irresistible urge to stretch his legs. A leisurely stroll would do him the world of good. After all, he was now a man of leisure. A flâneur. The only worry was that he ran the risk of being spotted by a workmate on their lunch break. After weighing the odds, he opted for a bracing walk in the woods, where meeting anyone he knew was most unlikely. His colleagues seldom strayed further than the nearest Burger Queen or McGuffin's. And so, head bowed, he made his furtive way into the trees, into the trees...

Once at a safe distance from civilisation, Lucien stopped in his tracks, closed his eyes and stretched out his arms so that his body was now perfectly cruciform. Fingering the foliage on either side, he slowly turned his face towards the seemingly benign warmth of the sun. Peace on earth to one and all! Something scuttling through the undergrowth disturbed his meditative serenity. He feared it might be a big wild boar, complete with terrible tusks and terrible claws – the whole hog. In the event, it turned out to be Rex, a type of bulldog belonging to Cédric, who – he now recalled – always went home at lunchtime to take his beloved pet for walkies. How could this have slipped his mind? Rex gambolled towards him, as though reuniting with a long-lost friend, snuffling greedily at his groin and wagging his tail – what there was of it. A strident whistle, and the hound scampered away into the bushes. Lucien took this opportunity to hide behind a tree, but Rex was soon panting and slobbering at his feet again, where he had deposited a bright yellow ball. He picked up the ball, threw it as far as he could, and sprinted in the opposite direction. Looking round, he saw Cédric, and in seeing him saw that he had been seen. He continued running until he was completely out of breath and could progress no further. This was when he began unravelling. Cédric was bound to tell someone at work that he had been spotted in the woods, behaving very oddly indeed. I'm no doctor, he would chuckle, but he was running remarkably fast for a sick man, that's all I'm saying. As a result of this indiscretion, he might lose his job. What right did Cédric have to deny him gainful employment; throw him on the scrap heap? He would not stand for it. He had rights too. Human rights. Do they owe us a living? Of course they fucking do!

Without realising it, Lucien had turned on his heels. When he caught sight of Cédric and Rex in the distance, he picked up the biggest branch he could carry and zeroed in on his newfound foe. How dare you! Who the fuck do you think you are, you dirty grass? Take that you cunt, and that and that, and that, and that and that, and that, and also that...

Flesh and blood is who we are, in the final analysis: Lucien contemplated his handiwork, like Francis Bacon in front of a handsome carcass. There was a pleasing unity now. A kind of merger had been achieved. Forensics would have a job telling man from dog. At least they would have a job, he mused, walking on. He was looking forward to the fireworks.

All was quiet in the deep dark wood.

Chapter Thirty-Eight
THE MAN WITHOUT QUALITY STREETS

(The dinner party / kitchen)

Standing at the far end of the kitchen, Astrid Strumpfhosen is deep in conversation with a walrus-whiskered man. Wearing sunglasses indoors, she could be a member of Baader-Meinhof or a Krautrock band. She is doing most of the talking, possibly relaying some vital information, but no else speaks German. When Maya breaks into song again, Astrid silences her. *Genug!* Everybody understands. Anaïs looks stunned by the sudden outburst.

A librarian-type – shades of Philip Larkin – comes in through the back door, a little out of breath, smoking a pipe.

'Ahoy!'

He is immediately followed by a much younger man.

'Ahoy!'

'Everybody,' says the moustachioed one, switching to English, 'this is Lucien.' He slaps him on the back, ruffles his hair. 'He's had a tough life. I met him when he was on the run from the police. He came to work with me for a while in my pop-up avant-garde supermarket, ASDADA. We used to sell silly ideas, like cutting tall people down to size in the name of equality. Anyway, he's one of us... Ah, here come Djamel and Arthur. Ahoy!'

Alexis is intimidated by Astrid – they have exchanged the odd word at Le Hareng Rouge – but also fascinated. She must be in her late sixties, from what he can gather, but wears a black catsuit like a woman half her age. He admires her grace and poise as she slips out through the back door leading to the *escalier de service*, the backstairs formerly reserved for domestic staff. The man with the pipe follows her.

'Ahoy!' he says, looking round.

Chapter Thirty-Nine
A BODY REELS SOFTLY

'Shall we begin?'

Septimus Smegma did not register. There was a vintage looking glass behind Artemisia, the renowned cartomancer, whom he visited regularly. When he peered above her shoulder he appeared in the foxed mirror, mirror on the wall. It usually gave him such a thrill. Today, however, all he could make out was the chair on which he was sitting. An empty chair, as far as he could see. He blinked, leaned forwards; narrowed his eyes. Nothing. He removed his spectacles, slid them back on. Still nothing. Septimus cleared his throat as a prelude to enquiring if, perchance, *she* could see his reflection. Artemisia swivelled round and back again, a big grin on her face.

'I'm not going to sugarcoat this,' she said, trying nevertheless to look as reassuring as possible. 'You're simply not there. It's quite extraordinary!'

Septimus remained silent. Any respite from the drone delivery of his soporific, supercilious, self-centred soliloquies was most welcome. Yet she felt obliged – professionally speaking – to say something, *anything*.

'Fernando Pessoa blamed the inventor of the mirror for poisoning the human heart.' Artemisia's frozen smile remained unreciprocated. Pointedly so. 'This failure to reflect may be symbolic,' she ventured, relaxing her facial muscles, trying another tack.

'Of what?'

'A general lack of reflection.'

'Care to be more specific?'

'Well, all that puerile hocus-pocus you mistake for spirituality.'

'That's a bit rich, coming from someone who's been publicly accused of putting the sham in shaman.'

'Sha*wo*man,' she corrected. 'Perhaps cruciverbalists are destined to become puzzles to themselves,' she conjectured, thinking aloud.

'I'll have you know that I'm also a published author,' he retorted haughtily.

'Oh yes, I forgot,' she laughed but checked herself, realising he was dead serious. Like Dorothy Parker, Septimus loved *having written*. Writing, for him, was merely a prolegomenon to the public performance of his ego – a manner of penis extension. Attending a couple of his numerous readings had made this painfully clear to her.

Septimus stared despondently into his biscotti frappuccino. After a while, he looked up, a carnivorous smile illuminating his hitherto somber mien. Artemisia knew what was going on. He was reminiscing about his youth. He always was, despite his overt aversion to nostalgia. That was the official line; this was his safe space. The glory days! Truly magical times when spending long afternoons dancing in front of the mirror could abolish the boundary between life and art, threatening to topple the whole system in the process. *Bliss was it in that dawn to be alive,* he whined, screwing up his face, *but Toby Young was very heaven!* Artemisia had never paid attention to his reptilian features before, but now that she had, she could not help picturing him wolfing down a live guinea pig or tearing off his human mask. The mask was the oleaginous façade; the carefully curated hipster persona. The reptile underneath was the ruthless slumlord, the *Telegraph* reader, the petty Brexiteer. The tension between the two was so great that something had to give. Artemisia thought of those carefully curated pictures of Mr and Mrs Smegma she had come across online. The more he smirked in them, the more depleted she appeared, as though he were sapping her life force. She wondered if he might be some kind of vampire. That would explain the mirror thing.

'I suspect the libidinal relationship you habitually entertain with your body image has broken down.'

'What on earth are you insinuating?' Septimus was incandescent with rage. On social media, he would have blocked her straight away, no doubt about it.

'Shallowness runs deep when you're young. You fall in love with everyone. Any guitar and any bass drum. You slide down the surface of things. Style has so much substance... You've never really grown up, have you? Just grown old.'

Septimus made to leave, but Artemisia followed him to the door.

'Have you seen my new acquisition? It's an original Archinard.'

She pointed to a framed pen-and-ink drawing that brought to mind Michaux, Dubuffet, Krasner, even Blinko. There was a meticulous method to its miniaturist madness – an insane intricacy that sucked you into its bewildering busyness.

'It doesn't represent anything in itself, anything at all in fact, but it has the uncanny capacity to accommodate anything in general. The doodles keep shapeshifting into new configurations, as if they were alive. I really don't know how he manages to achieve that effect. People see all sorts of different things in it, maybe things that are in themselves. It acts like a mirror to the soul. Leonardo da Vinci would have had a field day staring into it. What do you see?'

Septimus definitely saw something – something he had found profoundly unsettling – but it had vanished before he was even able to process it on a conscious level.

'I really couldn't say. It was like a subliminal image.'

'Come, Septimus. Let's see what's in the cards for you.'

She returned to her desk. Septimus sat down on the other side, making a big show of his reluctance to comply. His attention was drawn to the lyrics of a haunting song emanating from the room next door:

The paint is cracked

And the paper peels
The poster falls
And a body reels softly.

Artemisia shuffled the deck, then fanned out the tarot cards face down. She waited for him to pick the cards, one by one, by letting the palm of his hand hover above them like a metal detector, but Septimus motioned her to go ahead. He looked on as she slowly revealed the spread.

The Devil.

The Magician.

The Wheel of Fortune.

Death.

'And now for the reckoning... So, that's 15 plus 1 plus 10 plus 13, which makes a grand total of 39. 3 plus 9 equals 12 and 12 is...'

She handed him a card.

'The Hangman,' he muttered.

The music suddenly stopped, and, to his astonishment, all his tenants – past and present – filed into the room, filling it up.

'Mirrors are the doors through which Death comes and goes,' said one of them, a veritable force of nature with an unfeasibly bushy beard. He resembled an ogre from a very dark fairy tale. 'Are you coming or going?' The man did not wait for an answer. He pulled him out of his chair, threw him over his shoulder like a sack of spuds, and walked out of the room. As they exited, Septimus caught sight of a blue island in the misty midst of the drawing. That was the subliminal image he had glimpsed.

The other tenants all looked up at the ceiling, expectantly.

A trap door opened: Septimus dived headlong, dangling at the end of a rope, strung up by his feet like Il Duce. *Le sot dans le vide.*

Artemisia stood on a chair, held his topsy-turvy head in her hands, and kissed him full on the lips.

'You're sealed with a kiss,' she said, before slitting his throat in one swift movement with a zombie knife. She brandished the bloody blade. 'Ahoy!'

Someone put on 'Let's Lynch the Landlord' by Dead Kennedys. The party was already in full swing.

Chapter Forty
UN SANG D'ENCRE

(The dinner party / dining room)

'You're so cute,' says Anna Coluthon, 'I could just eat you up.'

'*Qu'est-ce qu'il est chou, ce petit Titus,*' says Perrine Jouët.

'*Oui, il est vraiment à croquer,*' says Ordalie de Nananaire. '*Je pourrais le manger tout cru.*'

Hégésippe Turpin-Goulet observes the young women bending and bonding over the pram, like three good fairies at a christening. Millicent Beaufort joins them, all smiles; more cooing ensues. She tucks in her infant son, then turns to Anaïs Chevalier – tonight's babysitter – who carefully wheels Titus away. An extravagantly moustachioed servant in full livery opens the connecting doors leading to the dining room. Océane Ciboise emerges, wearing a black cocktail dress, to announce that dinner will now be served – cue cheers from some of the guests. She snaps her fingers at a passing waiter: *'Lucien, veuillez accompagner Madame Beaufort jusqu'à sa place'.*

'Si Madame veut bien me suivre,' Lucien says, obsequiously.

Millicent walks the length of the interminable table, feeling the gaze of all the other guests, standing huddled together in the living room behind her. At the table's end, Lucien stops, turns round, and executes a little bow before retracing his steps. Crispin awaits, his hands resting on the back of a mahogany chair Millicent slips into. Odilon de Blancmange clears his throat, about to make another public announcement, but his wife, Blandine, gets in there first: 'Sit wherever you like, *à la bonne franquette*'. The sound of countless mahogany chairs suddenly being scraped on parquet flooring is deafening. Conversations grow much louder.

'Is it oysters for starters?' Athelstan enquires, almost shouting.

'Yes, with lemon confit,' Océane confirms.

'Sounds promising.'

'They're delicious, you'll see. There's also lobster – lobster Colette – if you prefer.'

'What a cruel dilemma!'

'You can have both, darling... *Djamel: Monsieur prendra des huîtres et du homard.*'

'*Bien, Madame. Je vais le dire à Arthur.*'

'Are you, like, really hungry?' says Manuella.

'Famished,' says Teddy Huskinson, deploying his starched napkin, the kind you can tie around your neck if need be.

Ninon Neenaw feels a hand squeezing her thigh, under the table.

'*Désolé! Je pensais que c'était ma serviette,*' says Hégésippe Turpin-Goulet with characteristic aplomb.

Donatienne swaps seats with Mina Harpenden, to avoid having to stare at her estranged husband all evening. Being reacquainted with his Y-fronts was already quite enough.

Georges Davos smiles at Mina, hoping she did not witness his wardrobe malfunction.

'My English isn't very good.'

'*Mon français non plus.*'

'My tailor is rich,' he says, sounding like Maurice Chevalier.

'*La plume de ma tante,*' she retorts, sounding like Jane Birkin.

A lofty waiter brings Athelstan his lobster.

'I'm jealous,' says Saskia Selkirk. 'Why do you get served before everyone else? Nepo baby!'

Athelstan snorts; Océane winks.

'I hear Adam Wandle has lived in France almost all his life,' says Tacita Rimini-Thompson. 'I had no idea, what with Mordenism and all that.'

'Yes, that's an important aspect of his work and personality,' says Loren, taking a sip of the Dom Pérignon she sneaked in from the other room. 'He often quotes a letter Arthur Ransome wrote to his mother: "I think of England as a sort of dream country".'

'England and nowhere. Never and always,' Archie West declaims, with faux grandiloquence.

'That one too,' says Loren.

'Interesting,' says Francis Scopitone. As Carson McCullers writes, "we are homesick most for the places we have never known". It seems to me that there's an element of that in his case... I'm working on a book about the places people wish to retire to – their vision of Paradise. For some, it's going home, back to their homeland, their roots. For others, it's back to nature, or a heliocentric move to the Algarve or Costa Brava. Brits who come to France are often looking for a version of their own country as it was – or as they think it was – thirty or fifty years ago. It's a form of time travel.'

'I often think of all those people,' says Victorine Gribiche, 'who, throughout their working lives, dream of an idyllic setting, where, at last, they'll be able to start truly living – but never make it for some reason or other. They die before retirement, or are no longer able to move due to ill health. They get what they want once it's too late. I sometimes wonder if dementia isn't some kind of reaction to this sick joke.'

'Go, go, go, said the bird: human kind / Cannot bear very much reality.' Archie West is pleased with himself, the earlier fracas in the hallway all but forgotten. A waiter tops up his glass. He looks round to thank him.

'Arthur!' he gasps, before keeling over.

Chapter Forty-One
LA PLAINE EST VIDE

Patrick Berkman was finessing his latest social media missive. He stared at the screen, fingers poised over the keyboard: 'You should be ashamed'. He added an exclamation mark before deleting the entire message, replacing it with 'Shame on you!'. He stared at the screen, his eyes screwed up in concentration until he had a brainwave: 'Shame!'. Yes, that was it! Shame!

People had no idea how difficult it was to move in circles where emails were always prefaced with *I hope you're doing as well as can be in spite of,* or even *amidst, everything.* People did not realise how difficult it was for a writer to be doing well *despite,* and indeed *amidst,* everything.

Shame! It encapsulated everything because everything was an utter disgrace in late-stage capitalism. You had to be in a state of permanent indignation – out and out outrage – at the state of the world. You had to rampage on the page, the socials, everywhere. It was exhausting but essential in these dark times.

We are the unacknowledged legislators of the world, he thought, tying up the laces on his expensive trainers. He hesitated to open the front door, for a group of boisterous kids had congregated just outside, in the hallway. They often did. Moving into a ground-floor flat had been a big mistake. He felt trapped.

When Patrick[26] and his girlfriend Siobhan first came to France from Dundrug – 'Ireland's Las Vegas' – they had settled in the fourteenth *arrondissement*, near Pernety. Two years later, they decided to downsize in order to live the Left Bank dream in the sixth. Their studio apartment was very cramped, but on weekdays – when tourists were not queuing outside – they would treat themselves to an overpriced coffee or two at Le Flore or Deux Magots. They bought books at Shakespeare and Company and read them in the Luxembourg Garden, where Patrick admired the joggers for making no concessions to modern sportswear. They were his kind of joggers. Like them, he began sporting a lengthy scarf, which resembled a neck brace once he had wrapped it all the way round. He continued to affect this Latin Quarter style for his daily jog when they moved out to Montreuil in search of more space – *une pièce en plus* – now that Siobhan was with child. Many creative types were migrating there, but Williamsburg it was not. As soon as he strayed from the gentrified enclaves, Patrick encountered the indifference, resentment, and even open hostility of the local population. He was made to feel he did not belong there, just as they had been made to feel they did not belong in France. *Ici, c'est comme au bled*

26 Born in Hampshire in 1969.

– he had heard that several times. It stayed with him. It resonated.

The kids were still loitering in the hallway. Patrick took a deep breath and opened the front door. He avoided making eye contact and ignored the jibes levelled at his neckerchief, and hence (he got the message) his masculinity.

Moving to La Plaine Saint-Denis had felt like another step down, but the little one needed a room of his own and anything bigger in Montreuil was out of their reach. Besides, it was more convenient from the point of view of public transport. They lived right next to the RER (La Plaine Stade de France) and there was also a metro station (Front Populaire) you could walk to in under twenty minutes. He soon noticed, on Line 12, that almost everybody alighted at Marx Dormoy – the last stop that was in Paris proper, *intra-muros.* The fear of *déclassement* among young professionals was palpable. They were hanging on to Paname by a thread.

Although populous, La Plaine felt empty most of the time. People commuted from Paris or other suburbs to work for the corporations that had moved there in recent years, promptly departing at day's end. There was no hanging about. Patrick had read somewhere that the employees of an international phone company were advised to go out in groups, at lunchtime, in order to avoid getting mugged. At weekends, young white families on bicycles would appear, as though out of nowhere, heading for the boho El Dorado of the Canal Saint-Martin. They invariably fled the neighbourhood as soon as their children were old enough to go to school. Diversity had its limits. The use of a bicycle was a dead giveaway anyway; a sure sign they were not really integrated – people here always zipped along on e-scooters.

Save for a few insalubrious *pavillons*, soon to be demolished, the most ancient buildings were barely twenty years old, and many had sprung up in the past decade, making the place almost unrecognisable from one year to the next. The area was unburdened with history. Most of the Africans, who used to repair cars illegally on rue des Fillettes, had moved on following the construction of Campus Condorcet. Patrick only spotted two of them today as he jogged past at a fair clip. He jogged past the TV stations, the empty canisters and deflated balloons (always black, for some reason) discarded by the nocturnal nitrous oxide abusers, the shantytown shacks of the homeless, pounding the pavements pitted with gobbets of spit. He began noticing strange graffiti – EAT THE RICH, LANGUAGE IS MURDER, LORD BIRO – and soon realised that the people he could hear running behind him were actually running after him. As soon as he recognised the voices of the kids from his building, Patrick started to jog faster and they all screamed at once, quickly outpacing him. He disappeared in the ensuing melee just as a new email pinged into his inbox: *I hope you're doing as well as can be in spite of everything*. What would surprise forensics was not so much that his assailants had stripped and dismembered him, but that they had also *devoured* parts of his puny body.

Chapter Forty-Two
LEAVING THE 21st CENTURY

(The dinner party / dining room)

Archie West is slumped over sideways in his chair, like Marat in his bathtub. Arthur lifts him off his feet, effortlessly; clutches him with one arm, whistles with two fingers. Djamel and Lucien rush over to help. Archie is carried away, with Blandine in tow. It is a shocking tableau, for sure, but one that somehow lacks verisimilitude. Most of the guests remain strangely unmoved. Some are struggling to even look remotely concerned. They cannot quite believe what has just happened before their very eyes. Try as they may, they cannot quite believe in Archie West, whose performance – neither dramatic nor 'deeply humane' – was singularly lacklustre. In truth, he resembled some kind of rag doll or mannequin rather than a convincing version of his authentic self. You could just tell his heart was not in it – that his commitment to death was only half-hearted.

Archie was here and no longer is, but for how long, and what difference does his presence or absence really make?

With her furrowed brow, Millicent does seem genuinely worried, though.

'Oh, I hope they haven't woken up Titus,' she whispers to her husband. 'Can you go check on him?'

'Reality doesn't always feel as real as it should, does it?' says Blandine, who comes back bearing the good news that Archie is reviving backstage. Much ado about nothing, it seems.

Loren gets up to present the main courses – all four of them – which she carefully curated over several long weeks in conjunction with Océane and, latterly, Alexis. Saskia likes the sound of the turbot *à la grenobloise* with sea herbs and wild garlic. Loren's evocation of the roast venison with figs and black cherries garners a great deal of support. Hégésippe even punches the air. *Yes!* Crispin returns just as Loren embarks upon a potted history of the *poule au pot façon grand-mère.*[27] He is followed discreetly by several policemen and women.

'No sign of Titus. Anaïs must have taken him for a stroll in his pram to send him off to sleep. I went down looking for them but found Archie sprawled out on the pavement. Blood everywhere.'

'Is he dead?'

'Very much so.'

'Oh my God! What happened?'

'Not sure. Lucien and Djamel were in here, apparently, and didn't see anything. They left Archie with Arthur,

27 With the obligatory reference to Henry IV of France.

who's gone AWOL. I called the cops and they're on his trail now.'

'A manhunt – how exciting!' says Francis Scopitone, eavesdropping on the conversation.

'The *hachis parmentier*,' Loren explains, 'isn't a glorified shepherd's pie, oh no – I'm saying this for the benefit of my compatriots.' A few cheers and boos. 'It's *confit de canard* in a divine potato *purée* – don't you dare call it mash – made with *crème fraîche*, garlic, and, most importantly, gallic flair. It is rather plain in aspect, but proves very special indeed, you'll see. One for the connoisseurs.'

She sits down. Djamel and Lucien start taking orders.

'Good work, Loren.' Francis gives her the thumbs-up. 'Did you go to Ha'penny's party last week?'

'Ha'penny?'

'My sister,' says Tacita Rimini-Thompson.

'Right – no.'

'Couldn't get on board with the menu,' Francis continues. 'Don't get me wrong, the food was delicious but I'm just not comfortable with a French chef dabbling in Moroccan cuisine. It's cultural appropriation with disturbing neocolonial overtones – the kind of thing that puts me right off my food.'

Loren, who is unwilling to get sucked into this conversation, remains silent.

'I can't write at the minute,' he sighs. 'How can you write when the planet's on fire? How can you indulge in futile word games when that orange clown squats in the White House? Do I even have the right to write any more? I'm male, cisgender, straight, able-bodied and, perhaps worst of all, white. That's the most shameful identity possible – and not only because it's tragically unfashionable, although there is that too. Do you think I have the right to write, Loren?'

'You know full well what I think. The world needs to be written, that is to say unwritten, not rewritten.'

'What does that even mean?'

'There you go again! Why do you need to impose meaning upon everything? It's a disease, a form of – what's the word? – pareidolia. The world is: isn't that enough for you? For me, art is about affirming the world, not changing it, trying to make it conform to some political agenda or other. If literature aims to do anything, it is precisely to erase ideology – everything that obfuscates, covers up reality; prevents us from getting as close as possible to things in themselves, and that, quixotically, includes language. It is an affirmation of what is, is what it is.'

'Have you partaken of the *poule au pot* yet?' Saskia enquires.

'Yes,' Anna says. 'It's unbelievable! I reckon it's the most tender, most succulent meat I've ever tasted in my whole life.'

'It's like feasting on a newborn's flesh,' Mina concurs, never missing an occasion to shock. 'What you say is all well and good, Loren, but what concerns me is that you seem to be parroting these terrorists by way of Wandle's anarcho-autism.'

'Exactly,' says Francis. 'If your views on art and literature aren't ideological, I don't know what is, frankly.'

'You know what?' Théodule says, 'I sometimes think you've written too many articles for *The End Times* and *L'Inhumanité*. You've become one of them.'

'What do these fucking terrorists want, anyway?' Hégésippe slams his fist down on the table. 'Solange de la Turlute, Titterington-Jones, Perlimpinpin, Lepiador, Smegma, Berkman... Who's next? How many more heads and ponytails are they going to chop off? How many more yachts are they going to sink? How many more sensitivity readers tarred and feathered? How many more gardens desecrated? What the fuck do they want?'

'Yes, pray tell us, Loren,' says Théodule, 'because it just looks like senseless killing to me.'

'You're right, it is senseless killing and, in a way, that's the point. It has to be thus.'

'What do you mean?' says Francis.

'There you go again. You really must seek help for your OCD.'

'Seriously, though, Loren, enlighten us.' Hégésippe is at the end of his tether.

'It's a crusade against *la gauche caviar*. You've always had your upper-class Kropotkins or Guevaras, but that was of little consequence so long as they co-existed with an organised working-class movement based on trade unions and the heavy industries. Today, however, the radical left is largely in the hands of bourgeois bohemians, which means – since you insist upon looking for meaning everywhere – that those who support the system and those who wish to overthrow it belong to the same class. As turkeys don't vote for Christmas, most of these communist aristocrats, champagne anarchists, and privately-educated numpties will never cross the Rubicon. Far from threatening the status quo, their opposition to the system actually ensures its survival. They are, in effect, collaborators. The terrorists have drawn the conclusion that the only solution is to eliminate the blockage in order to make change possible once again.'

'And we are the blockage,' says Francis.

'Precisely.'

'Writers, of course, are just the thin edge of the wedge. Soon, they will branch out into actors and other categories. *Ce n'est qu'un début...*'

Loren is interrupted by Odilon, who reminds her it is high time to announce the dessert – an *île flottante* 'created' by one of France's most fashionable confectioners – which is already being served. Following a brief speech and a toast to Crispin and Millicent, she invites the guests to have their 'just desserts'. A grave-looking police inspector of indeterminate age sidles up to her and addresses the room. He breaks the news that Archie West has, sadly, passed away. Graffiti, daubed on the pavement beside his prone body, suggests he was defenestrated.

'The inscription reads' – the inspector fishes out a crumpled piece of paper from his raincoat pocket – '"*Le sot dans le vide*".' He pauses, scrutinises the guests one by one, before resuming:

'We are attempting to locate the whereabouts of the three waiters, as well as the chef, who have all gone missing. They are presumed to be on the run, rats deserting a sinking ship.'

The inspector takes his leave. A hush falls over the table.

'Oh no!' Millicent cries out, interrupting the eternal silence of infinite space. 'Oh no! Oh no! Oh no!' She stares wide-eyed at the plate in front of her, a horrified look distorting her features. 'Titus! Where's Titus?' With a sudden retch, she throws up all over her pudding. Millicent then jumps up and rushes out of the room, pursued by her husband.

The other guests turn their attention from the door to the floating islands on their plates. The meringue, adrift on *crème anglaise*, is perfectly blue.

ACKNOWLEDGEMENTS

Pages 16-17: ‘set up at last, preparing to die’ is a quote from Elizabeth Hardwick’s *Sleepless Nights*, 1979.

Page 17: ‘I need to maintain a degree of discomfort in the world’ (which recurs on page 21) was inspired by Rachel Cusk: ‘To continue creating, a person perhaps has to maintain an essential discomfort in the world’ (‘Making House: Notes on Domesticity,’ *The New York Times Magazine*, 31 August 2016).

Page 21-22: the quotation comes from Gaston Bachelard’s *The Poetics of Space*, 1958.

Page 23: ‘patina of opaque non-disclosure’ is lifted from Tom McCarthy’s essay, ‘Blurring the Sublime: On Gerhard Richter’ (*Typewriters, Bombs, Jellyfish*, 2017).

Pages 29-30: ‘fine-tuned to a level of shell-shock sensitivity’ is copy-pasted from Sam Mills’s novel, *The Quiddity of Will Self*, 2012.

Page 30: 'the slumbering monster on the other side – its fresh breath of eternal rehashing' is adapted from Maurice Blanchot's 'Death of the Last Writer' in *The Book to Come* (1959; translated by Charlotte Mandell): 'There is, in every well-made Library, a Hell where live the books that must not be read. But there is, in each great book, another hell, a centre of unreadability where the entrenched force of this language that is not a language, fresh breath of eternal rehashing, watches and waits'. See also pages 69 and 285.

Page 31: *'Le silence a été assassiné. Il n'y a plus de silence nulle part'* comes from François Mauriac's *Bloc-Notes*, 1963.

Page 34: 'We are torn between nostalgia for the familiar and an urge for the foreign and strange. As often as not, we are homesick most for the places we have never known' – Carson McCullers, *The Heart Is a Lonely Hunter*, 1940. See also page 308.

'Grasping its hideous head with both hands, he strangles a particularly perplexing sentence while dodging the sting in its flailing tail' was inspired by this sentence in Annie Dillard's 'A Writer in the World', *The Abundance*, 2016: 'Half-naked, with your two bare hands, you hold and fight a sentence's head while its tail tries to knock you over'.

Page 35: 'It is not down in any map; true places never are' appears in Herman Melville's *Moby-Dick; or The Whale*, 1851.

Page 36: 'Is it her body I hold in my arms or the sea?' is taken from Ann Quin's *Passages*, 1969.

Page 37: 'How was he able to drink up the sea?' is a nod to 'How were we able to drink up the sea?' from Friedrich Nietzsche's *The Gay Science*, 1882.

Page 38: 'Such things happen in one second and last forever' is adapted from Virginia Woolf's 'All these things happen in one second and last forever' in *The Waves*, 1931.

Page 39: 'It conjured up a world where the advent of music was inevitable' is based on the following passage from Michel Butor's essay 'The Space of the Novel' in *Selected Essays*, translated by Mathilde Merouani and edited by Richard Skinner: 'If the novel is to provide anything like a complete representation of human reality, to reflect it, and thereby have an effect on it truthfully, it needs to speak about a world where the advent of music can not only happen, but is inevitable...' (Vanguard Editions, 2022).

'...you had to allow the words to wash around you' appears in Roald Dahl's *Matilda*, 1988: 'Sit back and allow the words to wash around you, like music'.

Page 40: 'Many men are human beings above and fish below. Yet each one represents an attempt on the part of nature to create a human being' is from Hermann Hesse's 1960 prologue to *Demian*, 1919.

Page 41: 'from swerve of shore to bend of bay' is lifted from the opening of James Joyce's *Finnegans Wake*, 1939.

Page 50: 'For last year's words belong to last year's language / And next year's words await another voice' comes from T. S. Eliot's 1942 poem 'Little Gidding', collected in *Four Quartets*, 1943.

'like a librarian's shush caught in a shell' is based on 'like a shush caught in a shell' from Sam Mills's novel, *The Quiddity of Will Self*. See also page 288.

Pages 51: 'It must be the heat. Or some rare disease. Or too much to eat' comes from the song 'I Feel Pretty' in *West Side Story*, 1957. Lyrics by Stephen Sondheim.

'She is tired, she is weary. She could sleep for a thousand years' occurs in 'Venus in Furs', a song – written by Lou Reed – that features on *The Velvet Underground & Nico* album, 1967.

Page 52: 'I am not even enough of a presence to become an absence' is stolen from Sam Mills's *The Quiddity of Will Self*.

'I simply am not there' appears in Bret Easton Ellis's *American Psycho*, 1991.

Page 70: 'I'm a cell of one' comes from B. S. Johnson's *Christie Malry's Own Double-Entry*, 1973.

'He had a great enthusiasm for devilment in those days, I'll grant you that. The theft of toilet-rolls from public lavatories, pens from post offices; the obscene telephone calls...' is based on the following passage from Joe Orton and Kenneth Halliwell's *The Boy Hairdresser* (written in 1965 but first published in 1999): 'Donelly had a great enthusiasm for anarchy. The theft of toilet-rolls from public lavatories, pens from post offices; the obscene telephone calls, the cards inserted in Praed Street windows giving the addresses of vicars' aunts and aldermen's widows, and the time he had loosed a rat on a crowded dance floor'.

'He'd give a wrong time, stop a traffic line' is a reference to the Sex Pistols' 'Anarchy in the UK', 1976: 'I give a wrong time, stop a traffic line'.

Page 71: '...if the world couldn't be beautified, at least it could be destroyed' was inspired by Len Gutkin's *Dandyism: Forming Fiction from Modernism to the Present*, 2020: 'If the world cannot be made beautiful, it can at least be destroyed'.

Page 73: 'Jack is in his corset, Jane is in her vest. And me, I'm in a rock 'n' roll band' is from Lou Reed's 'Sweet Jane', which first featured on the Velvet Underground's *Loaded*, 1970.

'*unexpress* the expressible' comes from Roland Barthes's *Critical Essays*, 1964 (tr. Richard Howard): 'We often hear it said that it is the task of art to *express the inexpressible*; it is the contrary which must be said (with no intention of paradox): the whole task of art is to *unexpress the expressible,* to kidnap from the world's language, which is the poor and powerful language of the passions, another speech, an exact speech'.

Page 76: 'God is what's left when nothing is left' is borrowed from Toby Litt's *A Writer's Diary,* 2023.

'You are suspended, weightless, in a pause in time' is lifted from Michael Bracewell's *Unfinished Business,* 2023: 'After an hour or so, he was suspended, weightless, in a pause in time that was meaningful and poetic and enabled him to see immense distances'.

Page 85-86: '...while someone else was eating or opening a window or just walking dully along' is from W. H. Auden's 'Musée des Beaux Arts', 1939.

Page 93: 'A poke at life' references Deborah Levy's *August Blue,* 2023: 'Perched between her lips was a fat cigar. Glowing at the end. It was a poke at life. A provocation'.

Page 95: 'L'Île bleue' – music by Gianni Ferrio, lyrics by Christine Fontane, sung by Monique Pianéa – was the theme song of *L'Île mystérieuse,* a popular six-part series, based on Jules Verne's novel, broadcast on French television in 1973.

Page 104: 'Painting the impossibility of painting' echoes Bram van Velde's 'I paint the impossibility of painting' in

Charles Juliet's *Conversations with Samuel Beckett and Bram van Velde*, 1995.

Page 105: '"Like" and "like" and "like" – but what is the thing that lies beneath the semblance of the thing?' appears in Virginia Woolf's *The Waves*, 1931.

Page 106: 'The lights burnt blue. It was now dead midnight' references William Shakespeare's *Richard III*: 'The lights burn blue. It is now dead midnight'.

Page 107: 'books in piles on the floor propping up tables' is ever so slightly adapted from Sam Mills's *The Watermark*, 2024 ('There were books in piles on the floor which propped up tables').

'antiques uprooted from dark eras and savage circumstances' was plundered from Michael Bracewell's *Saint Rachel*, 1995.

Page 130: The 'still point of the turning world' comes from T. S. Eliot's 'Burnt Norton', 1941. The poem appears in *Four Quartets*.

Page 132: 'lithe black form' features in the Calypso episode of James Joyce's *Ulysses*, 1922.

Page 134: 'Soon, its boundaries will be the horizon' is a reference to 'My garden's boundaries are the horizon' from Derek Jarman's *Modern Nature*, 1991.

Page 144: 'Awesome is the God who is not' appears in George Steiner's *My Unwritten Books,* 2008.

Page 148: 'I sometimes think humanity is a vast wave, undulating' comes from *The Diary of Virginia Woolf Volume 3: 1925-30* (entry for Sunday 17 May 1925).

Page 150: 'shining in the dark like the eyes of innumerable cats' is borrowed from G. K. Chesterton's *The Napoleon of Notting Hill,* 1904. (The original is 'shine in the dark like the eyes of innumerable cats'.)

Page 151: 'Girls wearing party dresses of gauze and silk glided like exotic flowers on a lake' derives from *The Quiddity of Will Self* by Sam Mills. (In the original, the girls 'floated' instead of gliding and their dresses are 'made' of gauze and silk.)

Page 153: 'with tail on high' is from James Joyce's *Ulysses.*

Page 154: 'Gurrhr!' and 'Mrkrgnao!' are both from James Joyce's *Ulysses.*

Page 158: 'Navigation was always a difficult art' hails from Lewis Carroll's *The Hunting of the Snark*, 1876.

Page 175: 'He was thinking of a desert island; of coral, treasure, and footprints in the sand' appears in Arthur Ransome's *Swallows and Amazons,* 1930: 'Titty was thinking of the island itself, of coral, treasure, and footprints in the sand'.

Page 191: 'He stepped back in awe – it seemed too perfect, far too beautiful' is a variation on a sentence in Ann Quin's short story 'Nude and Seascape' (*The Unmapped Country: Stories and Fragments*, edited by Jennifer Hodgson, 2018). The original is: 'He stepped back, it seemed too perfect, far too beautiful'.

Page 206: The 'small gilt-edged missal' features in Graham Greene's *Our Man in Havana*, 1958.

Pages 227: 'We all don't know nothing, he wants to scream, and we all don't bloody care' references Alternative TV's 1977 single 'How Much Longer'. The song was composed by Mark Perry and Alex Fergusson.

Page 257: 'Does the angle between two walls have a happy ending?' – J. G. Ballard, *Ambit*, Autumn 1967.

Page 293: 'the white radiance of Eternity' is from Percy Bysshe Shelley's *Adonais*, 1821.

Page 295: The 'terrible tusks' and 'terrible claws' appear in Julia Donaldson and Axel Scheffler's much-loved *The Gruffalo*, 1999.

Page 296: 'Do they owe us a living? Of course they fucking do!' is lifted from a song by anarcho-punk band Crass ('Do They Us a Living?') which features on *The Feeding of the 5000*, 1978.

'Flesh and blood is who we are' appears at the end of Poison Girls' song 'Persons Unknown', 1980.

'All was quiet in the deep dark wood' is from *The Gruffalo.*

Page 301: Here, I quote from The Jam's 'When You're Young', written by Paul Weller and released in 1979: 'You used to fall in love with everyone / Any guitar and any bass drum'.

'You slide down the surface of things' references a recurring line in Bret Easton Ellis's *Glamorama,* 1998 ('We'll slide down the surface of things'). It comes from U2's 'Even Better Than the Real Thing' on *Achtung Baby,* 1991.

Pages 302-303: 'The paint is cracked / And the paper peels / The poster falls / And a body reels softly' is from the song 'Tenant', written by Siouxsie Sue and Steve Severin. It appears on Siouxsie and the Banshees' *Kaleidoscope* album, released in 1980.

Page 303: 'Mirrors are the doors through which Death comes and goes' ('*Les miroirs sont les portes par lesquelles la Mort va et vient*') features in *Orpheus,* Jean Cocteau's 1950 film.

Page 307: 'England and nowhere. Never and always' comes from 'Little Gidding' in T. S. Eliot's *Four Quartets*: 'Here, the intersection of the timeless moment / Is England and nowhere. Never and always'.

Page 308: 'Go, go, go, said the bird: human kind / Cannot bear very much reality' is from 'Burnt Norton', also in Eliot's *Four Quartets*.

Page 312: 'Patrick started to jog faster and they all screamed at once, quickly outpacing him' references the following passage from Tennessee Williams's *Suddenly Last Summer*, 1958: '...Sebastian started to run and they all screamed at once and seemed to fly in the air, they outran him so quickly'.

'they had also *devoured* parts of his puny body' echoes 'They had *devoured* parts of him' in *Suddenly Last Summer*.

About Dodo Ink

At Dodo Ink, we're book lovers first and foremost. From finding a great manuscript to the moment it hits the bookshop shelves, that's how we approach the publishing process at every stage: excited about giving you something we hope you'll love. Good books aren't extinct, and we want to seek out the best literary fiction to bring to you. A great story shouldn't be kept from readers because it's considered difficult to sell or can't be put in a category. When a reader falls in love with something, they tell another reader, and that reader tells another. We think that's the best way of selling a book there is.

Dodo Ink was founded by book lovers, because we believe that it's time for publishing to pull itself back from the brink of extinction and get back to basics: by finding the best literary fiction for people who love to read. Books shouldn't be thought of in terms of sales figures, and neither should you. We approach every step of the process thinking of how we would want a book to be, as a reader, and give it the attention it deserves. When you see our Dodo logo, we'd like you to think of our books as recommendations from one book lover to another. After all, aren't those the ones that we take the greatest pleasure in?

At Dodo Ink, we know that true book lovers are interested in stories regardless of genre or categorisation. That's how we think a publishing company should work, too: by giving the reader what they want to read, not what the industry thinks they should. We look for literary fiction that excites, challenges, and makes us want to share it with the world. From finding a manuscript to designing the cover, Dodo Ink books reflect our passion for reading. We hope that when you pick up one of our titles, you get the same thrill–that's the best thank you we can think of.

www.dodoink.com
Tw: @DodoInk

dodo ink